Prais ～eries q/11

BINGO BARGE MURDER

"Chandler launches her first Shay O'Hanlon caper with panache. Coffee, romance, murder, and Dog all make for Minnesota nice-nice."

—*Lavender* magazine

"A solid first entry in the Shay O'Hanlon mystery series. Chandler writes with a wonderful sense of place, plenty of humor, and a crisp pace. The best part for me was the characters, which were so richly drawn that they felt like instant friends. This is a great read from the very first page!"

—Ellen Hart, award-winning author of
the Jane Lawless series and the
Sophie Greenway series

"Chandler's debut is fast and funny... crammed with memorably quirky Minnesota characters."

—Brian Freeman, bestselling author of *Immoral*

"Jessie Chandler delivers a fresh murder motive in this engaging debut mystery."

—Julie Kramer, author of *Stalking Susan*

"What do you get if you line up Shay O'Hanlon, a scrumptious police detective named JT Bordeaux, a computer genius drama queen, and a murder at the Pig's Eye Bingo Barge? If you said a rollicking, fast-paced blackout game of mystery and suspense, I'd have to yell—'BINGO!'"

—Mary Logue, author of *Frozen Stiff*

"A fun read with an emotional depth that sneaks up on you. The characters are interesting and quirky, and the location is unique and well-developed. I hope this is just the first of many adventures for this 'Tenacious Protector' and her pals."

—Neil S. Plakcy, author of the Mahu mystery series

HIDE AND SNAKE MURDER
"Jessie Chandler is the illegitimate child of Raymond Chandler and Dorothy L. Sayers. She's funny—and she's good!"

—Lori L. Lake, author of the
Gun series and the Public Eye series

"*Hide and Snake Murder* takes us to the beginning and end of the Mississippi, New Orleans and Minneapolis, capturing the quirky charm of both cities. It's a rollicking read with an entertaining cast of funny and fascinating characters. You won't be able to turn the pages fast enough."

—J. M. Redmann, author of the Goldie Award-
winning novel *Water Mark: A Micky Knight Mystery*

"Jessie Chandler makes me laugh. A talented storyteller with a deft hand at pacing, she writes rollicking, raucous adventures that are sure to entertain."

—Julie Hyzy, bestselling author of the Manor House
Mystery series and the White House Chef Mystery series

"Jessie Chandler doesn't just write twists in this novel, she writes twists within twists. *Hide and Snake Murder* is a unique story of zany friendship, tentative romance, and the deadly face of today's underworld."

—Elizabeth Sims, author of the Rita Farmer
Mystery series and the Lillian Byrd Crime series

Hide and Snake Murder

JESSIE CHANDLER

A Shay O'Hanlon Caper

Hide and Snake Murder

MIDNIGHT INK
WOODBURY, MINNESOTA

FIRST EDITION
First Printing, 2012

Book format by Bob Gaul
Cover design by Lisa Novak
Cover illustration © Gary Hanna
Editing by Nicole Edman

Midnight Ink, an imprint of Llewellyn Worldwide Ltd.

Library of Congress Cataloging-in-Publication Data
Chandler, Jessie.
  Hide and snake murder/by Jessie Chandler.—1st ed.
    p. cm.—(A Shay O'Hanlon caper ; 2)
  ISBN 978-0-7387-2597-0
  I. Title.
  PS3603.H3568H53 2012
  813'.6—dc23
                            2011052285

Midnight Ink
Llewellyn Worldwide Ltd.
2143 Wooddale Drive
Woodbury, MN 55125-2989
www.midnightinkbooks.com

Printed in the United States of America

For my great uncle Hank,
Major General Henry Rasmussen,
Ret. (US Army), who I hope
is romping with Lucky Dawg in
the greenest of heavenly pastures.
You were, and remain, our rock.

ACKNOWLEDGMENTS

Numerous nods of undying appreciation go out to many people, including Terri Bischoff, acquisitions editor and bearer of the dreaded whip of encouragement; Nicole Edman, my production editor, who has a keen eyeball for proper prose; Lisa Novak, my amazing, patient cover designer who did everything she could to make Doodlebug glow; Courtney Colton and Steven Pomije, who tirelessly work publicity; Katie and the rest of the sales crew who work so hard to get all Midnight Ink, Flux, and Llewellyn titles on shelves at bookstores and libraries; the proofreaders who hunt down all the missing or misplaced commas, periods, and lots, lots more; and last, but never least, thank you to Midnight Ink/Llewellyn Worldwide for allowing me to continue to have a venue that lets me share Shay and company with the world.

I could not continue to do this without the support of my wife and partner of almost seventeen years. Betty Ann, you rock. Thank you for all you do, every moment, every day.

Ellen Hart, you are, hands down, the queen of titles. Thank you for sharing this one with me. Lori Lake, Mary Beth Panichi, and Judy Kerr, you are the awesome threesome of brainstorming. It all started one dark and stormy June night!

Thank you to my Hartless Murderers, the BABAs, and all of my friends and family who read, re-read, and then once again went over this manuscript. The support, encouragement, and occasional thwap across the back of my head have been invaluable. I love you guys.

Ruta Skujins, this is a bittersweet moment. You helped me at every turn and gave me an outlet to sell my book at True Colors Bookstore, Minneapolis's last feminist book retailer. I'm so very sorry the store won't be around for book two. However, may our friendship and collaborations continue for a long, long time.

Pat and Gary at Once Upon a Crime Mystery Bookstore in Minneapolis and my ex-Borders cohorts: thank you for standing behind me.

Last, but never, ever least, a huge thank you goes out to friends and fans who took the time to pick up my books, read them, recommend them, and come and visit me at the crazy events I've been a part of in the last year. What a wild ride it's been, and may the ride continue on!

ONE

DEEPENING TWILIGHT GAVE THE trees surrounding the asphalt-covered trail in Minneapolis's Loring Park a skeleton-like appearance. The spring wind gusted intermittently, eerily shaking the naked branches. Molding leaves recently uncovered by melted winter snow gave off a dank odor that only added to my unease.

Dawg, my eighty-pound, white-and-fawn bulldozer, or rather, Boxer, pulled on his leash, veering off the path periodically to follow some interesting scent.

Cell phone in one hand, I checked it every few seconds for a new message. Baz, aka Basil Lazowski, an old schoolmate and an unfortunate family friend, had texted earlier in the day. He asked if I'd meet him at the park at seven thirty that night.

When I got the message, I had to think about his request. Carefully. On a good I-Think-I-Can-Handle-Baz day, I deliberately practice calming, deep-breathing techniques whenever he's within ten feet. On a bad No-Way-I-Can-Handle-Baz day, he was lucky to remain alive in my presence.

I hadn't seen Baz for well over a year. Last I'd laid eyes on his roly-poly carcass, he'd been passed out in his aunt's backyard, literally mooning the moon. He was a sick gambler, and when he ran out of money, look out. Throw some booze into the mix, and he'd bet away anything he could get his hands on. Clothes included.

Baz was most definitely a pain. But he did respect the fact I wasn't attracted to the male species, and he didn't give me any lip about it. And he was certainly good for the occasional laugh, usually at his own expense. After thinking it over, I decided I was in a reasonable place for dealing with him, so I'd agreed to meet up.

I'd arrived at the park on time, expecting him to be there. Instead, a second text instructed me to keep walking the path around the pond. It sounded odd, but that was nothing new for Baz. Now it was almost eight, and the place was strangely quiet for being right on the edge of downtown Minneapolis. I grumbled and groused to Dawg as we strolled along. He snorted at me—compassionately, I decided—whenever he managed to wrench his face off the ground.

As darkness descended, familiar park landmarks blurred. Objects that appeared harmless in the daylight took on ominous profiles. I had to admit, the place was freaking me the hell out.

I was about to give up and hoof it back to my truck when my phone finally chirped again. The text read:

> It's safe now. Walk to the east end of the park and
> cross the bridge. Meet me by the spoon.

Dawg's nose quivered as he meticulously sniffed the air. I said, "'It's safe now'? What's that supposed to mean?"

Dawg woofed low. His floppy upper lip had caught on one of his bottom teeth, making his face look lopsided. I swear they slapped his schnoz on sideways when they put him together in the puppy assembly factory, and they gave him a size-five tongue in a size-three mouth.

We left the path and made our way across the long, light-blue footbridge connecting Loring Park to the Walker Art Center's sculpture garden. On the other side of the bridge, the grass crunched softly underfoot. I was relieved to be out of the darkness of the park and into the yellow-orange glow of streetlights. We crossed the sidewalk and entered the garden itself. I peered into the gloom, my heart pattering against my ribs.

The iconic red cherry in the bowl of a huge silver spoon came into sight, looking black in the twilight.

Dawg nudged my leg with his head and slurped my hand, his not-so-subtle hint that he wanted a treat. Some help he was. I dug out a Snausage from a baggie in my pocket and tossed it. It disappeared into the dark, drooly cavern of Dawg's mouth with a snap of big white teeth. His tongue travelled rapidly around his lips, and he eyed me with a look. Yup, *that* look. With a shake of my head and an aggrieved sigh, I dispensed two more Snausages into his perpetually hollow belly.

"Come on, mutt." I gave the leash a tug and we circled the cold, inky water surrounding the sculpture and stopped at the end of the spoon handle. This was just too melodramatic. I crossed my arms, hugging my thick sweatshirt and navy windbreaker to me and shivered.

Dawg plopped his butt on my right foot and leaned against my leg. Wind whistled between both tree branches and the various sculptures spread around the area.

"Hey!"

The word echoed throughout the garden.

3

Already on edge, I shot forward, tripped over Dawg, did a half-somersault, and landed hard. I lay in the grass at the water's edge and gazed up at the round face of Baz the Spaz.

"What—the hell—are you—doing?" I wheezed, a hand on my chest trying to hold my hammering heart in. Dawg stood over me with one paw in my armpit and one next to my neck, snuffling my face with Snausage breath. I pushed him off me as I struggled to sit up.

"Sorry Shay, I didn't mean to startle you." Baz extended his hand. After a moment of debate about if I ought to slap it away, I grabbed it. He hauled me upright—quite a feat considering that at five-seven I towered over him by at least five inches. Every time I saw him, he reminded me of that kid's song, "I'm a little teapot, short and stout." His spare tire had expanded even more since I'd seen him last.

"What do you want? You've had me running around here for the last forty minutes."

"I had to make sure you weren't being followed."

I stood straighter and glanced around the garden before I caught myself. It wasn't hard to play into The World As Seen Through Baz's Eyes if you weren't careful. "Being followed? By who?"

"These two guys. I, uh … "

"Uh?" I repeated and gave him a raised eyebrow.

The fringe of blond hair surrounding his shiny pate fluttered in a puff of wind. "I'm in a spot, here, Shay. I need to get a hold of Agnes."

He lived with, or more accurately, mooched off of his aunt, Agnes Zaluski, not far my own Uptown address. Agnes was a good friend of Eddy Quartermaine, my landlord and surrogate mom. She and Agnes were members of the oft card-playing and occasionally crafty group, the Mad Knitters. They'd taken off two days before on a brief jaunt to New Orleans with Rocky, the mentally challenged all-around good guy I employed at the coffee shop I run, the Rabbit Hole. Rocky had been talking incessantly about their upcoming adventure for weeks.

I didn't think Agnes would've have departed without leaving Baz a way to get a hold of her if there was an emergency. "Doesn't she have a cell phone?"

Baz scrunched his nose up. "Are you kidding? You know that generation."

I did. Eddy wanted nothing to do with mobile devices either. It was frustrating.

"And she was a little ticked at me when she left."

Here we go. "Why was she ticked off at you?"

"I kind of asked her for some money—"

He clamped his jaw shut when he caught the expression on my face.

Dawg whined. Both Baz and I did a three-sixty, but saw no one. His skittishness was infecting me.

I heaved a breath and crossed my arms against the cold and the willies. "A little too much track time again?"

"The bet was a sure thing. Really. I don't know what happened."

Gambling was always "a sure thing" with Baz. When he wasn't at one of the two racetracks in town or at one of the local casinos making sure his bankroll disappeared, he worked for Ducky Ducts Duct Cleaning: We Clean Your Pipes Slick as a Whistle, Guaranteed.

"Anyway," Baz said, "she didn't leave me any contact information. I have to talk to her."

Eddy was a planner. She'd carefully outlined hotels, phone numbers, and travel times on a piece of paper and tacked it to a small corkboard on the wall in her kitchen. I said, "They're somewhere in

New Orleans, at the Hotel St. Mame or something. But why the subterfuge? Why not simply ask me for it on the phone?"

Baz squinted at me. "They're watching."

I rolled my eyes. "Who's watching? You make no sense." Even as the words left my lips, I peered around furtively again.

"Two goons. They trashed the house and kidnapped me and Wink."

"What?"

"The two—"

"No, the kidnapping part."

"Me and Wink—"

"Who's Wink?"

Baz eyed me. "Stop interrupting."

"Fine." My voice was tight. Baz was insane. Certifiable.

"Wink's a friend who comes over and plays PS3 with me."

I opened my mouth to make a crack about a thirty-something, balding man playing video games but snapped it shut at the expression on Baz's face.

"So it's two in the morning. Last night. We're in the middle of a serious battle. Halo 2. These two guys with guns busted in the back door. Practically took it off the hinges."

I raised a brow but didn't interrupt. Maybe he was hallucinating video games.

"One held us at gunpoint while the other trashed the joint."

"Trashed *Agnes's* joint? She'll have a heart attack if she comes home to that, you know."

"I didn't have time to clean. I've been hiding out all day." He gave me a you-are-too-stupid-for-words glare. "After they couldn't find what they wanted, they took us to this place in Brooklyn Center by Twin Lakes. By the railroad tracks."

6

I'd played in that area when I was a kid, leaving pennies on the rails for the trains to flatten. One time a friend and I were on the tracks and didn't hear the train until it was just about on top of us. Fortunately, we dove down the embankment just in time. The area was about as remote as you can get in the city.

"Then they shot Wink in the head. I'm pretty sure he's dead." Baz shuddered. "They said I was next if I didn't give it back. They'd put one right between my eyeballs."

Whoa. "They actually shot him? With bullets?"

Baz nodded and made a gun with his hand and pulled the invisible trigger. "Bang bang."

Now I definitely expected to see a couple monsters brandishing submachine guns.

Dawg whined.

I frowned at Baz. "And then?"

"The two goons told me I better get it back. If I squeal to the cops, they'll finish the job. They said they'd be back soon. Then they disappeared."

Holy crap. "What happened to Wink?"

"After they left, I used Wink's cell phone to call 911 and anonymously reported the shooting. Then I wiped my prints off it and threw it in the lake."

Man, was I an accessory now that I knew all this? Not good. Not good at all. "Was he breathing?"

"It didn't look like it. Most of the back of his head was in chunks a few feet away."

"God, Baz! Are you kidding me? You just left him like that?" The blood drained out of my face. I tried to take a couple deep, slow breaths.

"Well, what was I supposed to do? I couldn't carry him out of there!"

"No, but you could've waited for the ambulance!"

"Nuh uh. I wasn't about to hang around and let them haul me back to jail."

"Why would they?"

A look of pure guilt oozed across Baz's face, and I knew he'd done something dumb again. Nothing ever changes. Some of the fog in his story was starting to clear, as well as the full impact of the words he'd said just moments ago: *They said I was next if I didn't give it back.*

"Okay. What'd you swipe this time?"

"A stuffed snake. Nothing major."

The man was about to get himself killed, and he says it's nothing. While Baz cleared out linty ductwork, he occasionally gave himself a five-finger discount on items from the homes he worked in. Agnes bailed her nephew out of the clink more than once for his Making-Other-People's-Stuff-Mine obsession.

"What makes the snake so valuable they'd kill for it?"

"Some kid's favorite toy? There's diamonds sewed inside it? How do I know? It looked like any other kid's stuffed snake." If there'd been better light, I knew Baz's ears would be bright red and the veins in his neck would be standing out. With all the stupid things he got himself into, he was going to stroke out one day.

"Why didn't you give them the dumb thing, then?"

"I would've if I could've found it. The only thing I can figure is Agnes did something with it. That's why I need to talk to her."

I sucked air between my teeth and let it out slowly. "As soon as I get home, I'll call you with the number to the hotel."

"NO!" The word burst forth from Baz with vehemence.

8

Jeez. Dawg backed up, staring at Baz from between my legs. I knew how the poor pooch felt, but I didn't have anyone's legs to hide behind.

"If they shot Wink, who *knows* what they might do to an old lady. I'm afraid to go home. They could be watching my calls. If they find out where Agnes is, and if they think she has the snake with her, whether she does or not … She can be a pain, but I don't want her to get hurt."

Look at that. Baz did have a part of a shriveled heart in there somewhere. "Come on, Baz, why would they hurt her? They should be hurting you."

Baz gave me wounded look. "Because they're ruthless. Maybe they'd do something to her to get back at me. I dunno. And Eddy's with her. They could do something to them both."

The thought of Eddy in danger brought me up short. Shivers started deep inside, and I was more than ready to skedaddle. "What do you want me to do, then?"

Baz looked over one shoulder, then the other, and pulled me down so his lips were even with my ear. "I'll meet you at Sebastian Joe's about in an hour/hour-and-a-half and get the number from you."

"Fine." I straightened and gave Dawg a gentle tug. We followed Baz and his peculiar waddle back across the bridge. How much could I believe out of this klepto loon? Did someone really get shot last night? With Baz, you never knew the truth versus his version of reality.

———

On the short ride home, I mulled over the events of the last hour. From the sound of it, Baz dug himself deep this time. And may have gotten someone shot. That would mean murder, if it were true. Even as a kid, Baz made stuff up all the time trying to gain attention. Was he making up murder now? Regardless, something serious seemed to be going on.

A thought occurred to me then, and I caught my breath. If I gave Baz the information to the hotel where Eddy, Agnes, and Rocky were staying, and these two thugs threatening Baz got a hold of it, they could be in real trouble. I gripped the steering wheel tighter and glanced at the digital clock on the dash. It was eight thirty.

I pulled up to the garage and parked in the alley behind the Rabbit Hole, the coffee shop I co-owned with by business partner, Kate McKenzie. Kate was a pixie-like force of nature, a tiny tornado that didn't stop. Petite with a backbone of iron, she didn't put up with crap. She endeared herself to everyone she encountered, myself included. We'd gone to college together, and when the nine-to-five life didn't cut it for either of us, we collaborated and opened the Hole. We were lucky enough to lease the front half of Eddy's large Victorian house in the Uptown neighborhood.

Dawg followed me through the gate into his newly fenced-in backyard and scooted off to one corner to take care of business.

In Eddy's kitchen, the scent of her latest potpourri—vanilla and nutmeg—swirled in warm welcome. She lived in the rear half of the house while I bunked in a small upstairs apartment.

Eddy's carefully printed itinerary remained safely tacked to the corkboard on the wall. I snatched it down and jotted the hotel phone number on a scrap of paper, replaced the note, and stuffed the number in the pocket of my jeans.

Even if Baz the Spaz was lying, it wouldn't hurt to touch base with the travelling troupe and make sure everything was okay. I keyed the hotel number into my cell. After a transfer to their room, voicemail kicked in. I left a message after the babble of the electronic voice. Knowing Eddy, at nearly nine o'clock, they were probably out raising the roof in some French Quarter bar.

I decided it was time talk to my best friend, Nicholas Cooper, known to most as Coop. If I were straight, I'd have married him years ago. Coop was kind, considerate, and loyal to a fault. Coop, Baz, and I had gone through school together, so Coop was familiar with the craziness that accompanied Baz like the dust ball that trailed after Pig Pen. He'd have some interesting insight on this.

TWO

THE TRAFFIC ALONG WESTBOUND I-394 thinned as I left Minneapolis in my rear-view mirror. Coop had fallen into the world of online role-playing games like Warhammer and Dungeons & Dragons, and he had recently translated his interest from the screen and applied it to the real world. A few months back, the Hands On Toy Company started holding various role-playing game tournaments at their store in Minnetonka. Coop had turned from a curious player into a serious junkie. He'd lost a few of his peace-loving ways last fall when he thought he was a murder suspect in a crazy mafia and stolen nut mess. Since then, he'd become a lot more aggressive. Coop was still Mr. Peace & Love, but he was now willing to mix it up if shove came to punch. He even joined a co-ed broomball league over the winter—an ice sport much like hockey but played with special sticks and a small, soccer-like ball—with Kate and me. His first penalty was for roughing.

I pulled into the brightly lit parking lot. "You hang here," I told Dawg. He settled down on the front seat with a toothy yawn. The pooch was more likely to sleep through any nefarious goings-on than guard against them.

The building that housed the Hands On Toy Company and Game Room was so colorful it practically hurt your eyes. A New York sidewalk artist designed and painted the exterior. Eight multi-colored dragons soared thirty feet into the air on either side of the front doors and appeared to leap onto incoming patrons. The entrance itself, constructed out of lumber from defunct Iron Range mines, looked like the portal into an Indiana Jones movie. Hundreds of vividly colored splotches of paint flung haphazardly onto the walls completed the rest of the exterior.

The owner of Hands On, Fletcher Sharpe, was a generous Twin Cities philanthropist. He made his start in a rundown strip mall in Bloomington in the late Nineties, and eventually evolved the enterprise into a 70,000-square-foot heaven-on-earth for kids and the kid-like. Hands On was a very appropriate name because every toy and game available for purchase was on the sales floor ready for experimentation.

Inside, bright banners and swaths of neon-colored, gauzy fabric hung from the ceiling. A wide yellow, maroon, and purple-striped path wound through two-thirds of the store, curving through toddler toys to 'tween novelties into the teen games. Total distraction for the entire family. The last third of the building housed the Dungeon Game & Tournament Room and Café Hobbitude, an enclosed eatery designed to look like Frodo Baggins's Hobbit hole.

For once, I paid little attention to the assault on my senses as I followed the winding trail and emerged between the entrances to the Hobbitude and to the Dungeon. A regular-sized, round Hobbit door led the way into the eatery. Two huge blackened-wood medieval gates with heavy metal hinges and a lowered drawbridge protected the entry to the Dungeon. Suffice it to say Fletcher Sharpe dealt in multiple realities.

The air in the Dungeon was cool. Body odor, coffee, and Doritos drifted into my awareness. The only light in the Dungeon, other than the flame-like glow from torches on the walls, came from lamps recessed above groupings of two to four tables.

I caught sight of Coop at one of the tables with two linebacker-sized guys and a girl with long, stringy hair.

Play or Die was screen-printed on the back of his faded black t-shirt. He was wearing a bright-yellow Rabbit Hole baseball hat backward over short, bristly hair. He'd had to shave his shaggy, dirt-blond head after a run-in with some sticky pine pitch during one of his Green Beans for Peace and Preservation tree sit-ins. The group was trying to stop the removal of some pine trees for more probably unoccupied retail space somewhere in the Metro. If I remembered right, the Green Beans didn't succeed. But they sure tried hard.

The Green Beans were a group of dedicated tree-huggers who advocated peace instead of war. They were good people with honorable intent, but sometimes their good intentions got them into some tight spots. A number of members, Coop included, now had criminal records for trespassing, disturbing the peace, resisting arrest, disorderly conduct, and other various charges. Coop did try to avoid the cops as best he could. However, since I'd started seeing Detective JT Bordeaux, steering clear was sometimes hard to do. Thankfully, he'd finally gotten past his fear that she was going to haul him downtown for simply breathing.

I waited for the chatter to fade as the group became aware of my presence. Coop looked up, surprise on his face when he realized who was interrupting them.

"Hey, sorry. Coop, I need to talk to you."

"Sure, I was about to blow outta here out anyway."

Coop gathered his gaming paraphernalia and bade his co-players adieu. We were out the front door in a matter of minutes.

Coop, ever the card-carrying environmentalist, relied on his bike for transportation regardless of rain, sleet, or snow. He retrieved his ride from a rack next to the building. As we crossed the asphalt parking lot to my truck, he said, "So what's up?"

I bleeped the doors unlocked and Dawg's head popped into view. "I don't know what to make of this. You remember Baz, Basil Lazowski?"

"Baz the Spaz. Who could forget? Last time we saw him, his ass was pointed skyward, remember?"

"Hard to forget." I allowed myself a half-grin.

Coop hoisted his bike into the bed of the pickup and hopped in the passenger seat. Dawg greeted him with a slurp, then crawled into the back, panting happily.

I buckled my seatbelt. "Wait'll you hear this." I relayed my very strange middle-of-the-sculpture-garden meeting with Baz. "So a stolen stuffed toy, a possible murder, and Eddy and crew maybe involved without their knowledge. Which leads us to Sebastian Joe's," I finished.

Coop's jaw worked hard on a piece of gum he'd popped into his mouth. He was trying to quit smoking. Dawg rested his big head on Coop's shoulder and groaned as Coop rubbed the side of his face. "So Baz needs to talk to Agnes and see what, if anything, she did with the snake."

"And if Baz has the number, the bad guys could pry it out of him and figure out where Agnes, Eddy, and Rocky are. I'd rather not hand him the number, honestly. I'm probably being too paranoid, but they did theoretically shoot a hole in someone."

———

Sebastian Joe's Ice Cream Café on Franklin Avenue was an Uptown fixture. They'd been busy creating unusual, homemade flavors since the early Eighties. The place was my favorite ice cream joint, hands down.

I managed to parallel park in an open spot across from the store. After a sad whine of appeal from the backseat, Coop and I left Dawg and headed into the shop.

Sebastian Joe's always made my mouth water. The air was heavy with a mix of sweet ice cream and the tang of freshly brewed coffee. I gazed longingly at the bucket of Pavarotti-flavored deliciousness behind the glassed-in freezer as I passed by and followed Coop down a short hallway to the seating area in the back.

Baz was at a table in the corner with a bowl of at least three scoops of ice cream, stuffing his mouth as fast as he could swallow.

"Jeez," I said, "slow down or you'll choke to death."

"I'd be a lot happier dying doing something I love." He shoved another load in his mouth and mumbled, "Hey, Coop."

"Baz." Coop's face froze in a grimace of distaste. He didn't like ice cream and he didn't care much for the man eating it, either.

Baz took a breath. "You have the number?"

I said, "Why don't I give them a buzz? If Eddy or Agnes answer, maybe we can wrap this whole thing all up now."

He spooned another mound of ice cream into his mouth as he considered my words. "Dial."

Eddy, Agnes, and Rocky were staying at the Hotel St. Margaret. This time a man with a syrupy southern drawl answered. I asked him to put me through to Edwina Quartermaine's room.

As the phone rang, I watched Baz noisily scrape the bottom of his ice cream bowl with his spoon. I had a flashback to third grade, when he'd simply stick his face in his plate and lick it clean.

Voicemail kicked in after the fourth ring. I left another message asking one of them to call me, even though I hate leaving voicemail messages. Life was sure easier when people had cell phones. I wasn't to the panic stage yet, but the lack of response to my calls made me uneasy.

Coop, intently folding a postcard-sized advertisement into a paper airplane so he wouldn't have to look at Baz, said, "Why are these guys are after the snake? What makes it worth 'killing' someone over?" He floated quote marks in the air with his fingers.

"It's a stupid six-foot-long, neon-green stuffed animal. It's not even all that soft." Baz clattered his empty bowl on the tabletop.

I handed him a napkin with barely disguised disgust. He had a smear of chocolate on his cheek and a white drip of ice cream on his chin.

Coop aimed the plane over the top of my head and let it sail. It soared nicely until the wall behind me downed it. He said to Baz, "Who'd you swipe the snake from?"

Basil scowled at Coop's choice of words, making his small, close-set eyes even beadier. "I only intended to borrow it."

Right. Borrow, my ass.

"I did the duct job a few days ago, already turned in the paperwork. I have no idea whose house it was. Nice, I remember that."

Coop said, "That's the key. If you find out whose house it is, you'll know who's after you."

17

"Baz," I said, "maybe you should go have a chat with the cops."

"Forget it," he said flatly. "I'm on probation. If they find out I lifted something, it's right back in the slammer."

"Right where you belong," Coop said under his breath.

"Okay," I said. "We'll wait for Agnes or Eddy to call, and I'll see what they have to say. I'll let you know as soon as I hear anything."

Baz said, "Aren't you going to give me the contact info?"

"No way. You think I'm crazy? Like you said, if your playmates visit you again, I'm not taking the chance you'd hand the info over to them."

Coop barked a laugh. "I bet Baz would cave after being poked in the eye."

I caught Coop's gaze. Sadly, he was right. We left Baz staring morosely at his empty ice cream bowl and headed to the counter.

After Dawg enthusiastically welcomed us back, I gave him his small to-go cup of vanilla ice cream. He had that sucker slurped out in five seconds flat. After giving him some water to chase the sweet stuff, I pointed my truck toward Coop's place.

I glanced over at Coop, then back at the road. "What do you think?"

"I think the man's a complete jackass."

"He is. What should we do?"

Coop shrugged his thin shoulders. "Not much we can do. Wait and see what Eddy or Agnes have to say." He looked out the window and we rode in silence for a couple of minutes. "Give me your phone and I'll try the hotel again."

Coop waited in silence, then left another message. He hung up and handed my cell back. "How does that idiot manage to get himself into situations like this?"

18

"I have no idea. I figured after being socked around by that ex-WWF wrestler for stealing his heavyweight championship belt and landing probation instead of jail time he'd have curbed his habit."

Coop laughed. "Until someone chops off a few fingers or cuts his tongue out, he's not going to change."

"True enough. Thanks for tagging along."

"Any time."

I dropped off Coop with a wave and drove home.

Dawg and I trudged up the stairs to my place over the Rabbit Hole. The small one-bedroom unit fit the mutt and me pretty well. If we added anyone else to the mix, quarters became cozy, which I quickly realized when JT and I began seeing each other on a regular basis. JT had been at Quantico for the past six weeks attending the FBI's Law Enforcement Specialized Training Academy. She and I had been an item for a record-breaking five months. Up until she left, Dawg and I'd been spending an increasing number of nights at her house, which was far roomier and had actual pictures of interesting things hanging on the walls.

I opened the front door and stepped into the living room. A TV on a homemade wood-plank stand, a glass-topped coffee table, and an on-its-last-legs couch that had a tendency to poke unsuspecting sitters in the butt made up most of my living room. The two pieces of furniture I was rather fond of, my mom's antique roll-top desk and wooden swivel office chair, sat in front of the window.

Dawg followed me into the quart-sized galley kitchen, and waited patiently while I whipped up a peanut butter sandwich for him and a turkey sandwich for me. He gave me his patented "I'm a pathetic, hungry dog" look, upper lip caught on a lower tooth. Drool dripped from the corner of his mouth in a long string, slowly making its way to the floor.

After our respective snacks and one more visit to the backyard, I brushed my teeth and hit the sheets. Eddy still hadn't called back, so I tried one more time. If I didn't know her as well as I did, I'd have been worried. But she probably had Rocky and Agnes at some questionable Bourbon Street pub happily playing cards in a sleazy back room.

I clicked off the light. The mattress bounced as Dawg hopped aboard for the night. He plopped his heavy head on the pillow beside me, and the last thing I heard was his loud yawn.

THREE

Sophie B. Hawkins startled me out of deep sleep. The dim light of near-dawn filtered in around the curtains as I squinted at the alarm clock. Then the synapses in my brain started to connect and I realized it was my cell that was singing to me. 6:13 a.m. JT was right on time.

"'Lo," I mumbled, tongue sticking to the roof of my mouth.

"Hey, babe. How's my sunshine?"

Only a morning person could be so chipper at six in the fricking morning, but then it was seven her time.

"Sunshine yourself." I tried to swallow. "How're you?"

JT cheerfully said, "Had my ass handed to me yesterday on the Yellow Brick Road." When she'd first arrived at Quantico, she'd told me about the Yellow Brick Road. It was a hellish, six-plus-mile Marine-built trail through hills and treacherous woods. Any poor sucker who managed to finish received an actual yellow brick to commemorate the torture. JT had been delighted to attack the course. I had no idea how such physical punishment could make someone happy.

"Good to hear," I managed. Dawg whined and shifted so his warm head rested next to my cheek.

She laughed. The sound folded around me, a mixture of comfort and loneliness.

"I miss you," I told her as I rolled onto my side, awareness beyond the end of my nose beginning to kick in.

A sigh echoed through the airwaves. "I miss you, too." JT's raspy voice was like honey when she wasn't in cop mode, and the way she said those words did something to my heart. I had always been what one might call girlfriend-challenged, happy to bounce around trying out different babes but not willing to stick with anyone for too long. At this point, our relationship was still rolling, and I wasn't asking questions.

JT said, "I'll be home in eight days. It'll go by before you know it. What's new?"

I sketched out the details of the meeting with Baz, and tension built as JT absorbed my words. Dawg stood, circled, and settled back down with his chin on the curve of my hip.

After a pause, she said, "You don't have any names, no one I could run? Are you even sure there really is a dead body?"

"No on all counts."

"Call North Memorial and see if they'll tell you if someone was picked up in that area. I doubt it, but it wouldn't hurt. It'll be interesting to hear what Agnes says when you get a hold of her." She paused. "You could check with Harry, too. He's probably on street duty, but you never know."

I only knew the man as Dirty Harry. He was an MPD undercover narcotics officer who moonlighted with the homicide division occasionally. He and JT had worked a few details together and had collaborated periodically over the last few years. Tyrell, her current work partner, was out on leave, honeymooning in Tahiti.

"I will if I feel like things are getting out of control. I'm not sure what to believe when stuff falls out of Baz's mouth."

"No solo stunts." There was a clear note of warning in her tone. Last fall during Coop's unfortunate murder investigation, which had mob involvement, he and I had gone off and confronted the two killers without any law enforcement backup. JT was less that pleased with our actions and had let me know loud and clear.

I certainly wasn't planning any repeat performances. "I'll behave."

JT gave me Harry's phone number and I jotted it on a notepad next to the phone.

We chatted a few more minutes. Our separation had clarified my feelings for JT, and I surprised myself after we hung up by the very consideration of dropping the L-word on her. I knew I was falling for JT, but apparently I wasn't ready to admit it aloud. It seemed like whenever my relationships turned serious, they melted into big puddles of regret.

Google was a great thing, made even better as an app on a phone. In seconds, I was connected to information at North Memorial. A minute later, I hung up after being stonewalled by the receptionist. No name and no family relationship equals nada. So much for that.

I set the phone on the nightstand and closed my eyes. With dog-breath in my ear, I hovered on the abyss of snoozedom. Before I had a chance to slip under too deeply, the phone rang again.

"Hello?"

"Tank god, I deed help!" The voice was deep, very congested. My caller panted like a rabid dog.

I propped myself on my elbow. "Baz? Is that you? What—"

"It's be. They bade be tell em where Eddy lives. They thik she has da sdake."

My eyes popped wide open as his words sunk in. "Baz," I growled as I struggled to sit up. "What's wrong with your voice? What did you say to them?"

"Just dat baybe Agdes gave her da sdake."

He was a crazy man. "Why would you do that, you idiot?"

"I'm daglig from my fuckig feet in Agdes's garage, smardass. Sadistic batards." He trailed off, sucking in great breaths of air. "Worked a had free. Good thig I'm fat or by cell would've fallen out of by pocket. I could die haging here. Head's about to expode. Feet are turnig black. Hurry up ad get be down!"

I made it to my feet, and Dawg whined. "It's time to call the cops."

"DOE!" Baz howled. "I'b not goig back to jail. Beside, they told be they'd chop by dipples off if I squealed. Foget it. I like by dipples."

Too much information. "Calm down. I'm on the way, after I make sure everything is okay here." I hung up on the dingbat. Dawg let out a low woof and bounced off the mattress, flashing his Boxer grin. I couldn't believe Baz had handed over our address to those thugs. On second thought, I could.

I pulled on a sweatshirt, got a pair of cargos over my ankles, and grabbed Harry's number from the note pad and stuffed it in a pocket. I hopped into the living room as I tried to pull up my pants. Mid-hop, my left foot caught the leg of the coffee table. I went down in a tangle and landed on my side with a grunt.

Dawg barked and started bouncing up and down on his hind legs.

With a curse, I scrambled upright, buttoned my pants, jammed my feet into my shoes, and then realized my cell was still in the bedroom. I charged back in and retrieved it. Dog and I flew out the door, with me pausing at the last minute to grab the car keys. What was I going to do if they were in the house?

Dawg followed as I pounded down the stairs. At the bottom, to the right, a short hall led to the Rabbit Hole. The aroma of freshly brewed coffee wafted through the air. On the left, a set of floral, fabric-covered French doors led into Eddy's living room. When she was home, the doors were wide open, allowing her to monitor the goings-on in the Hole. She loved to lend a hand when the café got crazy.

I unlocked the French doors and slowly opened them. My heart, already pounding, started tripping quadruple time. Thankfully, everything in the living room appeared the same as it had the night before.

We hoofed it to the kitchen. Dawg, somehow sensing my stress, was now glued to my side, play-mode forgotten.

I skidded to an abrupt stop at the doorway. The back door was wide open, the pane of glass nearest the doorknob shattered. Sharp shards of broken glass lay on the linoleum, glinting in the weak light. Panic flooded me.

I grabbed Dawg's collar before he wriggled past me and cut his paws on the glass. How could I not have heard any of this? Even Dawg had been oblivious. Damn those well-built nineteenth-century walls.

Then my gaze caught the corkboard, and I nearly hyperventilated. Eddy's carefully written itinerary was gone.

FOUR

I DIALED COOP AND explained why I was speeding toward his place as if Lucifer himself were hot on my tail.

Those thugs could've still been in the house when Dawg and I roared into Eddy's apartment! I was a complete idiot. They could've duct taped us upside down just like Baz and then shot us both. Jesus. I guess I still hadn't learned that little think-before-acting lesson.

Ten minutes later Dawg and I screeched to a stop in front of Coop's apartment. He burst from the front door in the midst of pulling a shirt over his head. Coop was always a good sport about getting ready in a hurry.

Coop climbed in the pickup, and Dawg gave him a snoot full of tongue. I peeled out and headed toward Baz's as Coop used the hem of his shirt to wipe away the evidence of Dawg's affection.

He said, "Have you tried to call Eddy?"

"Not yet." I threw my phone at him. My stomach ached, and my head pounded in time to my hammering heart. If anything happened to Eddy ... or to Rocky or Agnes. I pushed that thought from my mind and concentrated on remembering where Baz and Agnes lived. Their house was near Glenwood Avenue and Penn, and it wasn't exactly easy to get from Coop's to there.

Coop punched some buttons and put the phone to his ear. After a moment he said, "Can you please transfer me to Edwina Quartermaine's room?"

The morning traffic was starting to get heavier. Without slowing, I weaved around a recycling truck.

After some long moments, Coop said, "Eddy, it's Coop and Shay. We need to talk to you right away. Please call Shay's cell, okay?" He disconnected. The message was similar to the last ones I'd left, and now, with Eddy's itinerary missing, the lack of response weighed heavily.

Pain throbbed above my right eye. "No one home again?"

"Nope. Maybe they stayed out drinking all night. It is New Orleans, after all."

"True. Boozing it up and playing poker. Eddy can sniff out a game in thirteen seconds flat."

Coop's mouth twitched in a ghost of a grin. "Right. Hurry up, lead-foot. We gotta get Baz down before his toes ooze out his ears."

I pulled to a stop in front of an aging yellow, story-and-a-half ranch-style house with a tuck-under garage. Baz's car, an older-model silver Taurus, sat on one side of the empty double drive.

Aside from the occasional car driving by, there was next to no traffic in the neighborhood.

Coop bailed out, and Dawg and I followed. Paint was peeling off the closed garage door in big yellow flakes. I hollered, "Baz! We're here! How can we get in?"

There was no reply, and for a moment, I wondered if Baz's heart had blown up under the stress of hanging upside down. Then a strangled-sounding voice yelled, "Just oped da fuckig garage door."

Dawg barked. He bounced around the driveway on his big paws, all revved up to play Let's Find the Stinker.

Coop grabbed the handle at the bottom of the garage door and heaved. There, in musty dankness, dangling on a rope from a rafter, hung Baz. His face was beet red. Gray duct tape wound around his torso. One arm hung below his head and the other was still taped behind his back.

I looked around for something to cut him down with while Coop grabbed Baz's shoulders and tried to wrestle him into a slightly less inverted position. Dawg danced around the two men, trying to figure out how to play their game.

I spotted a rusting box cutter on a worktable in the back of the garage and grabbed it. A ladder leaned against the wall, and I dragged it over and opened it up next to Baz.

The rungs on the ladder bowed from the weight of countless feet. Its wooden legs shifted on the uneven cement as I climbed toward the rafters and started sawing on the rope tied around Baz's ankles. The blade was dull, but with some elbow grease, the rope parted. Coop had hold of Baz's armpits, but there was no way he could hold up the man's dead weight. They both crashed with a heavy thud to the oil-stained cement.

Coop sprawled on the ground, arms and legs protruding from beneath Baz's rotund body. It would've been funny if I weren't afraid Baz had killed my best friend. I hopped off the ladder, grabbed Baz's loose hand and unceremoniously rolled him off of Coop, who let out a loud groan.

Dawg wiggled around, lapping Coop, then attempting to lick Baz, who weakly waved his arm in a losing attempt to fend off the shovel-shaped tongue.

"Oh—my god." Coop dropped his hand on his chest as he tried to breathe. "Baz, you need to go on a diet."

Baz had his thumb and fingers pressed into his eye sockets. "My eyeballs almost popped out."

I nudged Dawg out of the way and hauled up Coop. "We need to get out of here. Your new pals could show up anytime." I sure didn't want to be trussed up like a holiday goose and left for the Easter Bunny to find.

Both Coop and I helped Baz remove the duct tape wrapped around his torso. Most of the tape was stuck to his clothes, but his arms were a different matter. The air was punctuated with his curses as skin and hair came away with the tape.

"It's too bad you're so hairy, Baz," Coop commented as he yanked a long piece of tape from Baz's forearm.

Baz hissed in pain. "For Christ's sake, easy does it. I've got sensitive skin."

I said, "You don't have a sensitive bone in your body."

"I do too. You don't know how sensitive I am."

"Whatever."

Sensitive about what he could steal next was more like it.

"That's the last of it." I rolled the chunks of tape into a sticky ball and slapped it on the worktable.

"Help me." Baz held out both his mitts like a two-year-old wanting up. Coop and I exchanged a look, then pulled him to his feet.

"Thanks," he said as he shook himself. Raw red welts adorned his now nearly hairless forearms and even though he probably deserved it, I winced. Then my momentary feeling of goodwill fled as

Baz noisily blew his juicy nose in his hands and smeared the snot on his pants. Twice. I nearly threw up. "Baz, you're disgusting."

With a grimace of distaste, Coop said, "Let's go," and headed toward the truck. Dawg trotted along beside him.

Baz said, "What about me?"

I stopped and threw him a look over my shoulder. "Follow us in your car." Duh.

"Forget it. They know what I drive now. Maybe I could ride with you and Dawg could ride in back of the truck."

No freaking way was Booger Pants going to get into my pickup. I told him so and added, "Besides, it's illegal for dogs to ride in the bed in Minnesota unless they're in a crate. So either you can hop in back, or you can follow us. Your choice. Snotnose."

Baz's face turned into a pity-me mask. He even stuck his lower lip out. Shameless. He said, "Isn't *that* illegal? To have a person ride in the bed of a truck?"

"Nope, there's no law about that. Now come on or we'll leave you here."

Baz hobbled after me, chattering about dumb laws that wouldn't allow dogs to ride in an open pickup bed but would let people tempt death. He planted a foot on the bumper and attempted to heave himself over the tailgate.

After the third failed attempt, he croaked, "Help me."

I gave him a shove on the upswing. He rolled over the tailgate and landed with a thump, his feet sticking up in the air.

"I'd advise you to hang on, Baz." I left him floundering like an upside down tortoise and got in the truck. Coop squinted at me. "This is going to turn out bad, Shay. I can feel it in my bones."

"Me too." My foot hit the accelerator, and there was thud in the rear. Through the mirror, I saw that Baz was playing turtle again.

"Take it easy, Shay." Coop told me as he turned around and looked through the window. "You upended him."

"Not my fault, I told him to hang on. What the hell are we going to do now?"

Dawg let out a low whine and sniffed my ear.

Coop said, "We have got to get a hold of Eddy. And we need to go someplace Baz's buddies won't find us."

After a bit of driving and watching to make sure we weren't being followed, I pulled into a Perkins off Highway 100 in Edina. The sky was cloudy and it looked like it might rain any second. Dawg forced his big body past me when I opened the door and immediately ran over to the edge of the parking lot to take a leak on the shrubs.

I met Coop at the tailgate, and we watched Baz struggle to get out. Once he was safely on dry land, he said, "Thanks a lot for the hand, guys. And you didn't have to drive so crazy, Shay. I think my butt is black and blue now on top of everything else."

"Sorry, Baz. I did tell you to hold on."

He stomped toward the entrance.

Coop looked at me and brushed a hand over the top of his head. "He's making me crazy, and it's been less than an hour."

"I know." I took a deep breath. "The sooner we figure this out, the sooner we get rid of him. Go on in and order me a ham and cheese omelet, okay? Gonna try Eddy again and get Dawg settled back in the truck. If she doesn't answer, I'm going to call the New Orleans cops."

Coop scowled but gave a reluctant nod and followed Baz into the restaurant.

I pulled up recent calls and pressed the number for the Hotel St. Margaret. Another very Southern-sounding receptionist forwarded me to Eddy's room. No answer. Where the heck were they?

Dawg wandered over and sat on my foot. He leaned his heavy, solid body against my leg. It was one of our favorite positions. I scratched a spot behind his ears, and he gazed up at me with adoration. If only life were as easy as finding a convenient lift-the-leg spot and mooching treats.

My brain felt like mush. *Think, Shay.* I needed the number for the NOPD. I'd switched to a smart phone recently, and the gadget never ceased to amaze me. At this moment, the device was invaluable. I pulled up Google and keyed in New Orleans PD. Their website popped up, and I found a non-emergency number for the district I thought might cover the right area.

I leaned against the truck and absently played with Dawg's ear while the phone rang.

A rumbly male voice answered. "N'awlins PD Eighth District, Officer Fallon."

How did I even begin to explain this? "My name is Shay O'Hanlon, and one of my relatives is visiting your city with a couple of friends. I've tried to get a hold of them at their hotel numerous times, and they haven't answered. I'd like to report them missing."

"When's the last time y'all spoke to them, Ms. O'Hanlon?"

I tried to remember. Eddy had given me a buzz when they'd arrived Monday. Today was Thursday. "Monday evening about eight, I think."

"Where were they staying?"

"At the Hotel St. Margaret."

"Nice place. Has anyone from the hotel seen them?"

I hadn't thought to ask anyone that question. "I don't know."

"There's a lot of places here for folks to have a good time, Ms. O'Hanlon. Do you know what their plans were while they were here? Could you just be missing them when you tried calling?"

Eddy had mentioned touring some of the old plantations, but she liked to travel free and easy, without a lot of planning. "I don't know of any specific plans, but I left messages to call me back every time, and no one has."

Officer Fallon took a loud, slow breath. He drawled, "I'll transfer you to our Missing Person's Division. It's been well over twenty-four hours."

I waited through static, wondering if I'd been disconnected. Then a gruff voice said, "Missing Persons, Larson."

"Hi, Officer La—"

"Detective."

I cleared my throat and tried it again. "Detective. Sorry. Listen, Detective Larson, I think I have some missing people who need to be found." I launched into my story.

When I finished, Detective Larson said, "Give me the stats on each of them."

I gave him names, ages, and approximate heights and weights for all three.

The sound of clicking keys filtered through the phone. I imagined Detective Larson pecking away at a computer keyboard in a dismal gray police station.

Larson said, "I'll run it by Lieutenant Pomerantz and make a few calls, but all of them are of age, adults."

"But the two ladies are old, Detective. They're *not* on a bender."

"Uh," he grunted.

Great. While Detective Larson was certainly being polite, I could tell a brush-off when I heard one. If there wasn't any blood or dead bodies, these cops were going to do jack.

"I sure appreciate any help you can give me." I went on to spell out my name, recited my contact number, and then hung up.

Maybe I should call Dirty Harry. I pondered that as I rubbed the furrow between Dawg's shoulder blades. But what could he do? He wasn't in New Orleans. I'd hold off for now.

That decided, I told Dawg, "Time to get back in." I opened the truck door for him. His happy face faded into a pout as he slowly climbed onto the driver's seat. I leaned in and kissed him on the forehead. "Hang tight, buddy. We'll be back out soon, and I'll have a present for you."

His nub of a tail wagged twice, and he settled onto the seat with an aggrieved sigh. He was a patient mutt, and I was glad he'd followed Coop and me out of his brutal former life as a lowly junkyard dog.

When I walked inside, I could hear Coop and Baz, who were seated in a booth in the corner of the restaurant, yapping at each other. Wonderful. I was just dying to mediate the two of them. I had enough to worry about dealing with my own temper. I hurried over to them and slid in next to Coop, who was in mid-tirade.

"—and Baz, you are a stupid fu—"

"Shut up, Mr. Goodie Two Shoes—"

"I try and do what's right, unlike you, you two-bit thief—"

I elbowed Coop mid-roar. "All right you two, shut the hell up. We need to work together here, okay? Stuff your male egos back into your pants. We've got to figure out what to do now."

Baz, his voice dropping immediately to whine territory, said, "He started it."

Coop twitched his neck like a prizefighter although he never punched anyone that I knew of—not on purpose, anyway. He took a calming breath and tore his eyes from Baz to focus on me. "What'd you find out?"

"Next to nothing. The missing persons department took a report, but the detective made it sound like since they were of age, it was no big deal without blood or a corpse."

"Great," Baz said. "I'm going to die because we can't find a stupid stuffed snake."

Coop turned on him. "Don't you give a damn about your aunt? She could be in as much danger as you. I can't believe what a selfish son-of—"

"Oh, for Pete's sake. I'm going to the bathroom and I'm not coming back until you two can be civil to each other." I stormed toward the restroom at the front of the restaurant, passing a weary-looking waiter carrying a huge tray of food I hoped was destined for our table.

Poor Coop. He was usually the epitome of sanity, unless he thought the cops were after him, which actually happened with some regularity because of his membership in the Green Beans. The current situation required his rational side, and I needed him to get off the Bashing Baz platform.

I dallied in the not-so-rosy-smelling restroom harvesting a field of strawberries on my phone's farming app. I hoped by the time I was done the two boys would be over their little snit. Crops harvested, I tucked my phone away and was about to grab the door handle when it swung open with so much force that it hit the wall with a thud. I stepped back in surprise as Coop charged in.

"What—" I began, but Coop cut me off.

"Come on, we have to go. Now." He grabbed my hand and literally dragged me out of the restroom. The panicked look on his face shut my mouth. I allowed myself to be trundled out the front door and into the parking lot, with Baz trailing behind juggling three Styrofoam containers.

"What happened?" I asked as Coop let go of my arm.

"Eddy called me, Shay. Your phone was kicking into voicemail for some reason." Coop's voice was as grim as the expression on his face.

My heart about stopped. "What?"

Baz blurted, "Rocky disappeared."

My eyes widened. "What do you mean 'disappeared'?"

I was usually quite levelheaded, and I possessed a fair amount of common sense, with one big exception. When people or things I loved were threatened, I tended to see red and act without clear thought. My firm hold on rationality flew right out the picture window. I'd inherited this challenging trait from my alcoholic father, who was a shining example of how not to handle yourself in confrontations. In high school I'd been nicknamed the Tenacious Protector and earned the reputation of standing up for the nerds in class. Sometimes I went a little too far and landed in the hot seat in the principal's office, sporting ice packs on various body parts. Right now, I wanted to beat the crap out of Baz for getting us into this.

With effort, I drew a calming breath and held back the crimson tide. I blinked, and Coop, his face whiter than usual, and Baz with his load of containers came back into focus.

"Okay." I swallowed and ran both hands through my hair. "I'm fine. What did she say?"

"They found an all-night poker game—"

"I was right."

Coop said, "Yeah, you were. The game lasted almost twenty-four hours, and Eddy sent Rocky back to the room to get some sleep. Apparently it wasn't more than two blocks back to the hotel."

"But—" I began.

Coop held up his hand. "Let me finish. When Eddy and Agnes returned yesterday afternoon, one of the beds had been slept in, but Rocky wasn't there. They both figured he went out exploring, and they were so exhausted they crashed."

"Excuse us," I said to a couple with two toddlers trying to get to the entryway of the restaurant. We drifted toward the pickup and I said to Coop, "Go on."

"Eddy woke up last night about eight, and Rocky hadn't come back. She didn't think a whole lot of it, because it wasn't very late. When she got up this morning, he was still gone."

I shook my head in disbelief. Could Baz's thugs have gotten to them already? No way. The timing wasn't right. Was it? I squeezed my eyes shut for a long moment. "Did she call the police?"

Baz's head swiveled from me, to Coop, then back as I spoke, but he remained surprisingly silent.

Coop said, "Yeah. They took his information and said they'd look for him. Agnes and Eddy are staying near the hotel in case he comes back."

The uncontrollable need to take the reins and force everything back into its rightful place rocked me. "Coop, we need to go to New Orleans." My gut ached at my inability to fix this mess immediately, right now.

Coop gazed at me for a long moment. He nodded once. "I thought that's what you'd say. I didn't tell Eddy about Baz's issues. She got off the phone too fast."

Baz broke his silence. "I'll find somewhere here to hide out until the excitement dies—"

"You most certainly are *not* staying here." I whipped around to face Baz and advanced on him until my nose was almost touching his. "You're coming with us, you little weasel." I poked him hard in the chest. "If they have Rocky, we can use you to make an exchange."

"Shay!" Baz screeched. "You can't do that to me!"

The wave of rage reappeared in less than a heartbeat and bubbled dangerously close to the surface. "Listen, you asshole, if anything happens to Rocky—or anyone else—because of your irresponsible bullshit, I'll clean your fucking clock myself."

Coop's hand was on my shoulder. His long, thin fingers squeezed into my skin. "Shay! Easy does it. Calm down."

What a role reversal. I was usually calming down Coop. I shook off his hand and straightened, sucking in a lungful of oxygen. "Come on, then, let's go." I turned my back on both Coop and Baz, beeped the truck unlocked, stalked over, and crawled in.

Coop came around the passenger side, and after urging Dawg in the back seat, he slammed the door and buckled his seatbelt. He pulled a crumpled pack of Bubble Yum from his pocket, unwrapped it, and crammed two pieces in his mouth. He chewed violently for a moment, then muttered, "I need a smoke." Louder he said, "I know you're pissed, but we need you. Stay with me, here, okay?"

The engine rumbled to life. I put both hands on the steering wheel and willed myself back from the brink.

I resisted the urge to back over Baz's ass as he struggled into the truck bed, then I placidly drove out of the parking lot.

———

We wolfed down our now-cold breakfast on the way to drop Dawg off at the café. After explaining the essentials of the situation to Kate, she was more than happy to dog-sit. She also agreed to coordinate covering my shifts and having the missing pane of glass in Eddy's door repaired. I wanted to call the police and report the break-in, but after enough badgering, pleading, and tears from Baz, I relented. The thugs got what they wanted, and there was no reason for them to return.

I left Coop and Baz in the coffee shop and scooted upstairs to my place. I stuffed a change of clothes and some toiletries in a backpack and ran back down the steps. After some belly rubs and Dawg tongue, we drove first to Coop's apartment and then to Baz's house for travel necessities and boogerless pants.

As we drove from point A to point B, Coop called Delta and made reservations to New Orleans for the three of us, paying with my credit card.

After driving in circles to make sure Baz's new friends weren't skulking behind us, we killed time at the Mall of America's Magi-Quest, the world's largest live action role-playing game. Not my first choice of distraction, but Coop liked the place, and it effectively kept us out of sight until we had to be to the airport. I amused myself by periodically whacking Baz in the back of his head with my wand as we progressed through the game.

At noon we hung up our wands and drove to the airport. It took only a few minutes to pull into the long drive leading into the Lindbergh Terminal, now generically known as Terminal 1.

I pulled into the long-term parking ramp, followed the spiral to the third floor, and parked. We actually helped Baz out of the back end of the truck instead of watching him flounder his way to solid ground this time, and then we hiked into the terminal to endure security lines and await our flight.

Just before takeoff, I tried Eddy one more time. To my surprise, she answered. Relief flooded my veins.

"Eddy! Am I ever glad to hear your voice."

"The feeling's mutual. Coop told you about Rocky?"

"Yeah. We're coming down."

There was a pause. "I don't know that you need—"

"There is a need. We're at the airport, at the gate." Before she could respond, I plunged ahead. "In fact, there's a little problem up here that might be headed your way. I need you to change hotels."

"Change hotels? Why? What if Rocky comes back and we're not here?"

How much could I share without wigging her out completely? The full explanation needed to happen in person. I pulled a deep breath. "The short version is that Baz is in trouble again." I chewed on my lip a moment, then asked, "Do you guys have a stuffed green toy snake with you?"

"Why, yes. Agnes gave it to Rocky before we left. He loves it." I could practically hear the gears turning in her brain. In my mind's eye, I saw Eddy's brow furrow and one eye narrow in suspicion. "Why?"

"Baz took the snake from one of the jobs he was doing, and they want it back. Bad."

"That Basil." Eddy said. "I thought he learned something from that last mess he thieved himself into." She harrumphed. "Rocky had the snake wrapped around him when we saw him last. I imagine he'll still have it. Unless..."

40

My stomach clenched. "Don't even go there, Eddy. He's fine." I hoped I was right. "Anyway, do you think you can find another place to stay that's close to where you are now?"

"You bet. I'll go down and talk to the nice bartender. He knows everything, and he makes a darned fine Hurricane."

"And let the front desk know where you're going so they can get a hold of you if Rocky comes back. Eddy, I really wish you'd get a cell phone."

"Pshaw. Those things give me the hives. I'll call you on your fancy phone when I find out where we're going and leave you a message if you don't answer."

We disconnected, and by then it was boarding time.

———

In Louisiana, Coop flagged a taxi, and we crammed ourselves along with our bags into the back seat, with Baz between us. I checked my voicemail, but there were no messages. I pressed myself against the door and watched Coop do the same on the other side. If the driver hadn't had the front seat filled with various books on the occult and two stuffed voodoo dolls, I'd have asked if I could have ridden there. As it stood, I didn't want the driver to stick straight pins into either of the freaky-looking dolls on my behalf.

The man behind the wheel smiled wide, his teeth a brilliant flash of white against his dark skin. A fedora perched at a jaunty angle on his head and he peered at us in the rear view mirror through bloodshot, chocolate brown eyes. He said, "Name's Reggie. Welcome to New Orleans." He drew out *Orleans* and said it as Or-lee-ans. I was beginning to realize I had no idea how to pronounce the name of this town correctly. He continued, "Where can I take y'all on a fine day such as this?"

Baz blurted out, "The Café du Monde. I need some beignets."

We had time to kill until Eddy let me know which hotel they'd moved into, so I didn't protest. I had visited New Orleans once before, many years prior, but the memory was mostly hazy. Too many Bourbon Street Specials. The one thing I recalled with vivid clarity were hot, sweet beignets floating in powdered sugar at two in the morning. It wouldn't hurt anything to swing by there. My stomach growled at the proposition. It had been a long time since we'd eaten our cold Perkins breakfast.

"The Café du Monde it is," our driver announced, and we were off.

Forty-five minutes and a wealth of fascinating and horrifying New Orleans tales later, our driver and tour director deposited us at the corner of Decatur and St. Ann, in front of the imposing columned building that housed the French Market and the Café du Monde.

"That'll be forty bucks, my new friends." The driver handed me a white business card over the frayed front seat. "Y'all need a ride, you give me a shout, hear?"

REGGIE "THE EVERYTHING NEW ORLEANS" CABBIE was emblazoned across the top of the card in bright blue, with a cell phone number printed underneath.

"Thanks." I exploded from the cab like a cork popped from a bubbly bottle. As Baz worked himself out, I asked, "You have any money for the fare?" Once he'd extracted himself from the vehicle, he dug in his pocket and pulled out three dimes and a quarter.

With a shrug he said, "I used what I cash I had at Perkins."

Not only did I pay for his airfare, it looked like I was going to pay for his taxi ride and beignets as well.

"I've got it." Coop thrust a hand into his jeans pocket and pulled out a substantial wad of bills. The man was a computer genius, and since he'd started hawking his computer skills to the needy, his financial situation had much improved. It started when he helped some of the Mad Knitters—Eddy's pseudo-knitting, poker-playing and occasional cigar-smoking posse—with their computer skills. The mini business blossomed from there. Now Coop was designing customer rewards programs for bingo halls, hotels, and casinos.

He peeled off a fifty and passed it through the passenger window to Reggie. "Thanks, man," Coop said and slapped the roof of the car as the cabbie pulled away.

Baz was already headed into the café. "What are you waiting for?" he called over his shoulder.

"You should be waiting for us, doofus. We're the ones with the money." I itched to whap the back of his shiny head. Coop and I followed him into the café's open-air seating area beneath the signature green and white striped awning.

Round bistro tables and Fifties-style chairs with greenish-yellow vinyl sat beneath the canopy. White-aproned waiters wearing paper serving hats moved with astounding grace between the tables, serving up sets of three beignets to drooling customers.

We hoisted our bags and threaded our way to the end of the take-out ordering line, which, thankfully, wasn't overly long. The aroma of freshly cooked sweet dough and chicory coffee drifted through the air, and my mouth watered. For once, Baz had had a good idea.

Beignets procured, Baz, Coop, and I made our way to the curb as we munched on the sugary confection. Jackson Square, kitty-corner across the road, was the hub of artistic and impromptu goings on. The square bustled with painters, tarot card readers, and street performers.

I could see two psychics, a couple of magicians, an artist, a dark-haired ice cream vendor chick whose sizeable ice cream cooler was hooked to a blaze-orange moped, a hot-dog vendor, and a Statue of Liberty mime. The mime was dressed from head to toe in shimmering green and stood motionless on a gold-painted wooden crate about a block away. Statue mimes fascinated me, and I always wondered how they could hold out on scratching the inevitable itch.

Next to Lady Liberty, a punker chick with a pink Mohawk and fatigue pants sat on an upended five-gallon pail, drumming a hypnotic rhythm on three plastic buckets of varying sizes. A black-furred canine assistant gently collected tips in its mouth and deposited them in a bowl that lay on the ground in front of the mime's feet. Every so often, the statue would shift position, earning shrieks of delight from the children watching raptly from the sidelines.

I wiped sticky fingers on a napkin, tossed it in a nearby garbage can, and adjusted my backpack. Coop had already snarfed his own beignets down, and I could tell from his restless pacing and the white of his knuckles as he strangled the strap of his messenger bag that he desperately wanted a cigarette. "Hang tough, big guy."

He nodded and went back to walking the edge of the curb. We waited for Baz to wolf the rest of his snack down, which was going to take a while since he'd had the balls to get a double order. Powdered sugar coated his lips, and a white smear of the stuff somehow adorned his forehead. The travel bag between his feet was sprinkled liberally with powder.

Coop said impatiently, "Hurry up, Baz."

"I'm trying." Baz held the bag containing his goodies in one hand, and a half a beignet in the other. He shoved another bite into his mouth as soon as he swallowed the previous one. Suddenly, Baz made spastic motions with one hand and tried to say something. Beignet and powdered sugar sprayed from between his lips. I thought he was choking, and I pounded on his back.

Baz violently shook me off, his eyes wild.

Coop's "What the—" was drowned out as Baz blew the last of the chunks of donut from his mouth. He yelled, "Run!" and dropped the half-full bag of beignets. He left his travel bag on the sidewalk and sprinted across the road.

"What's his problem?" Coop muttered. He bent to pick up Baz's bag.

I caught sight of a huge mountain of a man and another guy steaming fill tilt toward us.

A half-second of frozen disbelief later I howled, "Holy shit, Coop, run!"

———

We charged across the road into Jackson Square, Coop juggling Baz's bag with his own. Baz was a quarter-block ahead of us, short legs churning. He was closing in on the group of magicians and the Statue of Liberty. The despicable duo was less than a block behind us. I could hear them shouting, but I couldn't make out what they were saying.

"Come on, Shay!" Coop hollered.

"I'm trying," I panted, pumping my arms hard, my backpack slamming against my shoulder blades with each stride. I was fast but no match for Coop's long legs.

Tourists looked our way, unalarmed, assuming our little chase was a part of the acts on the square. We zigzagged around clumps of trees and milling people.

I shouted, "I'm sorry!" to one woman I clipped. Baz was almost to the statue performer, and we were closing the gap. Loud voices echoed behind us. I wasn't sure if the bad guys were catching up or if vacationers were angry we'd stampeded through them, but I wasn't about to slow down to find out.

I blinked, and Baz disappeared.

Coop bellowed, "Hey! Baz!" and we both slowed about twenty feet from the performers, searching the crowd for the top of the fat little man's glistening head. Four of the vendors had closed ranks and stood on either side of Liberty. The tempo of the drumming sped up to a pounding staccato rhythm, helping to increase the size of the audience. Our pursuers were caught in the rear of the swelling crowd. Before we could take off again, the black dog working the audience for tips appeared in front of us. He barked and grabbed my pants leg in his teeth and pulled.

"Damn it, let go!" I tried to shake him off, terror oozing up my spine. The dog used his weight to drag me forward, toward the gap between the audience and Lady Liberty.

One of the magicians who'd set up next to the mime stood a few feet away. With small black eyes and a pointy black goatee, he looked like a cross between Johnny Depp the pirate and Johnny Depp of *Edward Scissorhands*. He moved toward us, and said under his breath, "Go with it."

Go with what? I shot a look behind us again. The two villains had shoved their way through about half the gathered crowd. They'd be on us in seconds. Coop gave me a skeptically raised eyebrow and shrugged. No time to argue. I allowed the dog to pull me toward Liberty. The drumming rose to an even higher, louder pitch. The dog released me once we got to the center of the open area and trotted off to the side.

People had started clapping in time to the rapid-fire beat, raising the noise level until the only thing I could hear was an all-consuming, thunderous roar.

Another magician, dressed in a Dr. Seuss top hat and sporting a billowing black cape, stepped between the crowd and us. He raised his arms, and effectively created a wall from the audience with the ends of the satiny cape attached to his wrists.

Invisible speakers boomed with the sound of the magician's deep, hypnotic voice. "Welcome to the Great Jackson Square Disappearing Act, where we make people go … " He snapped his fingers. "POOF!"

He paused a long moment, and in that time, the dog moved in and nipped my pants again, pulling more gently this time. I grabbed Coop's sleeve and allowed the mutt to lead us past the mime. The only thing that so much as twitched on the frozen performer were her eyes, which followed our progress.

Dr. Seuss continued his pitch, but I ceased hearing his words. White noise took over.

I hadn't realized the ice cream vendor had moved her moped and cooler behind the performers, next to the wrought iron fence surrounding the square until the dog let go of my pant leg and trotted over to her.

"Bags over there, mates." Her cheerful voice had a melodic accent, and it took a moment to place it. Australian. She jerked her thumb in the direction of a powder-blue plastic storage bin hidden behind one of the artist's set-ups. Coop and I flung our bags into the container.

With lightning speed, she lifted up the entire top of the cooler and said, "In you go." The tank-like freezer was about three feet in height, four feet wide, and about six feet long. Coop and I peered inside, and instead of ice cream, a frozen-looking Baz lay against the far wall, the expression on his face one of shock and amazement.

With no time to consider anything, we dove into the deep freeze. Baz grunted when Coop landed half on top of him, and Coop groaned when I rolled into the container and crashed into him. I didn't think we were all going to fit, but somehow we did. Our ice cream dream babe shut the top, latched it, and opened the foot-square ice cream retrieval hatch so we could breathe. Muffled sounds from outside filtered into the cooler. It was obvious when the crowd exploded in a joyful frenzy that the show was over.

A booming voice filtered clearly into the cool, shadowed interior of the cooler. "Thank you for watching the Great Jackson Square Disappearing Act, where you never know who will vanish next!"

The freezer began to rock as our savior fired up the moped and motored slowly away. I heard her say a number of times, "Sorry, mates, all out of ice cream. No worries, I'll be back tomorrow."

Sounds of the rowdy crowd faded as we swayed back and forth in our sardine can. At least the interior was cool.

Coop wheezed, "Shay, I love you, but can you slide a little to the left?" I shifted, and he moaned in relief. "My nuts will never be the same."

"Sorry." I wiggled closer to the ice-cold wall. "What just happened?"

Baz said, "I'm not sure if we were an accidental part of that magical act or what, but these guys saved our butts."

The cart hit a sizeable pothole. We bounced against the cold, hard bottom, and jostled back and forth. Suddenly Baz let out an inhuman cry. "My wip is stuck to da wall! Ow ow ow ow!"

For the next few minutes, Coop and I enjoyed an orchestra of Baz's pain-filled howls. I made very sure to keep my lips and tongue as far from the cold gray metal as I could.

The cart slowed, and we made two consecutive sharp turns. The bright light that filtered through the open serving-hole darkened, and the cooler came to a stop. Fifteen seconds passed, and then the sound of latches connecting the top to the base of the freezer echoed as they were undone.

Baz whimpered.

I whispered, "Don't move. Your lip will stay there without the rest of you if you try." I almost felt bad for him.

Then the top of the cooler was removed, and our rescuer's head appeared. She looked to be about twenty-five.

"Crikey, you must be some kind of friends for this treatment."

We stared up at her. Coop said, "What are you talking about?"

"Yeah, wha you talkin' 'out?" Baz sounded like Arnold from *Diff'rent Strokes*.

She looked at Baz. "Is your lip stuck to the metal? Oh my, where are my manners? Let's get you out of there. You with the lip, hang on." A warm, tanned hand reached in and closed around my icy fingers. She helped me out of the ice cream freezer, and I jumped to the concrete floor.

We were in a dimly lit area the size of a basketball court. Various ice cream vending contraptions sat against one wall. In front of those, four mobile hot dog stands waited for use in the center of the floor. Another wall was divided into six postage-stamp-sized changing areas. Two worktables were lined up in front of a six-foot makeup counter that overflowed with beautifying or face-altering accoutrements. Round vanity lights surrounded a mirror mounted above the table.

Coop climbed out, and then Ms. Australia said to Baz, "One minute, mate, and I'll have you loose."

She strode over to a one of the tables and grabbed a bottle of water. The Australian was a little shorter than I was, but stockier in all the right places. The old me might have said *Hey, baby, after this, let's hook up*. Now I just thought it instead of acting on my impulses. I guess my relationship with JT really was good for me.

"Here you go," she said. She slowly trickled water between Baz's lip and the metal wall of the cart. After a minute, Baz said clearly, "Oh, thanks. Thank you."

He wobbled and nearly fell on his face getting out of the cart, but thanks to a fast hand from Coop, he maintained what was left of his dignity.

Ms. Australia said, "I suppose I should introduce myself. I'm Gabby Green, and I bet you're wondering what just happened, eh?"

Coop rubbed his hands together to restore circulation. "You could say that."

Gabby Green leaned against the ice cream cart, her iridescent blue eyes crinkling at the corners. "You'll find out soon enough."

As she spoke, one side of the tall, rolling doors slid open. One of the magicians, the bucket drummer, and the Statue of Liberty entered the warehouse. Liberty deposited the powder-blue container that presumably held our bags near the door.

The black mutt bounded along beside them until he got an eyeful of the three of us outsiders. He galloped toward us, yipping in delight.

Liberty said, "Dave! Come here."

The dog leaped joyously and bounded back to Liberty. That voice... then it dawned on me. "Oh my god, is that you, April?"

Liberty grinned a very non-mime grin. "Shay O'Hanlon, how are you?"

———

I'd met April and Mary McNichi a number of years earlier when they were first starting out as an act playing small dives in Minneapolis. They bailed six years back and headed to a warmer climate. They pair spent some time in Key West performing during the Sunset celebration and eventually settled in New Orleans a year after Katrina hit.

"And that's what we've been up to," April finished as she rinsed the last of the gunk from her hair and face in a sink attached precariously to the wall. She vigorously rubbed at her now mostly green-free hair with a towel.

The rest of us had gathered around one of the tables. Mary had her chair balanced on its two back legs as she stroked Dave the Dog's head. I was waiting for her to tumble end over keister. She said, "Why are you guys running from those two goons? It was lucky Houdini," she pointed at the magician still in the Dr. Seuss hat who sat slouched on a bar stool, "realized you three were running from something more than the calories in a beignet."

Gabby said, "We simply moved up our little disappearing act a wee bit. It's the finale of the day."

Baz asked, "Do all of you work together?"

Houdini took off his striped hat, stuck his hand inside and pulled out a large gold coin. He flipped it in the air, snapped his fingers, and the coin disappeared. Cool.

"Not all of the performers out in the Square do." His voice rumbled from somewhere below his knees. "A while back a few of us decided it might be more profitable to gang up, so we rented this," he indicated the space with a sweep of his hand, "and came up with a number of acts we could do together throughout the day." He shrugged. "It's been working okay."

April threw the towel aside and sat next to Mary. "Back to you. What's going on?"

I sketched out the bare minimum of what had happened in the last twenty-four hours. "We have two major problems. We need to find the stuffed snake and get it back to the goons, unless they do have Rocky. If they do have him, then we trade Baz here—"

Baz barked, "That's NOT part of the deal."

I looked at him with narrowed eyes. "If that's what it takes … "

"Enough!" Coop said around another mouthful of gum.

I shifted my gaze off Baz on onto April. "And we have to find Rocky."

Houdini slid off the barstool. "What's he look like?"

I said, "He's about five-three, maybe 180. In his early forties, I think, but acts more like a kid. He always wears an aviator style cap. The kind with the ear-flaps."

Houdini nodded.

"He wears that hat no matter how hot it gets." An ache formed in my temple, and I absently rubbed it with two fingers. "The current hat is blue plaid. He's pretty round. He used to always wear this awful down-filled green winter coat all the time, and I mean *always*. But now he's replaced it with a Twins jacket."

"The guy loves baseball," Coop added. "And has one hell of a throwing arm."

"Yeah," I agreed. "He does. The jacket's varsity style, like kids in high school wear, and it's navy blue with cream-colored sleeves. The Twin's logo is huge. Fills up the entire back."

"Shouldn't be too hard to find someone in a blue plaid aviator hat and Minnesota Twins jacket around here who goes by the name Rocky. I'll hit the network." Houdini shucked his cape and tossed it on the table.

"Hang on a second," Coop said. Houdini stopped. "He's … " Coop looked at me with his eyebrows raised. I knew exactly where he was going.

"Special," I said.

Coop said, "He's not crazy, but he is challenged. Don't know what his disability is exactly. He lives on his own back home. What else? He's not too great with strangers. Has some communication quirks."

Gabby chuckled, and her laugh was very reminiscent of JT's, low and appealing. She tapped a knuckle against her lip thoughtfully. "He reminds me of … what's the name of the lass who always works Royal? 'Dini, you remember, the little clown who does the balloon wallabies?"

April said, "Gab, how many times do we have to tell you it's *animals*, not *wallabies*?"

"Hey, they're all round and chubby." A good-natured smile tugged up the corners of Gabby's mouth.

Houdini strode to the doors, the heels of his tall black boots clicking sharply against the cement floor. "I'm on it." He let himself out and slid the door shut.

Baz asked, "What's the network?"

"It's the performer's network," Mary answered. "We—even the performers who aren't part of our cozy little association here—are comrades in arms, so to speak. We watch out for each other's backs."

I looked at my watch. Almost 7:15 p.m. It was later than I realized. Eddy still hadn't called. I was hungry, wired, tired, and rattled. If we could get some answers, and pretty freaking soon, I'd feel a lot better.

I opened my mouth to speak when my cell rang. Eddy's smiling face filled the screen.

Eddy said without preamble, "We're at the Jardin Royal. They're still figuring out a room. And that boy has still not shown up. The front desk at the other joint is keeping an eye out. I gave them this number in case he does."

"Okay. We'll see you soon."

I hung up and looked at April. "It's been great catching up, but we really need to get to the hotel."

Gabby asked, "Where are they staying?"

"The Jardin Royal," I said.

"Not far. Would you like another lift? I've time if you'd like."

Baz looked over at the ice cream cart. "I really don't—"

"You will if you don't want us breathing down your neck." Coop told Baz.

"Okay. Fine." Baz crossed his arms, trying and failing to appear belligerent. "I'd love to ride in your cart again, Gabby."

We bid our farewells after swapping cell phone numbers with the McNichis and Gabby. Gabby grabbed a towel and swabbed the bottom of the ice cream cart as dry as she could. I was glad she was good about thawing out her freezer on a regular basis, or we'd have been stuck in way more melted ice and frost than the few drops my pants and shirt soaked up. This time we much more carefully settled ourselves inside the freezer, and Mary handed us our bags.

The cart bounced and jounced along the street for ten or fifteen minutes, and finally came to a stop. The moped engine stilled, and then the latches clicked open. Gabby's face appeared as she lifted the top off the cooler and set it to the side.

"Here you are, mates. Hurry now."

As I shook my legs out to restore circulation, I realized Gabby had gone around to the rear of the hotel and parked in the alley next to a big green dumpster. The aroma coming from it suggested the hotel restaurant recently had fish on its menu.

"Okay, my new friends, I hope things work out. We'll let you know if Houdini finds your friend." She put the lid back on the cart.

"Thanks much for the help, Gabby." I said.

"You're welcome." She finished reattaching the cover, and gave me an impromptu hug, held just a little too long to be simply friendly. She whispered, her breath warm against my skin, "If you're ever in town, I'd love to get together." Her meaning was crystal clear. A shiver ran down my spine. Thankfully, she stepped away, tucking a stray wisp of hair behind her ear, her eyes hot on mine. The temptation was palpable.

I broke eye contact. *No, Shay. You're not that person anymore.* But I wasn't dead either.

The moment passed, and Baz and Coop obliviously echoed their thanks. After another lingering gaze, Gabby motored off.

I forced my attention to our current situation, letting any thoughts of Gabby slip away. We snuck in the back door of the

Jardin Royal, and Coop and Baz decided to hang at a table in the bar while I talked to the front desk.

I waited while an older couple checked in.

The clerk greeted me with a smile. I said, "Can you tell me Edwina Quartermaine's room?"

The front desk attendants all wore black and yellow uniforms, and it reminded me of worker bees buzzing about. After keying in Eddy's name, he drawled, "I can't give you that information."

I was beginning to feel like swatting him. "Can you call the room and let her know she has a visitor?" I tried to keep my voice even.

The attendant stared intently at a computer monitor hidden behind the ledge of the glossy teak counter. Finally he said, "I can ring you through."

Jeez.

He handed me the receiver.

No answer. It was becoming the story of my life.

I left another message. "Thanks." I handed the phone back and turned away from the desk. I headed through the turn-of-the-century lobby toward the bar. Suddenly, someone grabbed my arm and swung me around.

"Shay! You're a sight for these sore eyes."

My heart stilled, then began to pound wildly in my chest. "Eddy!" I threw my arms around her.

After a rib-crushing hug, Eddy released me. "I know I shouldn't be, but I'm glad you're here." She reached up and patted my cheek.

Her dark-brown eyes looked sunken, and her ever-ready smile was absent. Salt and pepper hair shaved close to her scalp framed the smooth cocoa-colored skin on her face.

She said, "We've been walking the streets. That boy is nowhere to be found. I think I plumb near wore Agnes out." If Eddy was on a mission, watch out. I could hardly keep up with her myself when she was going full-steam-ahead.

Then I noticed Agnes behind Eddy. Talk about opposites. She was thin and taller than I was, even with her slightly stooped shoulders. She was as pale as Eddy was dark. Eddy's extra bit of padding made her huggable, whereas an Agnes embrace felt as if I was squeezing a pliable beanpole.

Agnes said, "Eddy sure did wear me out. First finding that all-night card game and then dragging me through the nastiest corners of the French Quarter. We're lucky you didn't get us killed when you kept waking up the street people asking if they'd seen Rocky."

Eddy glared at her. "Did you have a better idea? No. If it's been up to you, we'd still be sitting at that poker table."

"I was on a streak—"

"Losing streak."

"Not until those last hands—"

"That's right. That's when I kicked your skinny butt."

"You didn't do any butt kicking, you old bat. That prissy man on your right took my last chip."

Eddy inhaled and was about to unleash another insult.

"LADIES!" I shouted. Agnes and Eddy were good pals, but picked at each other about anything and everything. It didn't really matter what the subject was, they could find something to yap about.

They glared at another a moment longer, broke eye contact.

I studied Agnes. "You look like you could use a breather." Dark circles ringed her watery blue eyes, and her face looked even more pinched than usual. Of course, one problem was that she imbibed a little too much vodka a little too often. She hadn't had an easy life, and I thought she deserved sainthood for taking Baz in after her niece—Baz's mom—skipped town with a door-to-door insurance salesman. That was after Baz's dad keeled over and expired at the racetrack one hot summer day, in the middle of betting away the family nest egg. The apple sure didn't fall far from the tree.

She waved a knobby-knuckled hand at me. "I really am concerned for Rocky. Don't you worry about me, I'm fine."

I said, "I know you are. Come on. Coop and Baz are in the bar."

We found Coop ogling a tanned young woman sitting two stools down from where he and Baz were perched. She had a pack of Newports sitting in front of her and was puffing away as she chatted with the bartender. I realized, after a second, that Coop was drooling over the cigarettes, not the girl.

Baz slumped dejectedly, one hand holding up his chin, and the other making repeated trips from a basket of popcorn to his mouth. He straightened up as soon as he caught sight of us and brightened perceptibly.

"Basil!" Agnes said. "What have you done now?"

Coop ripped his attention away from the pack of smokes and muttered under his breath, "Long fucking story."

Good thing Agnes had a hearing problem.

"Hey," Baz said as he slid off the stool. "Agnes. Wow, am I ever glad to see you." Watching Agnes embrace short little Baz was a sight. It looked like a she was hugging a rotund ten-year-old.

"And Nicholas. How are you, dear?" Agnes patted Coop's cheek.

"Doing fine. We need to have another dominoes rematch sometime soon. After we deal with Baz's problem." Dominoes was the latest Mad Knitters fad. While poker still held the number one spot as their non-knitting diversion of choice, they always liked to broaden their gaming horizons, as Eddy was fond of saying.

"Indeed we do, dear, indeed we do." Agnes fixed her eyes on Baz. "What's going on now, nephew?" She arched a thin, penciled-in eyebrow at him.

I spoke before Baz could answer. "Let's take this reunion to your hotel room." The last thing we needed was another surprise appearance of the despicable duo, especially before we'd completely briefed Agnes and Eddy on what was going down.

We exited the elevator in the middle of the second floor. The hallway was narrow but beautifully maintained. Eight rooms occupied each side, and six-paned windows let light in at each end. A red and black runner stretched the length of the hardwood floor. Antique wall sconces flickered next to each entry.

Agnes stopped in front of the third room from the end and unlocked the door with an old-fashioned key.

Two double beds and a table with three ladder-back chairs occupied half the space. The other half contained a sleeper sofa, a TV, and a small refrigerator. The carpet was a lush maroon pile and the walls were painted light sepia. An early-twentieth-century drawing of the French Quarter hung above the table.

Eddy and Agnes claimed two of the chairs while Baz took the third. Coop and I perched on the bed.

Agnes said, "Okay, Basil. What have you gotten yourself into this time?"

"Why does everyone think I'm always doing something wrong?" Baz grumbled.

I leaned back and propped myself up with my elbows. "It's like your calling card. Your state of being."

Baz sneered at me. "Oh you think you're all that—"

"Do not!"

"Do too. Ever since you got that prize for climbing rope the fastest in gym class in second grade—"

"At least I could do it. If I remember right, you couldn't make it off the ground."

"I have weak arms."

"Weak arms? I think your problem was you schmoozed one too many pieces of cake from the cooks."

"You're just jealous I got extra—"

"Children!" Eddy bellowed. "Shut up."

I snapped my mouth closed. Baz and I could be a little Eddy and Agnes-like at times.

In a quieter voice, Eddy said, "Basil, just tell us what's happened."

Baz took a deep breath. "Fine. Agnes, did you do something with that stuffed toy green snake I brought home the other day?"

"Oh," Agnes said. "Of course I did. I gave it to Rocky when he and Eddy came over to pick me up for the airport. He's been wearing it around his neck since we got here. Thinks it's quite something else. Why?"

"I need it back."

"For what? You grew out of stuffed animals in your twenties."

Stuffed animals in his twenties? What a great razzing point. I looked at Baz, waiting for him to answer, wondering how much he'd admit to his aunt.

"I, uh, borrowed it from a friend and they want it back."

"Basil, you know better than to lie to me." Agnes sighed sadly, and then asked in a resigned voice, "Who'd you steal it from?"

Before he could answer, my cell rang, jangling my already frayed nerves.

Expectant faces looked at me I pulled it off my hip and answered, "Hello?"

"Shay?" April McNichi's voice boomed through the speaker.

"Yeah, it's me. What's up?"

"Houdini found Rocky."

"Where?"

"Remember Houdini mentioning a girl who made balloon animals?"

"Yep."

"She goes by Tulip, and I think it's a match made in heaven. They are so similar it's freakish. Tulip's incorporated your boy in her act, and he's wowing tourists by reciting random facts and doing instantaneous mathematical calculations."

"Well, that sounds like our Rocky." My heart unclenched a little. Thank goodness he wasn't dead or hurt.

"Houdini is on the way to your hotel with him now. He should be there any time."

"I don't know how to thank you guys."

"Come see our act and give us a big tip."

"You can count on it." I disconnected.

I related the turn of events, and we all trooped down to the lobby to await Rocky's arrival. We settled into two Victorian sofas that faced each other and talked about New Orleans poker. In less than ten minutes, looking like a dark devil-angel, Houdini strode through the hotel entryway. Rocky followed him, the neon-green snake hanging around his shoulders. He was wearing his Twins jacket and blue aviator hat.

His face lit up like a kid at Christmas when he caught sight of us. "Nick Coop! Shay O'Hanlon!"

I heard Baz say, "He's got it!"

Rocky lurched toward Coop and nearly bowled him over. Then he launched himself at me. After I'd squeezed Rocky, I pushed him away and shook him gently. "Rocky, don't you ever leave without telling us where you're going. You really scared Eddy and Agnes."

Rocky looked over at Eddy with big eyes. His bottom lip started to quiver.

"Oh, young man, you come here." Eddy opened her arms and Rocky dove into them.

"I'm very sorry, Miss Eddy. I did not mean to scare you." His voice was tight and low.

Houdini said, "I'll leave you all to your reunion."

"Thanks, Houdini," I said.

He tipped an imaginary hat at me. "Anytime. *Adieu*," he rumbled, and then swooped out the door without another word.

I turned my attention back to the unfolding drama. "Shhh," Eddy was saying. "It's okay. Just let us know where you're going next time. Okay?"

Rocky nodded vigorously. Then he stood straight and the expression on his face melted into one of barely restrained glee. "I found a girlfriend!"

Eddy was the first one to recover from Rocky's announcement. "You did? What's her name?"

Rocky beamed. "Tulip. She makes twenty-six different balloon animals. She is very pretty and is four-feet-nine inches tall!"

Oh boy. I wondered if anyone had ever explained the birds and the bees to him. If not, I was going to volunteer Coop for that job.

Agnes rocked her way to her feet. "Let's go back up to the room so we can hear this story properly."

Upstairs, I took a minute to use the bathroom. It didn't appear the Baz's new pals had anything to do with Rocky, Eddy, or Agnes, after all. It was simply a coincidence that the women had been unavailable to return our calls. That was a huge load off my shoulders.

As I wiped my hands, I heard Baz shouting. I opened the bathroom door and stepped out into the middle of a tug of war between Baz and Rocky. Rocky's face was set in determination. "Agnes gave it to me." His hands were wrapped around the head of the snake, while Baz had a grip on the toy's tail.

"No!" Baz shouted. "I'll buy you another one. Just give me this one."

"No. You are a mean man. I don't like you!" Rocky yanked on the snake. Baz stumbled forward a half step and then set his feet again.

"Give me the goddamn thing."

Baz pulled hard, and Rocky pulled harder.

With an unmistakable rip, the snake split in half. Baz slammed into the door. Rocky sprawled backward across one of the beds. As amusing as the crashing humans were, they weren't the most riveting sight before me.

What rooted everyone to the floor in amazement were the crumpled bills and rolls of cash that spewed out of the snake.

For a frozen moment, no one said a word.

Baz picked himself off the floor and scooped up a bill. He sniffed it and looked at it from different angles. Then he proclaimed in an awed voice, "I'm rich."

Rocky, his eyes wide, whispered, "Doodlebug broke."

"Don't you worry, Rocky." Eddy patted him on the shoulder as she looked at the money scattered around the room with a scowl. "We'll find you another Doodlebug. Won't we, Basil?"

Baz scooted around on his knees, furiously grabbing the crumpled and rolled bills and stuffing them in his pocket. He paused, both hands full of greenbacks. "Oh sure. Not a problem. Not a problem at all."

"Basil," Agnes said sternly. "That is not your money. And why is it inside that ugly animal?"

"Don't know," Baz said, his pockets beginning to bulge.

A knock sounded on the door. I looked at Eddy. "Are you expecting anyone?"

She shook her head and stepped around Baz. Her hand was outstretched to open the door when a very bad feeling slammed me in the gut. I reached for her and yelled, "Wait!" just as she twisted the knob.

The door slammed inward with violent force, toppling Eddy backward into me. We went down in a tangle of limbs as three men with wicked-looking guns strode into the room.

FIVE

FROM ON THE FLOOR, Eddy and I stared at a hulk-like man who loomed over us, pistol pointed directly at my belly button.

"Everyone on the bed," barked one of the other two men. This guy had been with the frighteningly large man when they chased us at Jackson Square. Up close, the second man's hair was beyond pale, and his skin was so white it practically glowed. The guy's eyebrows blended right into his sharp features. I expected vampire fangs to pop out of his gums when he opened his mouth.

Heart in my throat, I peeled myself off Eddy and gave her a hand up. She squeezed my fingers once in reassurance, and we joined the rest of the cadre already huddled on the bed.

The third man, who I'd never seen before, was of Latin origin. He stood maybe five-eleven, with slicked back black hair and dark eyes. He was obviously in charge. He surveyed the room and said in a clear but heavily accented voice, "Hunk, pick up the money off the floor."

Hunk? Really? The large man kneeled stiffly to gather scattered bills.

"Donny," the Latino jerked his head toward the pseudo-vampire, "I think *el hombre gordo* has some *dólares* in his pockets. Can you help him give them back?" He picked up the two pieces of the snake.

Donny advanced on Baz, who shrieked, "I do not!" He was still on his knees, money in one hand and bills falling out of his pockets.

The man thrust the muzzle of his gleaming blue-black handgun right in Baz's face. With his other hand, he reached down and grabbed the edge of a hundred dollar bill peeping out of Baz's pants pockets.

"You don't, huh?" Donny's voice was higher than Minnie Mouse's. He poked Baz's cheek with the gun. "I think you better check those pockets again. You don't want Tomás here to get angry. They don't call him Tommy Tormenta for nothing."

Hands trembling, Baz started handing over his ill-gotten booty.

Holy crap. *Hunk*, *Donny*, and now *Tommy Tormenta*? Seriously? We were trapped in a B-rated comedy.

Rocky stared at the gun in Baz's face. "That is a very nice FN Five-seven semi-automatic pistol."

How on god's no-longer-green earth did Rocky do that?

Tomás's right eyebrow spiked and one corner of his mouth curled up. He said in a deadly tone of voice, "*Sí*, it is, and it would be a very good idea not to piss any of us off."

As Baz handed over the last bill, I looked at Agnes. She was almost as white as Donny, and sat primly on the edge of the bed, her hands folded in her lap. Coop's jaw muscle bulged every few seconds, but he wasn't chewing any gum. I tried to think of a way out of this, but with three armed men against two ladies-of-a-certain-age, one working-on-reforming pacifist, a certified idiot, a challenged man, and me … we were a little overwhelmed.

Tomás said, "Give me your cell phones. Then we go." He motioned toward the door with his gun, then leveled it at Baz's chest. "*Señor,* it would do you much good to hand it over now." He held out his other hand expectantly.

Baz, his eyes all squinty and mouth bunched up as if he were about to throw a tantrum, removed a phone from his pocket and slapped it in the palm of Tomás's hand. I half-wished Baz would go into a full-on meltdown. Maybe the distraction would give us a chance to do something.

Instead, Tomás turned his dark eyes on me. "Your turn, *señorita.*"

Hope fading fast, I narrowed my eyes and handed over my iPhone. Coop followed suit.

"And you two," Tomás addressed Eddy and Agnes. "If you have a phone, I suggest you give it to me right now."

"I hate those things," Eddy said, "and so does Agnes. Doncha, Aggie?" Eddy elbowed her, eliciting a grunt.

Agnes rubbed her side and nodded. "Wouldn't catch me dead with one." She looked Tomás in the eye. "And Rocky doesn't have one either."

Tomás nodded. He picked up the empty ice bin sitting on the top of the dresser and then walked into the bathroom. Water ran for a minute, then Tomás reappeared holding the dripping bucket.

"Say *adios.*"

I nearly cried as my spendy gadget went for a swim along with the others. He set the bucket back on the dresser. That was one sure way of taking care of our communication issues.

Tomás dusted his hand and said, "Let's go, then. Nice and slow. Donny, you stay with me. Hunk, you lead. And," he stared us down through hard, cold eyes, "I would not try to escape. Situations like this often turn deadly. Let's go."

"Wait," Agnes said. "I need my purse."

Donny laughed. "Where you're going, old lady, you don't need a purse."

Luckily, neither Agnes nor Eddy decided to comment on that. I tried to quell the fear and impotent rage battling for emotional supremacy inside me. All I could do was concentrate on breathing.

The armed trio guided us down the emergency stairs that let out to the alley where Gabby had dropped us off. Darkness had descended, and the air was now chilly. A black panel extended-van was parked next to the still-aromatic dumpster.

"Tie them up," Tomás said.

Paleface Donny rolled the side door open. Unlike a regular van with bench seats facing forward, one bench extended back from behind the driver's seat to the rear. A shorter bench faced it on the other side next to a sliding door. The interior looked like something a SWAT team might use. A long coil of clothesline lay on the floor of the van.

I scanned the alley for a means of escape but could come up with nothing that wouldn't endanger everyone else. Thank goodness Eddy was keeping her lip zipped at least. She had a propensity for belligerence. Just like someone else I knew. I was riding the razor edge of desperate, insane action or rational inaction, but somehow I was managing to hold it all together.

Hunk and Tomás kept their guns trained on us as Donny cut the cord into pieces with a pocketknife. Then he proceeded to tie our arms behind our backs and deposited us in a row on the bench facing the door.

As Donny slammed me onto the seat, Coop met my eyes. They were broadcasting a mix of panic and determination, searching for a way out as diligently as I was. If someone—anyone—should happen down the alley, I was more than ready to kick up a ruckus.

Once we were lined up like slaughterhouse rats, Hunk and Donny settled on the bench facing us. They both kept the business ends of their weapons pointed our way.

Tomás rolled the door shut, climbed into the driver's seat, and fired up the engine. He slowly drove down the alley and made a turn. The only windows in the van were in the front, making it next to impossible to see where we were going.

We made a couple lefts, and then a right. I tried to memorize the turns, but lost track after the fifth one. I'd make a sucky Girl Scout.

For a long while, no one said anything. The sound of the tires humming on the asphalt road echoed through the interior. I periodically attempted to wriggle out of the rope to no avail. Donny knew his knots.

Baz said, "I think I'm getting carsick."

Oh my god, please don't let Baz barf.

Hunk said, "I'll shoot you if you throw up. So don't throw up."

That shut Baz up.

After what felt like an hour but was probably closer to less than half that time, Tomás slowed the van, made a couple more sharp turns, and rolled to a stop. By leaning slightly forward and concentrating on my peripheral vision, I could see through the front windshield without catching the attention of our captors, who seemed to have relaxed a bit. The headlights lit up a big garage door attached to a brick building. He reached up to the visor above his head and pressed a remote. A moment later, the door rolled slowly up. As it shuddered and creaked its way to the top, the interior was lit up by the van's headlights. Directly in front of us was row upon row of stacked, rectangular boxes.

Once the door opened enough for the van to squeeze through, Tomás pulled in and pushed the remote again. The door slowly descended behind us.

Donny pulled up the lock on the door, slid it open, and he and Hunk scrambled out.

"Your turn," he ordered, waving the way with his gun.

One by one, we emerged from the van and huddled together in the dim light cast by two fluorescent light units suspended high in the air.

Rocky said, "I do not like it in here. I want to go home now. Thank you."

I suspected we all agreed with that sentiment.

Eddy said calmly, "Rocky, we'll get home soon, and when we do, we're going to go to Hands On Toys and get you a new snake."

The expression on Rocky's face turned instantly from fear of the unknown into unrestrained joy. "Oh, I do love to go to the Hands On Toy Company and Game Room. Thank you, Miss Eddy! Thank you!"

Hunk poked Rocky in the back with his gun. "Shut up, you retard. Get moving."

Rocky's face dropped and the look of fear was back loud and clear. I opened my mouth to let Hunk have it, but Eddy beat me to it.

"Don't you call him a retard, you big oaf," she growled.

Her comment was ignored as Hunk and Donny, on Tomás's order, herded us into a small office lit with a single flickering florescent light. The eight-by-ten room held only two chairs, one desk, and a well-used green filing cabinet.

Hunk said, "In," and waved at us with his gun.

"What do you mean, 'in,' like we're just a bunch of cattle?" Eddy's composure wasn't holding up as well as I thought. "Hunk, where are your manners, young man? You can't treat women of substance such as myself and my dear friend Agnes like this. Or the kids, either, for that matter. You're scaring us all, you big bully!"

She wound up and kicked the astonished giant square in the shin with the one of the pointy-toed cowboy boots she was wearing.

A terrifying howl of pain echoed through the building. Hunk hopped around on one foot, his injured shin cupped in one hand, the gun waving dangerously in the other. Donny watched this turn of events in amazement, rooted to the floor outside the door.

The sound of running feet approached the doorway, and Tomás stuck his head inside. "¡Mierda! What is going on in here?"

Hunk leaned against a wall, a hand on his leg, and the gun in his other hand trained on Eddy. His eyes narrowed in a mix of anger and pain. "Please," he begged, "let me shoot her. One bullet. That's all I need. One little bullet."

Tomás said, "No, that's not part of our orders. If you cannot follow orders, Hunk, you will be needing one of those caskets out there—which won't be long enough, so I will have to break your legs to make you fit."

Tommy Tormenta indeed.

"Caskets?" Baz said. "We're in a casket factory?"

"You're gonna each get your own real soon," Donny said in his amazingly falsetto voice. So that's what the stacked rectangular boxes were. Excellent. Just where I'd always wanted to bite the figurative, and very possibly literal, bullet.

"Donny," Tomás said. "Cut the ropes off them. Roy will be here soon, and he doesn't want them marked up."

Hunk limped out, glaring at Eddy, who glared right back.

Donny quickly sliced the clothesline off our wrists, then exited and shut the door with a solid thunk.

"Why'd they cut us loose?" Coop asked as he massaged his wrists.

I shrugged. "Tomás said he didn't want us 'marked up.' Maybe they don't want to hurt us after all."

Yeah, right.

There was some bumping and banging outside, and then someone snapped what sounded like a padlock shut.

Eddy shook out her hands. "Once I thought I was going to expire in the ladies room. Now we're in a building plumb full of dead people's beds and we're still alive. Let's not be giving up any hope, you hear? When something like this happens on *Law and Order*, the cops find the good people, save them, and kick bad-guy behind." She was silent a moment. "Well, most of the time."

"Yeah," I said, "But that's when the cops know they're supposed to be finding the poor, imprisoned victims. The police don't know to look for us." I glanced at Rocky. "I guess they could be looking for you."

Rocky said, "There were 174 murders in New Orleans in the last calendar year. I am hungry, and I want to go home now."

SIX

I SAID, "WHAT ARE we going to do? Baz, this mess is your entire fault. You are a one-hundred-percent selfish, brainless, pathetic fool."

"My fault? I'm not the one who—"

"You're the snake thief, dickhead," Coop said.

Eddy tapped Coop gently on the forehead. "Language, young man. But he's right, Basil." She settled into a chair with a sigh.

Agnes said, "Nephew, why do you think all that money was sewn inside the snake?"

He shrugged. "I dunno."

Coop levered himself backward onto the desktop and sat with his legs dangling over the side. "Well I don't think the snake swallowed it, so it being in there wasn't an accident."

Rocky perched next to Coop and mimicked Coop's swinging legs. Baz stood looking dazed in the middle of the floor.

The panic, fear, and anger I'd shoved aside since the goons had stormed the hotel room swirled up from my gut to my brain, filling my head with the roar of desperation. I tried to wrestle the welling insanity back into its cage and, with some effort, succeeded.

I wandered over to the filing cabinet and tugged on the top drawer. It rolled open easily. Manila file folders full of invoices for companies that made coffins and various coffin parts were arranged in alphabetical order. I slid out one of the bills: coffin lids ordered from Mexico. The top of the purchase order had the name of the casket company, METAIRIE COFFIN AND CASKET, INC., emblazoned across the top of the page in blood red. How appropriate. At least I'd know where I died if it came to that.

I flipped through a few more files and noted most of the supplies came from Mexico. That figured. I gave up, flipped an empty garbage can upside down, and sat.

Agnes asked, "Basil, where did you get the snake?"

He shrugged. "I turned in all the paperwork, and the paperwork had the addresses. All I remember is that it was somewhere in Minnetonka."

"Well, that narrows it down," Coop said with not a little sarcasm.

We lapsed into an uneasy silence.

———

Two hours later, the lock on the outside of the door rattled. We all watched the door swing open.

Tomás walked in, followed by a six-foot-tall, barrel-chested man in a neat, gray pinstriped suit. He rocked back on the heels of his tasseled loafers and folded his arms across his chest. A thin moustache clung to his upper lip. He wore his iron-gray hair buzzed in a crew cut. A police shield hung from his black leather belt, and the straps of a shoulder holster peeked out of the lapels of his suit jacket.

For a brief moment, I thought help had arrived. Until he opened his mouth. "So these are our troublemakers. Rounded up and ready for the slaughter."

Slaughter? Who said anything about slaughter? Jeez, even if they planned to off us, he could have used a less descriptive word.

Tomás laughed darkly. "Indeed. It was a challenge coordinating things between here and Minnesota, but it all worked out in our favor."

Agnes shook her finger at the man standing next to Tomás. "You're the nice police officer we talked to about Rocky, aren't you?"

The man grinned coldly. "Lieutenant Pomerantz, New Orleans PD, at your service."

Agnes glared at him. "You're not nice. I'm going to tell your boss about you."

The sharp bark of a laugh was the lieutenant's only response.

His name was so familiar. Where had I heard it before? Then the memory crystallized. The New Orleans detective I spoke with from the parking lot of Perkins. He mentioned he'd talk to a Lieutenant Pomerantz about my report. And here was the bastard in the flesh.

My tone was accusing. "You're with Missing Persons."

He locked his eyes on mine. They were a sickly mesmerizing ice-cold gray. "Quick, aren't you? I run the unit. And, oh my, it does come in handy when I need to make someone disappear. Terrible pity the skiff you Yanks were in overturned in alligator-infested bayou waters. Silly tourists. Such a shame. Maybe we can fish out a leg or an arm for a proper burial."

For a moment, all the air whooshed out of the room, and the only thing I heard was the buzzing from the fluorescent lights overhead. Coop said hoarsely, "What do we know that's bad enough for you to kill us?"

"If you could only connect the dots," Pomerantz chuckled. "I'm sorry to say it's late, and I have somewhere I need to be. *Au revoir.*" He spun around and swooped out of the room. Tomás trailed him, and the lock clicked shut again.

"Holy shit," I said. "We've got to get out of here."

Coop levered himself off the desk as he looked upward. "Yes, we do."

I followed his gaze. White tiles hung suspended about ten feet over our heads. The room had a drop ceiling, unlike the exposed beams and girders that made up the skeleton of the gymnasium-sized warehouse.

Eddy stood. "Boost me up."

I'd settled back on my garbage can, and at Eddy's words, bounced up like a super ball. "Don't even think about it, Edwina Quartermaine."

Before I could argue further, the door opened. Hunk walked in, the gun in his hand. "Time for a little boat ride."

When none of us moved, he grabbed the person closest to him by the hair. The hair in his fist was attached to my head. I yowled. The back of my head crashed against his sternum. He wrapped a boulder-sized forearm around my neck and pressed the gun to my temple. "I said move!"

"Hey!" Rocky shouted. "Don't do that to my friend Shay O'Hanlon!" Before anyone could react, he rushed Hunk.

Coop caught Rocky around the middle right before he crashed into us. The barrel of the pistol dug deep into my skin. I tried not to hyperventilate.

"Easy, Rocky." Coop grunted as he held the squirming man in a bear hug.

"Let me go! Let me down, Nick Coop!"

I could feel Hunk's chest expand and contract rapidly against my back, his breath hot on my ear. "You keep that crazy munchkin away from me, or I'll pop her now."

Coop hauled Rocky from the room, giving us the widest berth he could. Agnes, Baz, and Eddy followed him out.

Hunk loosened his hold on my neck. He clamped a huge hand on my shoulder and hissed in my ear, "You try anything, and I'll cap your ass so fast you won't know what hit you." Then he shoved me out of the office.

The van was where they'd parked it, except now there was a long, flattish boat lashed to its top.

Donny's little-girl voice floated from the other side of the vehicle. "I've got it tied down, Hunk."

Tomás said, "Donny, come zip-tie their hands. Make them just tight enough so they can't get out but not enough to cut the skin. I'll see you two after you've taken care of this little problem." He disappeared around the van.

Donny wasted no time securing us once again. I cringed as he roughly yanked Agnes and Eddy's arms back. I swear I've never felt as powerless as I did at that moment, watching Eddy being manhandled like that.

Hunk gave me a shove and growled, "Get in."

We returned to our previous positions in the van, except this time Donny climbed into the driver's seat while Hunk remained in back with the gun on us.

Donny pressed the garage door remote. The pulleys creaked and groaned as the door rose. Hunk leaned against the van wall, keeping his gun pointed in our general vicinity.

My shoulders pressed against the side of the van. I arched my back, trying to keep pressure off my wrists. Coop was on one side of me while Baz sat on the other. Eddy and Agnes were beyond him, with Rocky tucked between them.

Hunk slouched down and stretched his long legs out, his weapon steady as a rock.

We needed a Hail Mary maneuver ASAP or we were going to wind up as fish gumbo.

SEVEN

DONNY HAD TO BE the slowest driver on the face of the Earth. Or time was moving at less than a snail's pace. I figured it had to be closing in on midnight by now.

Hunk said, "Donny, come on, man. This is boring."

"I'm going as fast as I can. Settle down."

Hunk let out a pained sigh. He glared at us for a moment then pulled a cell phone from his pocket with his free hand and turned it on. Every so often, he rested the phone on his knee and surveyed his hostages. It looked like he was in the middle of a hot game of solitaire. I was surprised he felt comfortable enough to mess with it. Apparently, he didn't think our threat level was high enough to be concerned about. Jerk.

Each time he got caught up in the game, the business end of the gun in his beefy hand dropped ever so slightly. Then a bump in the road would jostle him back into awareness, and up the weapon would come. This process repeated itself a number of times.

I closed my eyes as ideas churned through my brain. There had to be a way to use his preoccupation against him. If I slammed my foot down on one of Hunk's knees in the stretched out position they were in, maybe it'd snap in half, or at the very least hyperextend. That would hurt like hell.

The next time the muzzle tilted down, I nudged Coop. He slowly leaned toward me, and I whispered in his ear, "Tackle him." Beyond that I had no idea what we were going to do, but we had to do something.

Coop nodded almost imperceptibly and his body tensed. I bounced my knee against his thigh. One, two, and on the third whack, he exploded from his seat like a rocket from a bottle. With a roar, Coop slammed into Hunk, who grunted in surprise. I whooped and tried to balance without using my arms and stomped as hard as I could on Hunk's knee. My foot grazed the top and came harmlessly down beside his leg.

The van careened from side to side as Donny twisted in the driver's seat to see what was going on.

Incoherent shouts echoed through the interior. I lost my balance and fell headfirst into Coop's bony butt. My dead weight hit Hunk's legs. Violently shooting stars filled my vision. There was a split-second resistance, and then one of Hunk's knees gave out.

An inhuman scream filled the space.

My right elbow smashed into something hard. I added my own howl of pain to the din.

Multiple muzzle-flashes of gunfire lit the dark interior of the van, and the noise was deafening. Coop still flailed against Hunk, trying to pin the man to the wall of the van. Not an easy task without arms.

The van swerved and tipped precariously sideways. Then the world reversed in an instant. My head ricocheted off something, and pain exploded behind my eyes. This time I bypassed the stars altogether as blackness swallowed me whole.

———

I slowly became aware of Eddy's terrified face above me, barely discernible in the darkness. Suddenly I fell into a time warp and I was seven years old again, screaming in pain as Eddy dragged me from the twisted wreckage of my mother's car. Blood from a gaping head wound streamed down her face and dripped on my cheek. I sucked in a huge breath and yelled, "MOM!" at the top of my lungs—and then someone was roughly shaking me.

"Shay. SHAY! Calm down, girl. You're all right. Everyone's okay." Eddy's voice seeped into my awareness.

I thrashed even as cognition returned. I wasn't seven. I wasn't in the wreckage of our broadsided tan Ford Falcon. My mom's dead body wasn't sprawled beside me and Eddy's son, Neil, wasn't lying mangled in the back seat.

Hysteria retreated, and I gasped for air. I realized Eddy straddled me and felt her hands on my shoulders.

"I'm—" I struggled to sit up, but she was in the way. "Okay."

She climbed off but remained kneeling in the gravel next to my stretched-out form.

"Oh." My stomach nearly rebelled and my head swum. I sucked in a couple of desperate breaths and forced them out, trying to calm the queasiness.

The bright moonlight hurt my eyes. I squinted and looked slowly around. The van was upside-down in a low ditch. I was near the edge of the road about ten feet away. The scent of burned rubber and spilled automotive fluids filled the air.

I passed a hand over my forehead and my fingers came away sticky. The bony ridge above my right eye hurt like hell.

Then I realized my arms were no longer bound behind me. "What? How?"

"That Agnes is a 108-year-old Gumby. She managed bend herself into a pretzel, get her hands in front of her, and pull out a fingernail clipper that was in her pocket. Didn't take long to cut everyone loose after that," Eddy said as she rubbed my back.

As I blissfully overindulged in the simple process of breathing, my brain and stomach slowed their spinning. Coop and Baz came scrambling around the far side of the upturned van, followed by Agnes and Rocky, all of whom appeared to have survived the crash in one piece.

Coop skidded to a stop at my feet. "Is she okay?" he asked in a tight voice.

Eddy said, "Ask her your own self."

"I'm right here, and I'm fine." I felt something trickle down my cheek.

"Hey," Baz said. "You're bleeding."

Rocky crouched down on my other side. "Here, Shay. You must put pressure on a wound for it to stop bleeding. If it doesn't stop after twenty minutes of firm, direct pressure, we must seek medical attention." He whipped off his battered hat and slapped it to my forehead.

If I didn't die from my head wound, the germs on Rocky's beloved hat were probably going to do me in. But I didn't have the heart to make him take it away.

"Where're Hunk and Donny?" I asked, trying to peer around one of the earflaps that blocked my line of sight.

Agnes said, "We pulled them out of the van and dragged them over there." She pointed in the general direction of the upside-down vehicle. "Then we tied them to the tree."

"How did you manage that?"

Baz startled me by chortling. "Between bullets, broken glass, and—"

"My fist." Coop's voice held a note of wonder as he flexed his hand and winced.

"And Coop's fist," Baz agreed. "We didn't have any problem."

"How long have I been out?"

Eddy looked at her wristwatch. "Ten minutes, maybe."

Holy crap. I hope I didn't have brain damage. I tried to place events in order, but my mind wasn't cooperating. "What exactly happened?"

Rocky said, "You and Nick Coop were like an action movie!" He wriggled excitedly. "Nick Coop jumped on Hunk. You …" He trailed off with a frown. "I am not sure what you did. But then there were explosions." He mimicked the gunshots. "And the van went this way," he leaned to the right, "and that way," he leaned to the left. "Then you tipped over and Hunk screamed. Everything was upside down. It was amazing!" He nodded. "That was almost as fun as riding the Wild Thing roller coaster at Valley Fair. It is 207 feet tall and reaches a top speed of 74 miles per hour. It is also green, like my Doodlebug."

"Yeah," Coop said. "I'm not sure 'amazing' covers it. I can't believe no one got seriously hurt. I'm sure we'll feel it tomorrow though. Anyway, when you took Hunk's knee out, I don't know if he meant to pull the trigger, but he blasted a hole in the wind-shield, a hole in the passenger seat, and nicked Donny."

My eyebrows lifted.

Rocky bounced on his knees next to me. "A bullet went right through the top of his ear!"

"Yeouch." I cringed.

I got my feet under me and stood, not-so-accidentally dislodging Rocky's hat from my forehead. "Okay, now what?" I asked as I dusted my hands off. A wave of dizziness spread through me. Through a nauseated haze, I heard Eddy say, "I think we should start walking the way we came." She pointed down the dark road. "If any cars come, we can flag them down."

"Wait a minute," Agnes said. "We might want to see if we think the car is being driven by someone nice."

"Wise," Coop said.

That's how, forty-five minutes later, we wound up in the back of a pickup truck full of stinky sheep, driven by a farmer kind enough to detour into New Orleans proper on his way to an early morning livestock auction in Baton Rouge.

EIGHT

We arrived at the Jardin Royal well after three in the morning. On the way to the hotel, we all agreed it would be suicide to stay in the room from which Hunk and company had hauled us.

Eau de sheep followed us through the entrance. The front desk guy struggled not to wrinkle his nose at the stench and was all too happy to get us out of his lobby. The hotel had one suite left that slept six, and Agnes paid cash for it, slipped the clerk a fifty, and gave a fake name. The man hastily handed Agnes a key and directed us to the third floor.

On the way up, we made a pit stop in the original room and cleared it out. Thankfully, we were able to retrieve Eddy, Agnes, and Rocky's luggage and the bags Coop and I brought along as well as Baz's, so we could all change into something a little less aromatic.

The bucket with the cell phones had disappeared, though. I couldn't even take my waterlogged iPhone in for repairs.

After some heated discussion, we decided not to bring our incident to the attention of the local police. Who knew who was on the take and who resided in whose pockets? As soon as we were functioning in the morning, I was going to call and make airline reservations to get us out of the Big Easy.

I showered, and Eddy cleaned out the cut on my eyebrow and proclaimed it "just a scratch, quit your yelpin'."

Once we'd all settled down to sleep, the silence was punctuated by Baz's steady snore. I tossed one way, and then another, thankful I was alone on a rollaway. My brain kept replaying scenes from that fatal accident so many years ago that claimed the lives of Eddy's only boy and my mother. Every time I was about to drop off, a flashback flickered in front of my closed eyelids. Thankfully, the darkness and exhaustion finally won out, and I dropped into unconsciousness.

The eight a.m. wakeup call from the front desk came entirely too soon. I rolled out of bed and hit the bathroom before anyone else had a chance to move. I showered again, hoping to rid myself of the last vestiges of ewe. By 8:18 I was out of the bathroom and on the in-room phone with April McNichi, who, after being appropriately dismayed at our latest brush with trouble, tried like a madwoman to arrange return tickets for everyone and get us all on the same flight out. I assured her we'd pay her back as soon as we were able. Our luck seemed to be rolling with the punches, and April managed to get us six seats on an evening flight back to Minneapolis. We gratefully spent a few more hours sleeping before we had to head to the airport again.

It dawned on me all the contact information I had for JT was lost with my cell. Thank goodness I'd jotted her numbers down at home. The woman was probably fit to be cuffed because she hadn't heard from me for two days. Not much I could do at this point, I unhappily decided. Besides, how would I explain New Orleans, the kidnapping, the coffin factory, the car-wreck, and the rescue via sheep-truck?

———

At 7:45 that evening, we landed safely on the tarmac at MSP.

A half-hour later, after a bathroom break and some over-priced snacks, we headed out into the parking ramp and crammed into my truck. Agnes called shotgun, leaving Rocky and Eddy squashed like sardines in the back. Baz and Coop crawled into the truck bed along with all of our luggage. Eddy slid the small rear window open for them.

"You know they're going to keep coming after us," I said. "We escaped becoming alligator chow once, but who knows what'll happen if they get their hooks into us again."

"You're right," Eddy said. "Maybe we should talk to the boys in blue here in Minneapolis."

Silence filled the truck.

Then Agnes said, "We sure are in a pickle. If whoever is behind this had at least some of the New Orleans police department on their payroll, don't you think there are going to be some police officers on it here, too? After all, Hunk and Donny said they were up here in Minneapolis before they were in New Orleans."

"True." Coop's face was framed by the open window. "Cops are corrupt pigs."

"Hey." I twisted around in my seat to shoot a look at Coop. "JT's not a pig, and she's not corrupt."

He held up a hand. "She's the exception."

"What about Doyle?" I asked. Doyle Malloy worked MPD homicide, and we'd grown up in the same neighborhood together. I'd call him, but I knew he was up north right now working some big case.

Coop mumbled, "Doyle's a dumbass dork."

"Nicholas Cooper," Eddy said. "I'm going to rinse your mouth out with soap, young man."

"That I'd pay to see," Baz said as he nudged Coop out of the way, his face filling the rear window.

"Sorry, Eddy," Coop said, shoving Baz to the side and reclaiming the opening. "But it's true."

Doyle was Doyle, and he took some getting used to. Maybe it would be best to feel things out a bit more before we approached him.

This was an appropriate time for a change of subject. "Agnes, we could drop you off up at our cabin until this mess gets straightened out if you'd like."

"Are you kidding me? This is the most excitement I've had since Eddy hauled the Knitters to Canterbury and one of them jockeys lost his race and got shot at by the owner. No way are you guys leaving me behind. Besides, someone needs to keep an eye on that nephew of mine."

"No one shot at anyone, Agnes," Eddy said. "That was the starter's gun."

"There is no starter's gun. It's a bell."

"Bell, my wrinkled behind!"

"It was!"

Oh my. "Enough, both of you." I gave them each a look in the dim light.

"What do you mean, someone needs to keep an eye on me?" Baz grumbled.

"If someone had kept an eye on you," Eddy said, "We wouldn't be in this mess. And stop pushing at each other back there. One of you are gonna fall right out onto your head."

"Okay," I said. "We need to figure out just who's after us."

Eddy said, "We have to find out who Basil took the snake from. Start at the start. That's how they do it on *Criminal Minds*." She clapped her hands once and rubbed them together. It was something she did when she was about to immerse herself in trouble of some kind.

Coop said, "Baz, we need the location of the house you stole the snake from, and hopefully the owner's name."

"That information will be at the office."

"Then we have to pull a Bingo Barge on Basil's office," Eddy said.

"No way." I tried to look back at Eddy, but she was hidden in shadow behind my seat. Last fall, among other illegal acts, we'd broken into a floating bingo barge on the Mississippi trying to prove Coop innocent of murdering his boss. I wasn't itching to repeat the experience.

"We go on in and check things out." She was only warming up. "We need to do some investigating, here," Eddy said. "Got to get the address and then check out the joint. If we do a little poking around that house, we might find some clues as to why this is all happening. Where do you work again, Basil?"

"At Ducky Ducts in Crystal."

I have no idea how Baz kept a straight face telling people the name of his employer.

"Where in Crystal?" Eddy asked.

"Small office in the back of a strip mall between West Broadway and Becker Park."

Coop said. "I can't believe we're thinking about breaking into another business. I have enough problems with the law without sh—, uh, stuff like this." He sighed heavily. "How late are people in the office?"

Baz said, "Usually the receptionist, the accountant slash secretary, and Rich, the boss, hang around until five. Sometimes one of the other ducklings are there picking up jobs or dropping off paperwork 'til after seven. But it's past eight-thirty. Everyone should have cleared out by now."

"Wait a minute," I said. "Ducklings?"

"That's what Rich calls us duct service people." Baz's voice held a note of contempt.

Coop said, "Man, how low do you have to go to actually consider employment with these people? Ducklings?"

I caught Baz's shoulder lift in the rearview mirror. He said defensively, "It's a paycheck."

Agnes said. "It's high time we run the show instead of the show running us." She waved her hand. "Let's go."

I backed out of the parking space and began the long spiral to the bottom of the ramp. We were off to Ducky Ducts, on a date with destiny. Hopefully it wouldn't be the kind of destiny that involved a jail cell. Or winding up horizontal in one of those Louisiana coffins.

NINE

I PULLED INTO THE Ducky parking lot shortly after nine.

Eight bright yellow vans sat patiently waiting for morning and their "ducklings" to come and take them to the next appointment. Emblazoned across the back doors of the vans was the Ducky Ducts clever tag line: WE CLEAN YOUR PIPES SLICK AS A WHISTLE, GUARANTEED.

How embarrassing to drive around with that on your figurative ass.

"All of the vans are in," Baz said. "Rich's car and the secretary's minivan are gone."

"Whoever's coming, come on." I opened the door.

Agnes thrust a wizened, veiny hand at me. "Give me the keys. I'll be the get-away driver. Rocky's my second-in-command." As I dropped the keys in the palm of Agnes's hand, I wondered if her driving skills were any better than Eddy's.

Rocky hopped into the passenger seat, beaming as if the gift of a lifetime had dropped from the sky. "I will be a very good second-in-command, Agnes. There are lots of famous second-in-commands like Spock and Clone Captain Rex."

"Right," Agnes said, clearly having no idea who they were.

The cool night air slid down the back of my neck. I shivered, glad to have my sweatshirt on, even it if the front was still decorated with powdered sugar.

"I'll hang out at the door," Eddy announced as I gave her a hand out of the back of the truck. "Let you know if anyone we don't want to see shows up."

"How are you going to do that?" Agnes asked.

"I'll scream."

I smiled wryly to myself.

"Baz," Coop said as he looked at the entrance door, "Is there any problem with you going into the office after hours?"

"No, I don't think so. We come in late when we're stuck at a job longer than we were supposed to be to drop paperwork off. It's never been a problem."

Last fall's leaves and rocks from crumbling asphalt crunched under our feet as Coop, Eddy, and I trailed after Baz toward the office door. Baz stuck his hand in his front pocket and rooted around in there long enough I wondered if he was playing with himself. Then he pulled out a ring of keys and opened the door.

Coop and I followed him inside while Eddy planted herself in the doorway. Baz flipped on the lights. The office was windowless and small. It appeared tidy. An oak-veneer-covered reception desk with a flat screen monitor and keyboard was the focal point at the front of the twenty-by-forty-foot space. Three smaller IKEA-style desks sat behind reception. Stainless steel shelving units five levels high filled an entire wall from floor to ceiling. They were loaded with cardboard storage boxes.

Another room was connected to the office by an arched doorway. From the light spilling out, it appeared to hold whatever supplies were needed to accomplish the cleaning of one's pipes slick as a whistle, guaranteed.

The sound of an automated air freshener doing its thing made me jump. Then a pleasant scent settled over us—a cross between cut grass and sunshine. "What is that, Baz?" I asked.

"Midsummer Morning. The boss wanted a smell that associated the company with being clean and fresh. He thinks it keeps customers coming back."

If the name of the place wasn't Ducky Ducts, the scent alone might indeed sway me to use their services. Interesting psychology.

Baz walked over to the middle desk. The top was covered by three large file trays, each with a label: Jobs To Do, Jobs Completed, And Jobs To Redo. The to-do bin was a couple inches high. The completed files spilled out of their slot and towered precariously eight inches over the top edges. Someone needed to get to work on their filing. I was impressed to see the re-do file tray was empty. Maybe Ducky Ducts actually did a decent job the first time out.

Baz grabbed a mound of paperwork and started sifting through it. If either Coop or I knew what we were looking for, we'd have helped. As it stood, we were forced to twiddle our fingers while Baz discarded one file after another beside the wire container.

I gazed idly around the office. A huge yellow rubber duck with a bright orange bill was painted on the wall behind the desks. "Come on Baz, hurry up."

"I am hurrying," Baz said, his head bent as he shuffled through the papers. He set the last one down and picked up another handful.

"Here it is!" Baz opened the top of a manila folder. Coop and I crowded around him as he ran a stubby finger along the page. The finger paused below an address in Minnetonka. The name above the address sent my mind reeling. Coop actually backed up a step and said, "Oh, crap."

Baz looked from one to the other of us, confusion evident on his chubby face. "What?"

I looked at him, now positive he was from a galaxy far, far, away. "Don't even tell me you haven't heard of Fletcher Sharpe."

He shrugged. "I've heard of him. He has a lot of dough, right?"

"Jeez, Baz," Coop ran a long-fingered hand across his stubbly jaw. "You've heard of the Hands On Toy Company, right?"

"No shit," Baz said. "So what?"

"He owns it," I said. "He was voted Most Philanthropic Minnesotan for the second consecutive year by that magazine…" I snapped my fingers as I tried to pull the name from my brain. "What's it called?"

"The *Twin Citian*, I think." Coop said. "The guy's donated millions to local charities. He's the Twin Cities answer to T. Boone Pickens."

Hopefully Fletcher Sharpe wasn't Minnesota's answer to Bernie Madoff. I sank into a chair next to the desk. "Any kid worth his salt would be absolutely crushed if Sharpe is doing something he shouldn't. So would half the business community."

Coop said, "I'd really hate to see another well-known and mostly well-liked local businessman topple like Denny Hecker and Tom Petters. Sharpe's always been an awesome guy."

Both Denny Hecker and Tom Petters were at one time pillars of sorts in the Twin Cities area. Hecker owned at least twenty-six car dealerships, a restaurant, and a car-rental agency. He went on to defraud GM and others, winding up with a decade-long prison sentence. Petters bought out Fingerhut, purchased Polaroid, and added Sun Country Airlines to his collection before going belly-up on fraud charges and pulling a multi-million dollar Ponzi scheme. He was cooling his jets in federal prison for at least fifty years.

I had no doubt the creation of Fletcher Sharpe's Dungeon Gameroom had something to do with Coop's glowing assessment. Regardless, we needed to figure out why a cornerstone of the community had in his possession a toy snake stuffed with hundred dollar bills. It was a shame Baz hadn't managed to hang onto any of the moolah. If we could unravel whatever was going on, we could probably make Tommy Tormenta and company stop trying to lessen our longevity.

"Baz," I said, "can I see?"

He handed me the duct cleaning work order for Fletcher Sharpe. I jotted the address down on a slip of paper and returned it.

"I miss my phone," I said. "I could pop that address in there, and wham—the directions would appear." I handed the work order back to Baz. "What are we going to do about our trashed cell phones?"

Baz placed the paperwork back on the pile and returned the stack to the bin. "What can we do? They're goners."

Eddy called from the doorway, "Hurry up, kids. Time's a-ticking."

"Come on, let's go." I said. "I have an idea."

TEN

SINCE COOP HAD BECOME Super Computer Man, he found he needed the Internet in many places that didn't have WiFi. He'd purchased an AirCard, which granted him Internet access just about anywhere.

I drove around for the next ten minutes trying to find an intact payphone. Guess that's what you get with the advent of cellular communication.

We hit the jackpot at the third gas station we checked. After a momentary flush of panic in trying to recall the phone number, I punched the correct buttons and placed a call to Kate at the Hole. I gave her the rundown of what had happened (minus the near-death experience) and asked her if she'd mind running to Coop's apartment for his laptop. She agreed, and I told her where my spare key for Coop's place was. I sensed she was about to turn blue and tip over from curiosity, but she wisely held back her interrogational tendencies. Fortunately, one of our employees was working, and he agreed to close for Kate. She said she'd meet us at the Lake Calhoun Pavilion.

Before I left the gas station, I bought two packs of gum for Coop, and coffee for everyone except Rocky, who was partial to grape pop. Coop immediately ripped the gum open and shoved four sticks in his mouth. Anything I could do to help keep him off the smokes was well worth it. I had a feeling we were in for a very long night.

———

I held my wrist toward the glow of the street lamp, frustrated because I couldn't easily make out the time.

"Shay," Eddy voice was low and comforting as she absently rubbed my back. "You looked at that two minutes ago. Relax."

We were all sitting around one of the tables left out by the Tin Fish, a small restaurant with to-die-for seafood. The restaurant resided in the old pavilion on the northeast shore of Lake Calhoun. Coop and Baz traded insults while Eddy continued an on-going argument with Agnes about the versatility of some obscure knitting stitch. Rocky, on his knees at the edge of the concrete dock, peered into the black water lapping gently below.

It felt like it was taking Kate forever.

The lake vegetation that had been frozen solid for the last six months was now thawed enough to restart the decomposition process, and the night air held the tang of dead fish. Just like our dead bodies would smell if we didn't get things figured out soon.

I kept an eye out for Kate's old VW Bug and heaved an impatient breath. "Okay, you guys. What's next?"

Conversation ceased, and five sets of eyes locked expectantly on me, including Rocky's weary gaze from the water's edge.

"We need a game plan."

"Yes!" Eddy amped up. "A little reconnoiter and reconnaissance mission."

Agnes harrumphed. "Give the old gal a dictionary and she starts using big, ten-dollar words."

Baz said, "In this day and age, those are hundred-dollar words."

Coop chuckled. "Good one, Baz." They high-fived. What?

"I did not learn those words from a book." Eddy sounded insulted. "I got them right off the TV, from a rerun of *Remington Steele*. Or was it *Hart to Hart?* That series finally came out on DVD, you know."

I said, "I think we should see if Kate would mind bringing Rocky home. He should be safe there."

Eddy nodded. "I agree. The boy's tired." She nodded toward Rocky. Sure enough, he'd fallen asleep sprawled on the cement. Poor guy. He'd been through enough in the last couple of days to last a lifetime. Then I recalled his new girlfriend. We'd left the Big Easy so fast he hadn't even had time to say goodbye. I made a mental note to get a hold of the McNichis and see what we could do.

Before we could delve any deeper into our investigation, I heard the distinct and rapidly approaching click of dog toenails on cement. I whipped around just in time to get a face full of Dawg tongue. I wrapped my arms around his thick neck and breathed him in. He wriggled happily, then broke away and started the Boxer shuffle, bending himself in half and bouncing all over the patio.

Kate brought up Dawg's flank, and Eddy swooped her into a tight hug. "Are we ever glad to see you," Eddy told her without letting go. Kate McKenzie was formidable. She was small, but she didn't put up with much guff. She endeared herself to everyone she came into contact with, Eddy included.

"The feeling's mutual," Kate said. She looked at me over Eddy's shoulder, one eyebrow cocked in question. "I'm glad I'm able to help." Eddy gave her another squeeze and released her. Kate set Coop's computer backpack on top of the picnic table with a gentle thump. "Here you go." I could tell she was dying of curiosity but was doing a great job of biting her tongue.

Coop dove on the backpack and pulled out the laptop. In no time flat he had it turned on and booting up.

As we watched Coop work, Kate crossed her arms. "What happened to your head, Shay?"

I'd forgotten the bandage over my eyebrow. "We had some trouble in New Orleans, like I mentioned on the phone. Things got … a little physical."

Kate pressed her lips together as she watched Rocky gently snoring a few yards away. "He out of gas?"

I said, "That's one of the biggest understatements you've made in the last six months. Would you mind giving him a ride home?"

On the phone, I'd intimated some crazy thugs were after us and told her I'd explain everything soon. Now, instead of badgering us about what was going on, Kate simply said, in her amazing, continuing display of self-control, "Why don't I take him home to my house? There's plenty of room."

Coop nodded. "That's kind of what we were thinking. Keep him away from the Hole until we get this cluster sorted out."

"Done." Kate said. "Let's get him out of here while you ... do whatever it is you need to do." I was impressed Kate hadn't flat-out refused to do anything without hearing the entire story.

Even with Dawg's sloppy tongue for help, it took a long while to rouse Rocky. Finally, he and Dawg were loaded safely in Kate's Bug, headed to a soft, safe bed. I was envious.

ELEVEN

Coop finished looking up Sharpe's address on MapQuest, jotted some notes, and stowed the laptop in the backpack. "Let's get this circus on the road. I'd like to be in bed before four this morning."

I'd parked the pickup on the east side of the lake not far from the pavilion. We loaded up, and I cruised slowly around Calhoun. The parade of muscle cars, convertibles, tricked-out trucks, and crotch rockets that ceaselessly circled the lake throughout the summer months hadn't yet begun. I followed the street as it broke away from Calhoun and headed west on what would become Minnetonka Boulevard.

"I'm starving." I glanced wistfully at a darkened Chipotle across the street from a fire station. My stomach growled.

"Here," Agnes said as she fumbled around the inside of her kitchen-sink sized purse. She handed me a rumpled bag of peanuts from the flight home.

"Thanks." The six peanuts within wouldn't do much to quell the beast, but I wasn't in a position to be choosy.

"I think I have more in here." Agnes's voice was muffled, her head practically buried inside the bag. "Ah ha!" She emerged from the monstrosity and thrust her hand toward me. Clenched in her fist were at least half a dozen more bags of airplane peanuts.

"Thanks, Agnes." Warily I took a couple more of the crumpled packets. She must have raided the food cart on her way to the closet the airlines called a restroom.

Once the peanuts were divided equally, Coop navigated. We travelled on I-394 past Ridgedale Mall and farther yet to Highway 12. I took the sharp curve south, toward Lake Minnetonka. Many dips, twists, and turns later, Coop had me pull over and stop in a semi-secluded, residential area.

We were on a side street in of one of the many bays that formed the posh lake. The roads wound sharply, and numerous hills and valleys created a natural rollercoaster. The street we'd been following curved to the left up ahead and disappeared from view.

I shut off the engine and extinguished the headlights. The engine ticked in the cool night air. We sat in the dark, looking out at a large, wooded slope the size of a nice sledding hill. Perched at the top of the hill, a light-colored house nestled among naked trees that would soon sprout lush vegetation. The place was more modern than the classical mansions of a century ago, but not so new it would attract yuppie up-and-comers. A paved drive made a switchback on the way up to a three-car, attached garage. Most of the house was dark, but a very dim light leaked from one of the ground-floor windows.

"Baz," Coop asked, "this look like the place?"

"I think so." Baz leaned forward and peered out the window. "I remember that garage with the decorative stuff on the eaves." He nodded. "I'm pretty sure that's it."

Eddy said, "Basil, being pretty sure is quite different from being very sure."

"It's dark if you haven't noticed, and just a little hard to tell," Baz said defensively.

Agnes struck like lightning. A thwack echoed through the tight confines of the cab. "Ow!" Baz yelped.

"Basil," Agnes said, "you will not talk to your elders that way."

"Sorry, Eddy," Baz mumbled.

"I am not an elder," Eddy said.

Agnes said, "You are too, you old coot."

"I'm not a coot, either."

"Would you rather be a geezer?"

"You're a geezer. I'm—"

"Stop!" I said. Shoot me now. "If you two don't knock it off, I'll knock your heads together, you old farts."

"Old fart? I kinda like that," Agnes said.

Of course she would.

"Fits." Eddy patted Agnes on the shoulder. "You're like an old fart factory, Aggie."

"It's the Metamucil."

An awkward pause followed.

Coop cleared his throat. "Eddy, you and Agnes wait in the truck, and we'll—"

Eddy bristled. "Wait in the truck my flat left butt cheek. You're not leaving either one of us behind. Right, Aggie?"

"Right on, Knitter Sis." The sound of slapping hands filled the cab. The Knitters could easily become a secret society that cost your first-born grandchild and your left pinky finger for membership.

Eddy practically chortled. "Wish I had my lucky green sneakers on. Have you been watching *Dexter*? He's one cool serial killer. That man is slick. We pretend we're following Dex and away we go."

Away we go, indeed. I had a very bad feeling about this escapade. "We're here to see if there's any clue about why Sharpe has a money-stuffed snake in his possession. Nothing else. And Baz," I gave him a squint. "Hands off. We don't need you pilfering anything else."

"Hey," Baz held his mitts in front of him. "I learned my lesson."

That I doubted.

Coop said, "Okay, if we're all going to go on this field trip—"

"Duck!" Agnes shouted as headlights swept around the bend in front of us.

We all attempted the disappear-from-view scrunch-down I'd perfected in high school to avoid the flashlights of the cops who cruised city parks at night. As an adult, I appreciated their attempts to make sure no one was getting more than they bargained for during hot and heavy make-out sessions. Back then, I didn't feel quite so warm and fuzzy about it.

I held my breath as the headlights brightened the interior of the cab, then watched the shadows shift as the vehicle passed and continued on its way. I peeked over the dash. We appeared to be alone again.

"As I was saying," Coop said as he pushed himself out Eddy's lap, "Agnes, you and Baz come with me and we'll go around the house one way. Shay, you and Eddy go the other and we'll meet in the middle and compare notes."

"Fine," Baz said, and Agnes and Eddy echoed affirmation.

We climbed out of the truck. The trees would provide us some concealment, but it would've helped immensely if it were May instead of April. I kept a close eye on Eddy and Agnes as we carefully threaded between the trees and through the leafless underbrush up the hill. All we needed was someone to catch a foot on branches or a rotting log and tumble head over keister back down the slope.

 Moldy twigs and semi-soggy leaves made that much more difficult. After a couple near-slips, we arrived safely at the top of the slope and stopped just inside the treeline. I was breathing heavily. Eddy panted beside me. Coop and Agnes came up behind us with Baz at the rear.

What would be a beautiful lawn once things started greening up abutted the woodland and stretched a good fifty feet to the house. The place was an imposing two stories with a basement walkout.

From our vantage point, part of the front yard including a slice of the drive was visible, as was a fair-sized chunk of the backyard. A deck jutted out from the rear of the house in three terraced levels, each connected by a couple of steps and dropping lower until the third level sat about five feet from the ground to one side of the sliding-glass walkout. A set of four tiered stairs led to ground level.

From the backyard, the ground sloped upward on both sides and flattened out. Light glowed through gauzy curtains from a main-floor window.

Eddy said in a low voice, "See if you can tell if anyone's home, if any cars are in the driveway. That kind of thing."

"Edwina Quartermaine." Agnes put her hands on her hips, and insolently jutted her chin at Eddy. "Do you think we're stupid?"

"You want me to answer that tru—" Eddy began but was interrupted by Coop. "Ladies, cool your jets. Let's go. Quietly." He stealthily struck out toward the front of the house, followed by Agnes and trailed by Baz. I hoped it wasn't a mistake not to lock the Spaz in the pickup.

Eddy and I crept toward the lit window. The pace of my hammering heart picked up the closer we got. We crouched beneath the sill. I took a few deep breaths, trying not to hyperventilate. If we got nabbed ... I forced that thought out of my head. At least there were no alligators in Minnesota. Outside of the zoo, that is.

"Let's take a quick peek," Eddy whispered, cool as a snowball in January. I had to admire her backbone. I wondered how much watching the hour upon hour of crime shows had to do with her gutsiness. Or rather, her idiocy, depending on the outcome of this caper.

On the count of three, we slowly raised our heads and peered over the ledge. The curtain was cream-colored and filmy, just enough to create the illusion of blocking the view from outside.

A multi-colored lamp sat on the corner of a large desk, and cast a yellowish glow into the room. The lampshade was made of stained glass in the form of the roof of a Model T car. The base of the lamp shaped the rest of the car. It would easily have fit in the collectible toys section at the Hands On Toy Store.

The lamp cast its glow in a circle about six feet from the source. A computer sat idle and assorted papers and files rested on the desktop, with a chair tucked neatly underneath. Along one wall, two overstuffed chairs flanked a couch with chrome buttons running along the seams. A coffee table littered with assorted toys sat in front of the couch. A fireplace took up most of another wall. The room looked cozy enough. It also appeared unoccupied.

I tugged on Eddy's sleeve. "Let's go around the back."

We scooted to the corner of the house and followed the slight hill as it dipped downward. At ground level, two bay windows sat on either side of a sliding glass door. An eight-by-eight bricked-in patio area waited for warmer weather. Vertical blinds covered the windows and doors, blocking out our prying eyes.

An owl hooted. Both Eddy and I jumped. Eddy slapped her hand to her chest. "Gee whiz."

My own heart was thumping alarmingly hard.

"Come on, Shay."

I followed Eddy up the other slope and around the corner. Coop and Baz were standing next to the house, sniping at each other. Eddy and I hustled over.

"What's going on?" I whispered.

Coop turned on me, his eyes burning even in the dark. "This idiot," he said, poking Baz in the sternum, "let Agnes disappear."

"I did not just let her disappear, donkhead. You guys got around the corner before I did and when I caught up, she was gone. It's your fault."

"What are you two talking about?" Eddy glared at Baz and then turned her double barrels on Coop.

A pained expression settled on Coop's narrow face. "Agnes is gone."

Eddy's lips thinned. "What do you mean?"

A sinking sensation enveloped me. Why did things seem to get worse when they were already in the shitter?

"We left you and circled around toward the front of the place," Baz explained. "I stopped for a minute to try to get a look in one of the basement windows. They kept on going around the house."

"If you would have kept up with us this would have never happened." Even in the darkness, I could see the big vein on the side of Coop's neck pop out. I thought for a minute he night grab Baz by the throat.

"Then what happened?" I prompted.

"Just like that," Coop snapped his fingers, "poof, she's gone."

"The woman didn't disappear into thin air," Eddy said. "She's got to be around here somewhere."

"Come on." I started toward the front. There really was nowhere for an old woman to hide. The driveway was empty, there were no vehicles she could've ducked behind. The garage jutted out from the house, and past that, a small porch with a black metal swing led to the front door. It appeared the only entrances to the house itself were through the garage, the front door, or in the back through the sliding glass door on the deck and at ground level. Not a lot of options.

We regrouped in front of the porch.

"See," Baz said. "There's nowhere for her to have gone."

I looked at the front door. "You don't think … "

Three more sets of eyes locked on the doorknob.

"She would never … " Baz said.

"Oh yes she would," Eddy told him.

I met Coop's gaze. "Oh oh."

"Uh huh." He nodded grimly.

"Go try it, Coop," I said.

"Not on your life."

"Baz?"

He squinted his squinty eyes at me. "Forget it."

"Chicken shits." I slunk up to the front door and pulled my hand inside the sleeve of my sweatshirt. The handle twisted easily. To my surprise and horror, the door swung open on well-oiled hinges.

After a startled moment, Eddy said, "Time's a-wastin'. Come on." She swept past me into the dark interior. I sucked in a breath, and followed her inside.

The front door opened to a sizeable foyer right out of Fletcher Sharpe's toy store. As my eyes adjusted, I made out huge stuffed animals lining the entryway on one side. A giant giraffe, taller than I was, stood at attention closest to the door. Behind the giraffe, a life-size black bear reared up on its hind legs, trying to appear menacing but only looking huggable. Three pudgy cubs trailed along after her. On the opposite side, four antique carousel horses in various stages of preservation made me want to climb aboard for a ride. Farther down, a doorway led to the right and another opened to the left. Occupying the right half of the hall just past the doors, a staircase led to the second floor. To the left of the stairs, the passage continued out of my line of sight.

"I sure wish I had a flashlight," Eddy said in a stage whisper. Coop laid his hand on my shoulder, more to orient me to his whereabouts than anything. One look beyond him and I realized Baz was hovering at the doorjamb.

"Oh come on, ya big baby," I said. "Hurry up."

"Easy for you to say. You're not looking at two to ten in the slammer for a probation violation. And busting into someone's house on top of that."

I didn't bother to mention he was an accessory to our crimes whether he came inside or not.

Eddy said, "Basil, you keep watch out there and warn us if we need to skedaddle. Okay?"

"Yeah. I can do that." Baz seated himself on the top step.

By the time I turned back around, Eddy was gone and Coop was disappearing through the right-hand door. I hustled after him. Luckily, the windows on this level allowed enough light in to give a sense of trippable objects in our way.

I couldn't believe we were in a stranger's house, and that stranger happened to be one of the most well-known and well-liked executives in the city. If we got busted, we were going to be in some serious crap.

Eddy called quietly, "Agnes? Aggie? You in here?"

A gigantic, U-shaped couch sat in front of an equally humongous flat-screened TV. Hundreds of DVDs occupied a built-in shelving unit along one wall. Everything was very neat, and the room lacked the clutter of everyday life.

No Agnes.

The urgency of the situation pressed down on me. When would Fletcher Sharpe come home? I doubted he'd find any humor in discovering us in his house. And I didn't believe for a minute Baz would stick around to warn us of anyone incoming. He'd be too busy hauling his well-padded hiney back down the hill to the safety of the pickup.

"Go!" I whispered loudly. "Next room already."

Another door on the far end of the room was closed, and Eddy reached out to open it.

"Wait!" Coop yelped.

Eddy jerked her hand away. "What?"

Coop, in a slightly calmer tone, said, "You don't want to leave fingerprints, do you?"

"Oh yeah. Should've thought of that. Grissom would be disappointed." Eddy pulled her sleeve over her hand and opened the door. She stuck her head inside for a moment. The light flashed on, then off, and she reported, "Bathroom. With two more doors. A place with this many doors would confuse a person."

We followed her into a half-bath. I guessed one door opened to the hall behind the stairway, and light glowed through the other portal. Probably the study we'd peeped in through the window. A thought popped into my mind. What would the cops charge us with for peeping? Then I realized it really wouldn't matter. We were in way over our peeping heads.

Eddy left the bathroom and entered the study. Coop and I followed.

The view was pretty much what we'd seen on the outside. Now that we were inside, I could better see the toys lying on the coffee table. Two stuffed snakes similar to Rocky's, three fuzzy teddy bears, and a mean-looking gorilla rested on its glass-covered top.

Coop walked over and picked up one of the snakes. "Looks like the one Baz swiped." He squeezed it. "I don't know if there's anything but stuffing in here or not, but it feels oddly crunchy."

"You don't think … " Eddy sidled up next to Coop and scooped up a bear. She turned it this way and that, examining it and squeezing it between her hands. "It's sure a hard thing for a fancy toy." She stowed the bear under her arm and went back to calling Agnes's name.

Coop dropped the snake and pivoted to follow Eddy out the other doorway. "She's right. This place has more passageways than a mausoleum."

Nice descriptor.

We paused outside the study. We were in an area that opened up to the back half of the main hall. Another stairway heading downstairs was behind the upstairs set. I'd love to see this house in the daylight. Or with the lights on. Or even in the beam of a flashlight. Moonlight was overrated.

Hardwood floors turned into ceramic tile as we slunk single-file into the kitchen. A newspaper was spread open on a six-foot-long, butcher block-topped center island. An L-shaped counter took up two walls, and a stainless-steel gas stove and refrigerator spanned another. A closed door was directly to our right.

"Agnes," Coop hissed loudly. The only sound was our muted breathing and the tick of a clock somewhere. Agnes didn't answer.

Eddy sighed. "Jeez, she's not that fast. Where is she?"

"I—" A loud thump came from behind the closed door. We all jumped in unison.

"What the—" Coop muttered under his breath.

Another bang issued from behind the door.

"All right, that's it," Eddy said through gritted teeth. She strode right to the door and yanked it open faster than I could think. Another clang issued from the space. Coop and I, frozen in place, watched in horror as Eddy flipped the light on.

There, on the floor, sat Agnes. The neck of a liquor bottle was clenched in one hand, and can of peas in the other. A few other tins of vegetables rolled around the floor near her.

"Missed the chair, I did." Agnes hiccupped and took another healthy glug. "Good stuff. Want some?" She held the bottle toward us.

I found my tongue and croaked, "Holy shit, is she drunk?" I had trouble imagining how she got schnockered in a measly ten minutes.

"Agnes," Eddy boomed. "How many times do I have to tell you to stay off the potato hooch? You know what moonshine does to you after one swallow."

She must have had a bit more than one swallow to get herself in this condition.

Agnes's only answer to Eddy was a belch. Her eyes were glassy, and her features appeared crooked on her face.

"Where," Coop asked, "did you find that bottle?"

A gnarled hand pointed up above her head. Indeed, on one of the white wire shelves attached to the wall, between canned vegetables, about two dozen Progresso Sirloin and Vegetable soups, boxes of Uncle Ben's rice, and various pastas were a stash of five additional bottles of Grey Goose vodka. Fletch apparently liked his booze top shelf. Literally.

The scowl on Eddy's face was enough to send a shiver down my own spine, and I wasn't the one in trouble. She said sternly, "Aggie, get your wrinkly fanny off that floor. Nicholas, come over here and help me."

Eddy and Coop hauled Agnes to her feet. She towered unsteadily over Eddy. Coop kept a hand under her arm in case she decided to attempt to visit the floor face-first.

"You old fool," Eddy scolded as she tried to pry the bottle from Agnes's hand.

"Not a fool. I'm the one who found …" Agnes's voice trailed off as she tipped the bottle and swallowed down another gallon or so.

I said, "Let's get her out of here before we—"

"GIVE me that, Aggie!" Eddy had her hand above Agnes's on the neck of the bottle. The stuffed bear she'd tucked under her arm fell to the floor as she wrestled with Agnes for possession.

"No!" Agnes shouted. "Mine!"

"Give. Me. That. Jug." Eddy punctuated each word with a yank.

"Leggo, old hag. I foun' it."

I picked the toy up off the floor and wiggled it in Agnes's face. "Look, Agnes, a teddy bear, just for you."

"Oh. Cute." She swiped at him with her free hand, nearly upending herself. Without Coop's assistance, she'd have gone down.

"Aggie!" Eddy wrenched on the bottle. It flew out of Agnes's hand, through Eddy's, clobbered my forehead right above the same

113

eyebrow that had been banged up in New Orleans, and bounced onto the shelf behind me. I saw stars. Again. Then what felt like a river of wetness began to flow down the side of my face. Again.

"Oh no!" Coop let go of Agnes and lunged at me. He grabbed the bear from my hands and slammed it against my forehead. Déjà vu, with the substitution of a bear for Rocky's aviator hat. Out of the eye not covered by teddy bear fur, I saw Agnes pitch forward. Eddy caught her and staggered under her weight but somehow managed to keep them both upright.

Coop wrapped his arm around my head, and if there had been a pimple at the top of my noggin, it would have popped.

"Hey," I squawked. "Get off!" I tried to push Coop's wiry body away from me, but it was like trying to move Mount Rushmore.

"Shay," he said. "Stay still. You're bleeding."

"I'm fine, for Pete's sake. Let go."

"Nicholas," Eddy said urgently. "Scoot. We have to get out. Too many complications."

"I am *not* a complication," I ground out furiously from very near Coop's armpit.

Someone flicked off the light. I wondered how much of a mess the open bottle of booze was making, and whether or not I was leaving a trail of blood behind. Great. Now they had my DNA.

The four of us staggered out of the kitchen and into the hall. We were about to round the foot of the stairs and make a beeline for the exit when the sound of jingling keys echoed outside the door. Which was now closed.

Our impromptu train stopped short right behind the staircase, and we bumped into one another accordion-style.

The door had been open when we'd left Baz standing guard. Now the door was closed. I had a very bad feeling that Baz was not the one jingling his keys on the stoop outside.

The four of us backpedaled and ducked down behind the stairway to the second floor. My head was pounding. I inanely wondered if the increase in blood pressure was making the gash in my head leak more than it already was. I couldn't see with Coop's iron grip on my noodle, but I managed to twist enough that I got a glimpse of the foyer.

The sound of a key sliding into the lock sounded like an explosion to my partially covered ears. Then the door swung open.

A man stood in the doorframe, backlit by moonlight. Something behind him caught his attention and he turned away for a moment and spoke. I couldn't make out the words, but even if I hadn't been able to see him, the tone of his voice clued me in to his identity. Instantaneously, horrified chills suffused my back and goosebumps sprang up on my arms. The man wasn't Baz. It was Tommy Tormenta, and he wasn't alone.

TWELVE

"OH SHIT." COOP'S CHEST tightened against the side of my head as he spoke. "Downstairs," he whispered.

We tried to move quietly. Not easy to do when one very short old lady was staggering under the weight of a plastered senior citizen and another person was hauling me around by my head like a football he didn't want to fumble.

Coop whipped me about-face and half-dragged, half-carried me down the stairs into the basement. On the edge of panic, I wriggled enough to see that Eddy was doing an admirable job guiding Agnes down the steps in front of us.

At the bottom of the stairs, I was yanked to the right and hustled down a hall. I barely made out the fact we'd entered a spacious room, and then Coop was wrestling me down to the floor.

"Where are—" I began. Coop slapped his big hand across my mouth. He still held the teddy bear squashed against my head with his other hand. If the blood dried while the bear was being imbedded in my skin thanks to Vise Grip Boy, I'd never be able to pull the thing off. Footsteps echoed overhead and the faint sound of voices became louder.

My heart thundered in my ears. We were going to be dead in a matter of moments, and I wasn't even going to be able to see it coming.

The voices grew louder. I stopped breathing, squeezed my eyes shut. Waited for the impact of a bullet.

" … and that's what happened to 'one-legged' Hunk here." Tommy's accented voice grew louder.

I pressed myself against Coop, awaiting the final blow.

Someone turned a lamp on a distance from our hiding spot, casting a very dim glow around the object directly in front of us. I had no idea how they could miss four people huddled like shaking sheep awaiting the big bad wolf.

Tommy continued, "Donny's supposed to be on his way here tomorrow. Minus a piece of his ear, but that shouldn't slow him down too much."

The sound of something opening came from very near. I cringed further.

A voice I didn't recognize said, "Beer?"

Hunk said, "Yeah."

"Tomás?"

"No, *gracias*. Water, if you have it."

"I do."

Water began to run from a tap that sounded way too close. Then there was the unmistakable crack of an aluminum can being popped open.

How come they didn't see us?

"Thanks," came Hunk's gruff voice after a moment.

Coop's arm relaxed slightly and he removed his hand from my mouth while keeping the pressure on my forehead. Directly in front us was a free-standing, knotty-wood cabinet. It had to be a wet bar. I managed to see that Eddy and Agnes were on the floor next to us. Eddy's hand was over Agnes's mouth, and Agnes had a startled, deer-in-the-headlights expression on her face.

"The people you were supposed to dispatch to the depths of some bayou swamp have disappeared. They know what you look like." The voice hardened. "And they've seen the money in the snake. Zorra's not going to like this at all."

"Hey," Hunk said. "It's not like we just let them go. The bitch almost broke my knee."

That was some consolation.

"Zorra will deal with you when she arrives Tuesday. In the meantime, you both had better have these loose ends taken care of before the next shipment comes up. Hunk, I'll need all your resources for this one."

"I've got it covered." Hunk burped loudly.

"Hey, find some manners or I will cut off your avocados, *pendejo*," Tommy said flatly.

"Sorry, boss."

"There's too much at stake to make any more stupid fuck-ups," the man said. I wondered if he was Fletcher Sharpe.

"Tomás, your Juárez connection is complete?"

"*Sí*. The tunnel is done. Product is being transferred. The factory is prepared for the increased exchange."

Tunnels? Juárez? Sounded like smuggling. I recalled the money that exploded out of the snake during the tug-of-war between Baz and Rocky. This wasn't good. Not good at all. And Zorra. I'd have laughed at the ridiculousness of the clichéd name if I weren't so terrified.

"Well," the man said through a yawn, "let's get some sleep, and in the morning you two can figure out what you're going to do to clear up our little problem. Pick one of the bedrooms upstairs to use."

The light clicked off. Footsteps muted by the carpet passed and faded. We stayed still another two minutes. Creaking came from the floor above as the men moved around.

"Let's go out the sliding-glass door," Eddy whispered.

Coop still had me in a headlock.

"Okay." Coop tightened the grip on my head.

"Hey," I whispered indignantly as I attempted again to shove him away. "Let me go already."

"Nope."

I struggled to bat him in the stomach but the angle prevented me from making full contact.

"Stop it, Shay. I'm not letting go." From the tone of his whisper, there was no arguing. I gave up and let him drag me to the patio door. Eddy already had a dazed Agnes propped against the wall and was working the latch. Then the big glass door slid quietly open, and so did the screen. Agnes lurched out the door with Eddy on her heels.

Coop and I followed, stopping only long enough to shut the door behind us. I struggled to keep up with Coop's long legs as we hobbled across the lawn, no easy feat since I was unable to see. Coop had to loosen his hold on my head, but he didn't let go. I waited for a gunshot to ring out, but we hit the tree line and descended the slope without incident. Agnes and Eddy had reached the bottom and were just about to the truck.

Baz, only his forehead and eyes visible, peered cautiously from of the back end of the truck.

"What happened?" he asked as we approached.

"I could ask you the same," I growled.

Coop squeezed my head and said, "Give me the keys."

I dug them from my pocket and slapped them in Coop's hand. He pressed the unlock button. Eddy braced Agnes against the side of the truck with one hand and wrenched the door open with her other.

"What's wrong with Agnes?" Baz asked as he scrambled out of the bed.

"Don't ask," I told him as Coop pulled me around to the driver's side. I thought for a minute he was going to let me drive when he hurriedly yanked opened the door. Instead he popped the smaller rear one and crammed me onto the narrow bench seat. He grabbed my hand and pressed it to the bear. "Hold it on there," he said gruffly. I was certain the stuffed animal was now permanently attached.

Eddy nudged Agnes next to me and climbed in beside her. Baz practically leaped into the passenger seat. Coop fired up the engine and made tracks out of there.

THIRTEEN

"Is anyone going to tell me why Agnes is snoring back there and why Shay has a bear growing out of her head?" Baz asked as Coop flew around curves and screamed over hills.

"There was an incident," Eddy said. "Basil, why didn't you warn us someone was coming?"

An uncomfortable silence filled the cab. Baz said, "I was afraid they'd see me. They pulled up in a big black Escalade. I freaked."

Damn. I knew he'd bail on us.

"So what happened?" Baz wasn't going to let it go.

I said, "Agnes apparently slipped in the front door and managed to find Fletcher's stash of booze."

"Vodka?" Baz asked.

Eddy said, "You know it. That woman cannot hold her potato-based spirits."

"Oh, boy." Baz whistled. "And why is Shay wearing a bear?"

"I forgot to duck," I said.

"There was a slight miscalculation in removing the bottle from Agnes's grip," Eddy said. "Shay, when we get home, we'll get you fixed up good as new."

I cringed at the thought of having all the little fibers that were now implanted in my skin, covered with clotted blood, pulled off one at a time. I gave the bear an experimental tug and decided blood could be a substitute for glue.

Coop took the curve onto eastbound 394.

"Anyone behind us?" I asked.

"Nope," Coop answered after a quick check in the mirror. "What do you think they were referring to?"

"The guys in the basement?" Eddy asked.

"Yeah," Coop said. "The whole Juárez thing, tunnels..."

"Juárez?" Baz repeated. "Who is 'they' anyway?"

"Our friends from the Big Easy," I mumbled.

"No way. Hunk and Donny?"

"Hunk and some other guy. No Donny," Eddy said. "They said he'll be here tomorrow."

I asked, "Was that Fletcher Sharpe?"

"I don't think so," Coop said.

"No, it wasn't Fletcher," Eddy said. "His ads are always on TV for that toy store of his." She went on to relate what we'd heard. When she was done, a charged silence filled the air, broken only by Agnes's light snores.

"Man." I scrubbed the half of my face not covered up by fur. "This whole thing is unbelievable."

"No doubt." Coop's voice sounded hollow, tired. We all were.

My mind was having a hard time staying on track. Hopefully that was from exhaustion and not related to the vodka noggin knock. I forced my brain cells into some semblance of order. "We've got to get some rest. And, sorry folks, it ain't gonna be at any of our own homes."

"No," Eddy agreed. "We can't go anywhere near home. What time is it, anyway? I have to visit the little old ladies room."

That made at least two of us.

"1:03 a.m.," Coop relayed. "Let's go to Kate's place. She'll have enough room there to put us up for the night. Maybe we should just go to the cops."

"Oh right," Baz muttered from the back seat. "We don't know who's on the take, who's compromised, remember?"

"My goodness, Baz, such a big word for such a little guy," Coop said. "I didn't know your vocabulary included anything over five letters."

"Hey!" Baz said, his voice rising. "I'm not an id—"

"You spineless coward," Coop bellowed. "Running off to save your own—"

"BOYS!" Eddy's sharp voice brought the bickering to a screeching halt. "Whether we like this or not, we're in this calamity together. So stuff a sock in it."

We rode the rest of the way to Kate's without more than three words between us. Ideas echoed around my mind, rolling like a snowball down a giant hill. Should we go to the police? Baz, sadly enough, was right. We didn't know who might be on the take in this muddle of a mess. I really wished JT were home. It'd been forty-eight hours since I'd talked to her. She was going to be fit to be hog-tied.

Screw it, I decided. If I couldn't have JT, I'd take my second best option. As soon as my brain worked again, I was going to call Dirty Harry. If JT trusted him, so would I.

My brain ached, and the skin under the matted stuffed animal itched fiercely. I could hardly wait for surgical separation. Then I'd call Harry whether everyone else wanted me to or not. Desperate times, desperate measures. Decision made, I shut my eyes and fell into an uneasy stupor.

———

Kate lived in a three-bedroom, story-and-half bungalow not far from Minnehaha Creek, on Chicago Avenue just past True Colors Bookstore and Pepito's Mexican Restaurant. The thought of Pepito's made my stomach rumble, reminding me it'd been a while since our last feeding.

Coop navigated the narrow alley behind Kate's house and pulled onto a double-car-sized cement platform that masqueraded as a driveway. The house was dark, nary a light bleeding through any of the windows.

The sound of the engine faded into silence, and we emerged from the truck. I assured Coop I could manage to hold the bear to my own head without his assistance, and he reluctantly relented. Good move on his part, as my patience was wearing thin.

We trooped into the fenced backyard—carefully following the crumbling sidewalk for fear of stepping into a Dawg-sized dump—and huddled on the back steps. Kate's doorbell hadn't worked since the day she'd moved in. I raised my hand to knock. Before my fist met wood, Eddy's hand curled around my bicep, stopping all forward motion. "Wait," she whispered. "We don't want to wake up the neighborhood. Last thing we need is someone calling the cops." Good point. Kate was a sound sleeper, but maybe she wasn't REMing yet.

"I'll try her bedroom window." I hopped off the two-step stoop, carefully keeping the bear against my forehead. Gingerly I followed the edge of the dark mound I knew was a flowerbed in summertime but was now a mushy mess.

Kate's bedroom was in the corner of the house, and I was mighty happy one window faced the backyard. Who knew what the neighbors might do if they got an eyeball of some freak with a furry growth on her head skulking around.

A screen covered the window. I reached across the muddy abyss and tapped on the trim that surrounded the glass as a siren sounded in the distance.

I waited for some hint that Kate was alive and stirring. I sure hoped some do-gooder with insomnia wasn't watching and reporting suspicious goings-on to the authorities.

The curtains behind the glass didn't stir, and no lights came on. I tapped harder.

Still nothing. The ground under my feet sunk down as I stepped closer to the house. Too bad Kate had her windows replaced last summer. Her old ones were practically falling out, and I could've hollered at her through the cracks to get her butt out of bed.

Everything seemed calm, and the emergency siren had faded into the night. Gritting my teeth, I rapped harder. Suddenly deep woofs directly on the other side of the wall shattered the quiet. The noise practically vibrated the window. A light appeared.

"Kate," I yelled as loud as I dared. I didn't need her calling 911 because she thought intruders were raiding her yard. Dawg continued to bark as a silhouetted figure moved around the room. Then the light went out.

I knocked again.

Sudden movement startled me as the curtain flew back and I was face to barrel with a great big gun.

Holy shit! When did Kate get a gun, and why hadn't she told me about it?

In reaction, I stepped away from the threat, but the tennis shoe on my left foot was stuck in the squishy ground. I lost my balance, and my foot slid out of my shoe.

I tipped backward in slow motion, my one unoccupied arm desperately flailing for a nonexistent handhold. My butt thudded against the ground hard enough to make my teeth clack, and the elbow on my free arm was the only thing that stopped me from flopping full out on Kate's dead grass. The same elbow that had been abused in New Orleans. Ow.

Kate shoved the window open.

Brave girl. Actually, stupid girl, if I thought about it.

The barking was remarkably louder now that there was only a screen between the deadly weapon and me.

"Kate!" I yelled sharply.

A shadowy face replaced the gun barrel. "Shay?"

"Yes!" I hissed. "Don't shoot."

"You scared the bejesus out of me. What on earth are you doing? What's wrong with your head?"

The moment he'd recognized my voice, Dawg stopped barking. I could barely make out his wrinkly muzzle as he snuffled wetly at the screen, trying to figure out how to get through it to bounce on me.

"Let us in, and we'll tell you all about it." I heaved myself to my feet. Somehow, I'd managed not to rip the bear off my head. Which, in hindsight, was too bad. It would have been nice to have the ripping part over with.

Kate disappeared as I hopped on one leg to the flowerbed and retrieved my shoe. It made a sucking sound when I wrenched it from the mud. I clapped it against the foundation to try to get some of the clay-like stuff off.

The backyard light flicked on. The screen door screeched open, and voices filled the night air. I was about to pull my shoe on when Dawg shoved his way through the crowd and galloped straight toward me, ears flopping merrily, jowls slapping up and down in time to his strides. I hopped madly around, trying desperately to get my shoe on before impact. Then all eighty-some pounds of Boxer plowed right into me. My shoe sailed out of my hands and my butt reacquainted itself with the ground. My left elbow smacked the surface, but this time the force of the blow was cushioned by something soft, thank goodness.

Dawg straddled me, his entire body quivering in excitement. He licked my face. Good thing I didn't wear contacts because his big tongue would've slurped them right out.

"Dawg," I panted. "Off!"

I tried in vain to push him away. He was a star at doggy-school and usually responded to my slightest direction. Not this time.

Coop dragged the mutt off me. His affectionate attention shifted to Coop, who rubbed his face vigorously, causing his loose lips to flap up and down. After reacquainting himself with Coop, Dawg danced around in a circle, bounced straight-legged on all fours a couple of times, and raced toward the door.

"Happy to see us," Coop observed.

"No kidding." I swiped at a glob of Dawg drool that was on my cheek. After Dawg first came to stay with me, I'd stopped being grossed out at his bodily fluids either dripping on me or flying through space and landing with a splat on the furniture or the walls.

"I'll get the luggage." Coop extended a hand. "You get the bear removed."

"Thanks." I grabbed him with my left hand, surprised to find my right hand had held the bear to my head through the Dawg-attack. I was getting good at this.

I started toward the door.

Coop said, "What's on your elbow?" I stopped and pulled my sleeve around to face the light. A large mud-colored smear ran from my elbow toward my wrist. At first glance, I thought it was mud from the flower garden. Until the smell hit.

"Ugh. Son of a—that's *not* dirt." I held the sleeve away from my skin, my face frozen in horrified disgust.

Coop laughed. "The mutt's here for less than twenty-four hours, and you manage to find the poop." He guffawed, and my horror melted into a smile. Then I joined in semi-hysterical laughter.

Kate stuck her head out the door, and Dawg slipped in past her, intent on greeting the rest of his pack. "What are you two doing out there? You're gonna wake the neighbors, and then I won't be the only one pointing a gun at you."

Coop looked quizzically at me.

I raised the eyebrow on my unimpeded eye. "The woman's armed, and we didn't even know it."

Never assume you have Kate's number, because she was always full of surprises. This night needed to end, and the sooner the better. But I felt a whole lot better after having released some tension, even if it had to be at the expense of my crap-covered arm.

FOURTEEN

"Ow!"

"Shay, shut up and stop being a baby," Eddy muttered. I eyed her reflection in the mirror as she squinted at my forehead. One of her hands was full of bear and the other snipped more fur away.

We'd gathered in Kate's bathroom after bedding Agnes down in a spare bedroom and Baz on the couch, and relegating my sweat-shirt to the wash. Luckily, Rocky slept through our noisy arrival. Now he was probably going to awaken from my cries of pain. What could I say? Bear fur, congealed blood, and a forehead gash weren't a recipe for a simple fix.

Kate, who favored an over-sized Paddington Bear t-shirt and matching boxers for sleepwear, leaned on one side of the doorjamb while Coop occupied the other, both watching in amusement while Eddy worked. With one last scissor slash, the bear was free. She tossed the toy at Coop, who one-handed the blood-covered, partially-bald animal.

"Thank you, Lord," Eddy said. "I'm sorry this happened, Shay, but I didn't think I could take one more howl out of you." She wet a washcloth and slapped it above my right eye. "Hold this on there a minute. It'll make it easier to clean up. Cut's not too big, maybe an inch or two."

"So, Kate," I said, trying to be careful not to move too much. "What's up with the six-shooter?"

"After being held at gunpoint by mobsters during Coop's murder investigation," she elbowed Coop, "I bought it."

Kate was queen of the unexpected.

Eddy grinned. "Gotta teach me how to use that."

That was so the last thing we needed.

"So fill me in on what's going on," Kate said, neatly sidestepping Eddy's comment.

My eyes drooped shut as I half-listened to Coop relate what had happened in the last forty-eight hours, including our nocturnal visit to Fletcher Sharp's place. Eddy's low voice added a colorful tidbit every so often. My body hurt, my beloved iPhone was sunk, and the baddies were back. It hadn't been a good day. All I wanted was to curl up with JT and go to sleep.

Eddy gently took the cloth from my hand. In no time, she cleaned me up and had three Steri-Strips holding my battle wound closed.

We moved en masse from the bathroom to the kitchen. I grabbed the bear as I was steered out of the bath. The thing was heavier than it should be, and I wanted to know if this animal was filled with the same kind of stuffing as Rocky's snake.

The mint-green-painted kitchen was small by most standards and carried a hint of Kate's legendary cinnamon rolls. My mouth watered at the thought.

I swiped a paring knife from a butcher-block on Kate's counter and fell into one of the four ladder-back chairs that encircled the table. Coop and Eddy followed suit while Kate flitted here and there, putting hot water on for tea, her power drink of choice.

As if reading my mind, she pulled a tin-foil-covered cake pan off the counter and set it between us on the tabletop. She peeled the foil back, and there, in all its frosting-covered, chewy goodness, was half a pan of the sinful rolls. I considered grabbing the whole thing, running for the bathroom, and locking the door behind me. Then I decided if I wanted to live, I'd better share.

Kate laughed at the obviously ravenous expressions on our faces. "I take it you're all hungry."

She pulled plates out of the cupboard and forks from a drawer, whipped a huge knife from the butcher-block, and set to work cutting us generous pieces.

I stabbed the bear with my own small knife.

"Shay," Eddy said in alarm. "What are you doing?"

"Trying," I carefully tried to cut a hole in my ex-bandage, "to see if this has the same innards as the snake."

Kate froze, the butcher knife in mid-air, silently watching me gut the bear.

Sure enough, mixed with white stuffing were wads of crumpled bills along with rolls of currency. I pulled out a few of the clumps and rolls. They all contained fifty and hundred dollar bills.

I thought Kate's eyes were going to spring out of her head. Nothing like a little show-and-tell to turn someone into a true believer. Like Fletcher Sharpe's slogan, Everything Is Hands On.

"Oh, my god," Kate said. We sat in silence, looking at my bear massacre.

Coop said, "It wasn't a fluke. I can't believe Fletcher Sharpe would do something like this."

"Proof's in the pudding, as they say." Eddy picked up one of the rolls. She opened it and counted. "A thousand bucks in hundreds."

What was this? Money laundering? Payoffs? Theft? Drug dough?

"Kate," I said, "can you stow our little friend here somewhere safe?"

"Sure." She waited until we'd replaced the loot in the bear and disappeared from the room with it. She returned shortly. I wasn't even going to ask where she'd tucked it away. Sometimes less knowledge is much safer.

Kate shook her head. "There's no lack of excitement with you guys, is there?" She set gooey, cinnamon roll-mounded plates in front us, and we dug in.

I swallowed my third bite. "I'm going to talk to JT's undercover cop friend, Dirty Harry, and see what he thinks about this whole mess."

Eddy wiped the corners of her mouth with a napkin she'd grabbed from a holder on the table and said, "It's time to get some real muscle on the case. Call in the big dogs."

"I agree." Coop nodded, albeit hesitantly. His innate distrust of law enforcement was in full bloom. He sighed. "What else can we do? We're in a fix the size of Idaho here. Who's good, who's bad?" He tapped his fork on a tooth. "But what if he's on the take, too?"

We chewed some more, contemplating that as well as the Zen rush the cinnamon rolls were giving us.

I said simply, "JT trusts him."

"Then do it." The whistle of the teapot ramped up, and Kate pulled the pot off the burner with practiced ease. She poured hot water into two mugs, one for Eddy and one for herself. Three boxes of tea appeared in front of Eddy, along with her steaming mug. Then Kate pulled a couple of cans of pop out of the fridge and handed them to Coop and me before she settled herself in a chair. The woman was as efficient at home as she was at the Hole.

I popped the top of the can. This no-cell thing sucked. I asked, "Can I use your phone?"

Kate pointed at the wall, where a white cordless was mounted. Dawg was curled right beneath it on his home-away-from-home dog bed, snoring softly and occasionally passing some very foul gas.

After washing down the roll with a couple swigs of Diet Coke, I grabbed the receiver, gave Dawg a pat, and sat back down. My thumb hovered over the push buttons as it occurred to me I had no idea what Harry's number was. I said as much.

For a breath, no one said anything. Kate pushed her chair away from the table and stood. "Shay, doesn't JT have her cell with her?"

"Yeah, she does." I morosely propped my chin in my hand, very much ready to go to sleep and forget this whole thing. I was dangling at the unraveled end of my rope. "I don't know that number either. Who knows any phone numbers anymore? You program them in your phone and forget them."

Kate walked out of the kitchen without a word.

Coop shrugged. Eddy raised her eyebrows at me and shook her head.

Ten seconds later Kate returned. She tossed her cell at me. I barely managed to stop it before it skidded across the tabletop and onto the floor.

"Nice phone. What do you want me to do with it?"

Kate laughed. "Call JT, silly."

I'd forgotten Kate had possessed JT's number longer than I had. She'd had a torch for the woman for some time, but I was the lucky one who caught her.

After some random button pushing, I found the address book and scrolled down to the B's. Sure enough, there was JT Bordeaux.

Kate cleared the table as the line began to ring. It was 3:00 a.m. on the East Coast. At home, JT always slept with her cell right next to her head in case she got a call out in the middle of the night. I hoped she did the same thing at Quantico.

I counted four rings, and I expected the voicemail to kick in. There was a fifth ring, and then JT's sleep-groggy voice was on the other end.

"Kate?" she said hoarsely, her voice holding a hint of panic.

"Hey, babe, not Kate. It's me, Shay."

"Shay?" There were five full seconds of silence on the line. Then in a rush JT said, "Where have you been? Are you okay? Where are you? How come you haven't been answering your phone?"

I should've expected her reaction, but the concern behind the harsh tone warmed my soul and made me miss her so bad I nearly choked up. I could hear more mumbling behind her in the background.

"Wait a minute," she told me. I heard more rustling, then silence, then the sound of a hollow bang.

JT came back on the line, her voice echoing. "I'm in the bathroom. Didn't want to wake up my roommate." She went from sleep-dazed to razor-sharp in a remarkably short amount of time. "Tell me what's going on."

I was past being able to cherry-pick the events that wouldn't freak her out, so I laid it all out, the good, the bad, and the utterly terrifying.

When I was done, JT said nothing for what felt like forever, but was probably only fifteen seconds. She took and released a deep, measured breath. Then she said, "I thought something was wrong. I even talked to one of the guys here who runs the program to see what it would mean if I had to leave before I finished."

I swallowed hard. The last thing I wanted to do was put the career JT had worked so hard at on the line. "And?"

"And," she said, "if I leave, I forfeit the ride here, and I won't be asked back unless the reason for my departure involves a catastrophic accident, illness, or death involving an immediate family member. Or me. Jesus, Shay, I was afraid I was going to have to use that reason to come home."

"I'm really sorry, JT. I didn't have any way to get a hold of you." I felt terrible. Terrible for JT, for me, and even for Baz.

"Oh, Shay," she whispered. The ache in my chest intensified, and it had nothing to do with the cinnamon bun heartburn I felt coming on and everything to do with the woman on the other end of the line. I opened my mouth to tell her I was sorry to have scared her, and that I loved her so much my heart hurt when she was away, to say the words that were somehow scaring me less every day. But the winds of *amore* dissipated when her tone became brisk, now in cop-mode. "Okay. Do you have paper and a pen?"

Kate was way ahead of me on the note-taking front and had placed a pad of paper and a stubby pencil in front of my nose at some point in the conversation. She was amazing, always anticipating, always aware. I picked up the pencil with a smile of thanks. "Go ahead, JT."

"Here's Harry's number again. It's going to go straight to voicemail unless he's off duty, which he rarely is. Leave a message and he'll call you back as soon as he can. Then make copies of the number and give them to Coop, Eddy, and Kate. No way will *all* of you lose 'em." She rattled the phone numbers off, and I carefully jotted them down.

She continued, "And here are my contact numbers, just in case." She spewed off more digits.

I repeated all the phone numbers back to her to make sure I had them correct. "Look, JT, we're cool here. I don't need you to come home. I'll call Dirty Harry as soon as I'm off the phone with you, okay?"

JT heaved a sigh. "Tomorrow go to Wal-Mart or Target, or wherever they sell those pay-as-you-go phones. This way those bastards can't track you, if they have that capability. Program the phone numbers I gave you into them, and call and leave me a message on my voicemail with your new number."

My woman was brilliant.

"Listen—" I hesitated, wanting to say more, wanting to tell her what my heart was hollering at me. "I miss you." Wimp. Nothing but yellow-bellied sap sucker.

"I miss you too, babe. I really do. When I thought something might have happened—" JT's voice was suddenly huskier than usual, and she cleared her throat.

"Nothing did happen, so don't worry. I'll call you as soon as we get the new phones. Go back to sleep for ten minutes."

"Very funny. Call me."

"I will." I hung up, very aware of the thumping of my heart. I let out a breath, happy to have the call done with, but missing JT worse than ever.

Kate said, "I have to be to the café at five-thirty. I'm going to hit the sack for a couple more hours."

Eddy scooped up another cinnamon roll and deposited it on her plate. "If anyone comes to the café asking about any of us, you tell them you haven't seen us for days."

Kate agreed, and we hammered out sleeping arrangements. I'd share a bed with her, Eddy would bunk with Agnes, and Coop headed for the basement and a ratty futon.

We bid Kate a good night, and I keyed the phone on again and dialed Harry. The ringing kicked into voicemail. I told him who I was and gave him a very brief rundown of what was going on. I asked him to call me back as soon as possible, and gave Kate's house number. *And please*, I prayed to anyone who would care to listen, *let Dirty Harry not be on the take.*

FIFTEEN

I AWOKE TO SOMEONE prying my left eyelid open.

"Are you in there, Shay O'Hanlon?"

"Wha—" My brain felt like it had been pickled in some of the crude oil that had leaked into the Gulf. Comprehension was slow going.

"Hello in there!"

I weakly batted at the intrusion to my eyeball. Everything was blurry, out of focus.

"Wake up, Shay. It is 7:34 in the morning. You should be up bright and early to make the most valuable use of your day. It is late already!"

"Rocky?" I attempted to open my other eye. The room was bright, much brighter than my bedroom at home. The light hurt. I slammed both eyes shut.

"That is me. Rocky." His fingers were back, forcing my eye open again. An eyeball stared back at me from about two inches away.

"I'm awake. You can let go of my eyelid now."

The eyeball and fingers of torture retreated. I blinked a couple of times, and things blended into focus. I was in Kate's room.

Rocky sat on the edge of the bed next to me, dressed in his aviator cap and Twins jacket, even though we were indoors. He had an impish grin on his face and leaned forward until his nose almost touched mine.

"Are you awake?"

"I am now."

His round face didn't move, and he whispered loudly, "I have a secret."

My eyes crossed as I attempted to look at him. "What is it?"

Rocky gave me two raised brows and a smirk. "If I told you, it would not be a secret anymore."

I squeezed my eyes shut and pushed my head against the pillow. I wasn't good morning company on the best of days. I was about two breaths from growling, and I was doing my best not to lash out. It wasn't his fault his internal timer went off at six in the morning.

"You need to eat a nice, balanced breakfast every day, with a portion of the recommended daily allowance of thirty-two grams of fiber to help regulate your digestive system." He paused dramatically. "You know, so you can poop!"

I laughed in spite of myself. I don't know where he came up with his mandates, but he was usually right. I propped myself up on my elbows, thankful the fog was lifting off my brain.

"So what's your secret?" I asked.

Rocky sat up straight, crossed his legs, and then placed his hands one over the other on top of his knee. He said proudly, "I am in love."

Oh boy. "With who?"

"Tulip. The most beautiful animal creator ever."

Tulip ... Tulip. Then it came to me. The balloon maker in New Orleans.

"She is the prettiest flower in the world." Rocky's eyes had taken on a far-away, sappy look, and his face glowed.

What kind of a parent would stick a kid with the name Tulip? I supposed it was better than Turnip. I suppressed a grin. "Tulip is a lovely name, Rocky."

"We are going to get married one day and have two kids."

I wasn't ready to deal with love and the Rockster. Coop needed talk to him about the birds and the bees, because I wasn't touching that with a ten-foot pole. No pun intended. "Oh." I tried to think of a better response. "Don't you think she's a bit far away for a relationship?"

"No, we have Facebook."

I squinted at him. "Since when did you get a Facebook account?" I knew he didn't have a computer at his place, and he wasn't very tech savvy. Coop had tried to give him some basic web surfing lessons, but Rocky had zoned out after ten minutes.

A huge smile creased his face. "Kate got me all set up last night."

As I inhaled to speak, the phone on the nightstand next to the bed rang. I grabbed it. "Hello?"

A rusty-sounding voice said, "I'm looking for Shay O'Hanlon. This is Harry."

"Harry, hi. I'm Shay. Thanks for returning my call."

"No problem. Any friend of JT's is a friend of mine." Harry sounded like he was talking out of one side of his mouth. "You're having some problems."

"Yeah. But, ah, I'd rather not talk about it on the phone." It dawned on me anyone could tap into Kate's landline. Great. Now I was sounding as paranoid as Coop sometimes was.

"If you want to meet, you'll have to come to me."

"No problem. Where and when?"

Rocky, bored with my call, wandered out of the room. I was going to have to file the Tulip issue away for later visitation.

There was a few seconds of silence on the line, then Harry said, "Come to the corner of Dunwoody and Hennepin at nine-thirty. Dress down. Gotta go."

The line disconnected.

I rolled out of bed and looked at myself in the mirror on the dresser. My short black hair stood on end, and one side of my face was imprinted with a latticed stripe from the lace border on the edge of the Kate's pillowcase. The area around the three Steri-strip bandages holding my forehead together was starting to bruise. I sighed and trudged into the master bathroom. It was Frankenstein's shower time.

———

I pulled on a clean t-shirt and a pair of black jeans, about as "dressed down" as I was going to get. We were going to have to do some laundry soon. I followed my nose toward the kitchen, where some kind soul had put coffee on to brew.

Eddy, Rocky, and Agnes, who looked much less bleary, were all seated around the kitchen table. Coop leaned against the counter next to the refrigerator, his eyes at half-mast, holding an open can of Coke. At my entrance, he looked up and saluted me with his can. "Morning," he said wryly.

Agnes looked over her coffee cup. "I want to apologize for what happened last night. I shouldn't have wandered off—"

Eddy snorted. "Sure as a chicken has feathers, you shouldn't have wandered off. Scared us silly. And you should know potato juice always kicks your skinny butt. It practically dumps itself down your throat. Dum-dum."

Agnes stiffened. "Who're you calling—"

"You! Ya boozer." Eddy narrowed her eyes. "I don't go into strangers' houses and chug their alcohol."

"Oh, no? What do you call having one too many and falling out of Sula's window?"

"I tripped, and she wasn't a stranger. But she did make a mean Jäger Bomb."

This was a tale Eddy hadn't told me. "You fell out a window?"

Agnes cut her eyes toward me. "She sure did. Landed right on her head in the flower bed."

I looked at Eddy, whose lips were pressed tightly together. She said, "I'm just glad it was summertime and the ground was soft."

Rocky picked that moment to say, "Hi, Shay O'Hanlon!" He grinned, fork in hand, oblivious to the sniping he'd unintentionally cut short. The pan of cinnamon rolls was in front of him with maybe two bites left.

He said, "I love Kate's rolls. And cinnamon lowers cholesterol and inhibits bacterial growth and food spoilage. And tastes great!" He shoved the rest of the gooey roll in his mouth and chewed happily.

"Sit down, Shay," Eddy told me.

I sat. She stood, went over to the coffee maker, and poured a cup.

Eddy placed a chipped mug adorned with a Rabbit Hole logo in front of me. I took a careful sip and sighed as the dark liquid seared its way down my throat. "Where's Baz?" I asked.

Coop's glower deepened. "Still out on the couch."

Nice.

"Rocky," Coop said, "why don't you go and give Baz the eye treatment you gave me this morning?"

Nice to know I wasn't the only one who had their eyelids peeled apart as a wake-up call.

"No, thank you. I don't like Spaz Man. He's mean." Rocky slid the pan away and stood.

"Basil's not mean, Rocky. He's just a little misguided," Agnes said.

"I have to go Facebook." Rocky zipped out of the kitchen.

Agnes pursed her thin lips in disdain. "Facebook? That's all the kids talk about nowadays. Doesn't anyone talk with their real faces anymore?"

"Not when they can do it on a piece of technology." Coop rubbed his scruffy chin. "Rocky doesn't have a computer."

I said, "Kate let him use hers and set him up last night so he can communicate with his newfound love."

"Love?" Eddy said. "What love?"

"Tulip of the balloon animals." I took another sip of coffee, feeling the caffeine spread into my veins like hot lava.

Coop asked, "Tulip from New Orleans?"

"Yup. He's in love, and they're going to date via Facebook."

Agnes said, "My goodness, things have changed since I was young."

"You haven't been young for sixty years, Aggie." Eddy poked her arm. "Maybe Kate should give you Facebook lessons. Nicholas got me all set up, and I can friend you."

Agnes harrumphed. "I don't know a thing about computers, and I'm too old to start now. He tried. I failed."

Eddy said, "You might be old, but you still have a brain in there."

Agnes gave Eddy a sharp look. "Are you saying I'm old?"

"You called your own self old."

Agnes frowned. "Guess I did."

"Anyway," I jumped in before the conversation veered too far off the path. "We need to run to Target or somewhere and buy a couple pay-as-you-go phones."

I turned to Eddy and Agnes. "How much cash do you guys have on you?"

A strange look crossed Agnes's face. She said, "Oh … A few bucks."

I restrained myself from rolling my eyes. Eddy hated when I disrespected my elders.

"I have," Eddy said as she emptied her pockets on the tabletop and counted, "Two hundred seventy—"

Agnes interrupted her. "Where did you get all that dough?"

Eddy narrowed her eyes at Agnes. "Are you accusing me of something?"

"No, I was just asking. No need to get defensive."

"I won this money fair and square, Aggie."

"Didn't say you didn't."

"But you implied—"

"Ladies," I burst out. "Stop."

They tore their gazes from each other to look at me.

"I'm meeting with JT's co-worker, Dirty Harry—"

Eddy said, "Silly name."

I gave Eddy a look. "Why I was asking for money is this. Hunk and company probably already know my pickup, and if they don't, they can find out. I think we should rent a car, something unassuming, and if you pay in cash … " I trailed off, leaving the obvious unsaid. "And we'd have a heck of a lot more room. Coop and I can drop you off and we can meet back here when we're done."

Plan agreed upon, we left Dawg still snoozing on Kate's bed, Baz sound asleep on the couch, and Rocky chortling periodically in front of the computer screen.

———

We dropped Eddy and Agnes off at Enterprise Rent-A-Car and headed to Target in Edina. The sun was shining, and puffy white clouds floated high in the sky. I should be out running around Lake Calhoun or getting frisky with JT, not on a mission to buy untraceable phones.

Target was open when we arrived, and the place was busy even at this early hour. We procured two basic phones, and headed back to the car. I activated them, then called and left a message for JT, relaying the new numbers to her.

I pulled into Kate's driveway less than an hour later, and we'd just stepped from the car when a loud rumble filled the air.

Coop looked at me. "What is that?"

"I dunno. Sounds like a car with a glasspack, or a missing muffler, maybe."

The rumbling grew louder. A neon-orange Dodge Charger with black stripes and shiny black tires pulled into the drive and stopped next to my pickup. The rumble of the engine vibrated the cement beneath my feet.

My jaw dropped.

Eddy hopped out, beaming like a mom with a newborn. The passenger door opened more slowly, and Agnes emerged from the dark interior, looking a little pale but slightly smug herself.

Eddy patted on the hood. "What do you think of this little baby?"

Coop walked slowly around it, whistling under his breath the tune that usually accompanied clowns under the big top. He claimed it was "Entrance of the Gladiators," but I hadn't believed him until I Googled it myself. He was right.

I said, "Why?"

Eddy's grin stretched from ear to ear. "Gotta use a credit card at Enterprise even if you pay cash. So me and Aggie had to take a cab to this little place in North Minneapolis that would accept the greenbacks. It was called," she drew a large rectangle in the air, "Stan & Ione's Classic Rental Cars. 'We take cash.'" She eyed me. "You did say no credit cards."

Guilty on that count.

"And this was all they had left."

Of course it was.

"And it sure goes fast."

And that's why Agnes was pale. Eddy loved speed, whether she was in her old yellow truck or driving someone else's car. Whenever I rode with her, I regretted not having the forethought to take Dramamine, and I prayed for my very life the duration of the trip. It didn't help that Eddy's peripheral vision had gone to hell and she refused to admit it.

Coop trailed a hand over the glossy paint. "How much did this set you back?"

For the first time, an abashed look clouded Eddy's face. "Don't ask. It's Aggie's fault."

"I thought," I said to Agnes, "you had a few bucks. You *did* use a credit card, didn't you."

Eddy said, her voice well into accusatory range, "Are you deaf, child? I told you we had to go somewhere else. We didn't use a credit card. But Agnes whipped out a roll the size of a drug dealer's."

She'd definitely watched too many episodes of *Weeds*.

Coop said, "Did you win more than you let on, Agnes?"

"Perhaps." She didn't elaborate.

Maybe she lifted money from the bear. That would make me laugh.

Eddy said, "She was holding out."

A rare look of guilt crossed Agnes's face. "Okay, okay. Fine. I won a titch more than I mentioned."

Eddy said, "I still can't believe you didn't tell me—"

Agnes planted her hands on her hips. "You were losing."

"But—"

"I didn't need you begging me for more money to buy back in the game."

"Excuse me? How dare you! I never beg."

Here we go again. I said, "Ladies! Let's get this show on the road."

SIXTEEN

We sailed north on 35W in our glowing orange Charger. Since Eddy was the only approved driver on the rental contract, she was behind the wheel. After three minutes, Agnes looked seasick.

Eddy weaved around a garbage truck and two cars, then sliced back into the right lane. If we'd been in NASCAR, she'd be kicking booty.

It wasn't long before she squealed into a metered spot in front of Joe's Garage, a restaurant right off Loring Park. She shut the car off. "Shay, you and Coop go on and talk to this Harry. Agnes and I will have something to eat and wait for you in the Garage."

My mouth watered. Coop and I hadn't had a chance to eat anything that morning (Rocky had snarfed the remaining cinnamon rolls), and I was hungry. I heaved a sigh. Hopefully Harry would be there, and we'd pick his brain and get back to the restaurant fast.

Coop and I followed the sidewalk to the corner, past Café Lurcat, and around the bend to Hennepin Avenue.

Down the block, at the next intersection, a man in a trench coat holding a battered cardboard sign slowly walked up the off ramp, past the cars idling at the light.

Coop elbowed me. "There he is."

"I see him." He had a head full of short, dark hair that looked oily even from this distance.

The light changed to red again, and the man was about to hike past the waiting line of cars when he glanced our way. He aborted, came back to the corner and stood facing traffic, holding his sign so it was visible to the oncoming vehicles.

The closer we got, the dirtier the guy appeared. A frayed backpack sat in the weeds between the street and the parking lot.

When we were close enough, I said, "Harry?"

He turned to face us, his tattered coat billowing away from his legs in a gust of wind. The clothes beneath it were in no better shape than the coat, and the smell that assailed my nose made me catch my breath. He had on at least two shirts, and the tan pants he wore could've stood on their own. The shoes on his feet were run down at the heel, and the grayish-colored sock on his right foot was visible through a hole worn through the leather by his big toe. He was at least as tall as Coop.

An unlit, half-smoked cigarette dangled from one side of his mouth.

"You O'Hanlon?" he asked.

"Yup, and this is Nick Cooper, a good friend." I jerked a thumb at Coop.

Harry eyed us a moment. "Come with me."

He picked up the backpack, stuffed his sign inside, and crossed the street.

I looked at Coop.

Coop shrugged. "Better follow him."

We scampered across the road and trailed Harry as he headed for the back of whatever business was housed on the corner of Dunwoody and the ramp off I-94. The red brick building was covered with vines creeping skyward. Around the back a path was worn in the ground. We skirted two other buildings and wormed our way through a narrow opening in a hedge. I lost my sense of direction.

Harry stopped at a rickety shelter of sorts constructed in a small thicket of trees and thick brush. "Welcome to my humble abode. Have a seat." Harry disappeared into the structure.

A small fire pit was situated near Harry's "house" with two lawn chairs that were well past the point of use nearby. Coop and I looked at each other and shook our heads simultaneously. Standing was safer.

Grass and brush in the immediate area had been trampled into submission. Discarded booze bottles, crumpled fast food wrappers, empty cigarette boxes, and a mattress with springs poking through the covering lay in a heap on the edge of the clearing. The intermittent breeze periodically brought the smell of rotting garbage from somewhere close by.

Harry emerged butt first from the shelter, grumbling under his breath. As he cleared the entry, his hands were clenched in the material of a sweatshirt. The sweatshirt was filled with the skinny, dirty body of a man of indeterminate age. Long gray hair hung in clumped strands from his head, and the rest of him was clothed in threadbare blue jeans and black tennis shoes. He had an unopened, oversized can of beer clenched in his fist.

"Thanks for hanging while I was gone, Red. You gotta scram now." Harry gave the dude a healthy shove down the trail. Red staggered a couple steps, muttered something incoherently, righted himself, and disappeared.

Harry wiped his hands on his shirt and plunked down in one of the chairs. "Red keeps an eye on things while I'm gone. Otherwise other homeless guys try to take over my dream house." He stretched his legs out and crossed them at the ankles. The unlit smoke still dangled from his lips. "First things first. Not much I'm going to be able to help you with. I'm deep, and bringing you two here's a big risk. I can give you a little advice, but that's about the extent of it."

I held up a hand. "We understand. Anything is better than nothing at this point."

Harry studied me through narrowed eyes for a couple long moments. "So you have a problem with potential drug runners."

I shifted from one foot to the other. "Yeah. It sounds like the situation involves Juárez, tunnels, drugs maybe."

Harry rolled the cigarette around lips, moving it from one side of his mouth to the other as he considered my words. Coop intently watched, his eyes focused on the unlit stub. His cheeks bulged as he ground his gum between his molars.

"I have one that's only half gone if you want it," Harry told Coop. The man didn't miss a thing.

Coop tore his eyes from Harry's mouth and met his obviously amused gaze. "Ah, no. No, thanks. I'm trying to quit."

Harry chuckled. "Me, too. Figure as long as I don't light it, can't hurt. Like a security blanket."

That broke the ice and they both laughed.

Harry said, "Tell me what you know."

Between Coop and I, we gave Harry the rundown on the last few days. When we finished, he said, "You've been busy. I can see why you're worried about taking this to the police. Don't know much about Louisiana law enforcement, but I do know New Orleans PD struggled long before Katrina. The MPD's pretty solid, but there's a few rotten grapes in the bunch, specifically narcs."

He reached into his trench coat, produced a flask, and tilted it our way. "Tipple?"

Coop swallowed hard, and I watched his Adam's apple bounce up and down. He declined with a quick shake of his head. He wasn't a complete germ freak, but wasn't real fond of sharing his food and drink with other people.

Harry fastened his eyes on me. "Shay?"

"No, thanks."

Harry unscrewed the cap, tipped the container to his lips, and took two big swallows. "Your loss." He shrugged as he returned the cap and stowed the flask. "Juárez. Lot of drug-related stuff going on there. The Mexican end of things isn't my area of expertise." He took the cigarette from his mouth, pulled a box of Marlboro Lights from a pocket and slid it inside. "Gotta save what you can out here. Never know when you might find more.

"But I have a new contact," Harry continued. "Her name is Luz Ortez, and she's a recently relocated Mexican studies professor at the University of Minnesota. I don't know her well, but we've had a couple of meetings where she's come in to speak about cartels."

Coop asked, "Relocated from where?"

"Some university in Mexico City."

Score. I asked, "Would she be willing to meet up with us?"

Harry folded his arms against his chest. "I don't know. Don't see why not." He rummaged through one coat pocket, and then the other. "Ah, there it is." He whipped out an old-style flip phone.

Coop said, "Have you heard anything about Fletcher Sharpe being mixed up in drug dealing?"

Harry said, "Not specifically Sharpe. But nothing surprises me anymore. Seems like there was some word out about that toy store of his. Or maybe something about one of the guys who worked there." Harry's shoulder lifted. "Can't remember. But I can do a little checking around." The flask appeared again, and Harry took another snootful of joy juice.

Harry flipped his phone open. "Give me your cell number, and I'll give you a contact number for Ortez." I pulled out the slip of paper I'd written our new cell numbers on and recited them as Harry poked a thick finger at the small keys on his phone. Then he rattled off Luz Ortez's phone number, and I punched it into my cheap pre-pay phone. I'd forgotten how much time it took to punch each key multiple times to get to the right letter. Coop was right. We should've coughed up more money for one of the models with a keyboard.

"Tell her you got her name from Dirty Harry, and I think she'll talk to you. If she won't, let me know, and I'll see who else you can try."

We thanked Harry for his unusual hospitality, and he led us back to the intersection. We left him at the corner with his cardboard sign, and retraced our path toward Joe's Garage.

I eyed Coop. "What do you think?"

"I think we got a name we can start with."

"Rough way to live."

"No kidding." Coop shuddered. "I don't even want to think where he uses the bathroom."

I made a face. "I'll try the professor." The beeps from the phone sounded loud as I navigated my way to the contact list. I had to try twice before I figured out which buttons I had to push to place the call.

Voicemail quickly kicked in, and a Spanish-accented voice filled my ear. I left a message and hung up.

"Seems like all I've gotten lately is voicemail," I said as we crossed the entrance to Joe's Garage.

"That's what happens whenever you need something yesterday. Hopefully she'll call back fast."

Coop snagged a couple of menus from a basket attached to the wall. He handed me one. I spotted Eddy and Agnes vigorously waving from a table toward the back. We threaded our way between tables toward them.

———

My belly was soon pleasantly full eggs and home fries. While Agnes and Eddy argued over who was going to foot the bill, I excused myself and took care of it at the bar. Sometimes it was just easier that way.

I came back and braced my hands on the back of my chair. "Okay, ladies." I raised an eyebrow at Coop and added, "and gentleman. The bill's paid. Let's blow this shack."

That shut them up.

We trooped toward the front door with Eddy in the lead.

"Hey!" Eddy said once she was out the door and on the sidewalk. "Where's the car?"

We filed out behind her. The street in front of the restaurant was a one-way, with metered parking along the south side. There wasn't a single bright-orange car in sight.

Coop said, "Didn't we leave it over there, by the college?" The busy campus of the Minneapolis Community and Technical College was right up the street.

I nodded slowly, a doomed feeling lying heavy in my previously comfortably stuffed gut. "Yup, we did." Could anything go right? I walked toward the spot we'd left the car. As I neared it, broken bluish glass littered the ground.

"I told you, Eddy," Agnes said, sarcasm dripping from her voice, "that car was a little too flashy."

For once Eddy had no comeback.

We called the cops, who eventually showed up and took a report. I feared Stan and Ione's Classic Car Rental was not going to be very happy with us.

Coop said, "You think Hunk and Donny took the car?"

I thought about that. "No, if they knew we were driving that car, they'd have known where we were. If they knew where we were, they could've scooped us up when we walked out of the restaurant. I bet this is the work of some kid who's probably having the time of his life right now."

Eddy said grimly, "Until he crashes it."

Since Kate was working, I called my dad to see if he'd be able to come pick us up. A half-hour later, he rolled up in his boat of a car. While my dad may have been hit-and-miss in the fatherhood department, he wasn't lazy about his vehicles, and that only intensified after my mom died. His forest-green 1970 Olds Delta 88 was in pristine condition, its black interior beautifully maintained. He only drove the car when the snow had melted and enough rain had fallen to rid the streets of residual road salt from the winter.

"Peter O'Hanlon," Eddy said as she rounded the car and practically dragged my father out the door for a hug. She released him and gazed up into his craggy face with obvious affection. "Aren't you a sight for these eyes."

A roguish grin creased his stubble-covered cheek. He boomed, "Ms. Edwina, it's been too long."

Eddy and her son had lived next door when I was growing up, and our two families had spent a lot of time together. We shared many meals, and after we ate, my parents and Eddy would play cards while Neil and I raced Matchbox cars in the dirt outside or on the worn carpet in the living room. Sober, my father was warm and engaging; drunk, well, let's just say after That Night, Eddy bailed my father out many times, and she pretty much raised me as her own. Nevertheless, Eddy has always carried a certain fondness in her heart for my dad.

He took in the rest of us. "Hey, honey," he said to me with a smile.

"Thanks for coming, Dad." I was happy to see his eyes looked clear and sharp. He hadn't hit the bottle too hard yet today.

Dad zeroed in on Coop. "If it ain't the vegetable muncher. How's that no-smoking bullshit going?" My father was old school, which amounted mostly to guns, country, and personal freedom. His version of personal freedom included allowing smoking in his bar, the Leprechaun, although there was a statewide smoking ban for all indoor establishments, including bars. Even after being slapped with two fines, he hadn't put up the required signs or enforced the ban. Stubborn man. Guess I came by my own obstinacy honestly. Unfortunately, his version of personal freedom also didn't include homosexuality in any form. That caused some roof-raising arguments between us.

Coop said, "I'm going through too many packs of Juicy Fruit."

"Good for you, kid." Cigarettes used to be the common denominator between Coop and my father, but since Coop had been trying to quit, Dad, surprisingly, rallied behind him.

"And," Dad turned and squinted at Agnes, "who's this?"

Eddy introduced them, and Dad, at his most chivalrous, offered the front seat to Agnes. When he wasn't ten sheets to the wind, he was a pretty decent guy.

Coop, Eddy, and I settled in the back, and Dad peered at me through the rear view mirror. "Where to?"

With no better idea, I said, "The Leprechaun, please." If nothing else, it would be a place for us to regroup. With any luck, it would also keep us out of the reaches of Mr. Tormenta. I would have to be careful what I told my father, though, because if he had any idea people he loved were in trouble, he'd dive right into the fray with no second thought. I come by that trait honestly as well.

Eddy chatted with my dad, keeping things casual and upbeat as we travelled down Hennepin to Marshall. Northeast Minneapolis was gentrifying, bringing in trendy businesses that blended well alongside older establishments. The Leprechaun was one of those older establishments, and Dad had singlehandedly turned the place from a rundown dive to a profitable blue-collar haven.

Walking into the Leprechaun was like falling head first into the past. A haze of smoke and the smell of stale alcohol hit me with an almost physical force.

My father had spent many years working barges up and down the Mississippi, and the water was in his blood. The walls, lined with river-related memorabilia he'd collected throughout the years, included several pictures of his dad's logging days. An antique, polished-to-a-spit-shine oak bar took up one wall. Behind the bar, a large, mounted mirror with a gilded frame faced those who occupied the bar stools. The word LEPRECHAUN was etched on the surface of the glass along with a picture of a leprechaun, hat in hand, frozen in the midst of a jig. Exposed beams darkened with age and smoke ran the length of the ceiling from front to back.

A few customers sat at the bar, and they looked over at our back-door entrance, checking out who was crashing their party. A bartender I wasn't familiar with was engaged in conversation with a patron who looked like he was leaning a little too far off his stool. I usually recognized someone, but that wasn't the case today.

Dad said, "Shay, why don't you get these folks settled at the corner table, and I'll be back in a minute."

Agnes said, "This is a nice place your father has, Shay."

"Yeah, it is. He's put in a lot of hard work in it." Then it occurred to me maybe we should get ourselves on the same page as far as what we were going to tell the old man. "Hey, let's keep things easy and not worry my dad. He has a tendency to get worked up when he hears about, oh, problematic stuff."

Everyone nodded in agreement. I knew Coop and Eddy understood what I was talking about, and although Agnes hadn't witnessed my father in one of his righteous tirades, she went along without question.

My dad appeared from the back room. "So, what can I offer you all?" He looked at me. "Shay, your usual?"

I wished I could have about five of my usuals, which was a big, bad Fuzzy Navel, but I didn't dare impair my faculties any further than they were. I was already a step behind from the lack of sleep. "No, thanks, Dad. Just a Coke."

Dad nodded. "Cooper, a Bud?"

"I might be staying away from the smokes, but I'll take a Bud anytime. Thanks."

Before my father had a chance to ask Agnes, Eddy said, "I'll have coffee, black, and so will Agnes." Eddy cut her eyes at her. "Won't you, Aggie?"

Agnes glared at Eddy and it looked like she was about to let her have it. Instead, she said, "Coffee would be fine, Mr. O'Hanlon."

My dad boomed a laugh. "Last time someone called me Mr. O'Hanlon, the cigarette police were writing me a citation for a bullshit smoking ban violation. Please, call me Pete."

Obviously charmed, Agnes said, "Okay, Pete. Thank you, dear."

Dad headed for the bar, and I slumped back in my chair. "We're without a car, mooching off Kate, and have a man with the last name of Tormenta dogging us. What next?"

Agnes, seated next to me, patted my shoulder. "It's okay, Shay. Things could definitely be worse. We could be an alligator delicacy right now."

Good observation. That truth actually made me flinch.

My phone rang before I had another chance to wallow. The number was unfamiliar. I flipped it open. "Hello?"

"Hi," a throaty voice said. "Is this Shay O'Hanlon? Luz Ortez here."

"Yes, thanks for calling back! Can you hang on a second?" I excused myself and headed for the front door. I didn't want my dad to overhear anything and start asking questions. Once I was outside, I said, "I'm here. Had to get somewhere I could hear you."

"No problem. What can I do for you?" Her voice was friendly and her tone sounded curious.

I sucked in a breath. "I was wondering if I might meet with you today to talk about Mexican cartels. I was referred to you by Dirty Harry."

Paper rustled in the background. Then Luz said, "Dirty Harry. Nice man. Okay, have a meeting at two, but I should be free by two forty-five."

Excellent. "That would be great, Ms. Ortez."

A melodic chuckle came across the line. "You're not a student. Call me Luz. Do you know where Coffman Union is?"

"Yes."

"There's a Starbucks on the ground floor. Does that work?"

"You bet. I really appreciate you taking the time to see me."

"It's no problem. After my meeting, I'll need a break."

Too bad we weren't closer to the Rabbit Hole. I could've caffeinated her and gained a new customer in the deal. Once you had Hole coffee, you never went back to the old grind.

I thanked her again, and we disconnected. The sun-bleached brick wall was warm against my back. I closed my eyes. The past few days had been nuts. I needed someone to tell me things were going to stop spinning like a top, so I flipped the phone open again and dialed JT. I knew she wouldn't be able to answer, but hearing her voice when voicemail kicked in was like an invisible hug that wrapped me tight.

SEVENTEEN

At two-fifteen, Coop and I were on the road, headed for the East Bank of the University of Minnesota. I had called Kate and asked her to check in on Rocky and Baz. All was well for the moment.

My dad had invited Eddy and Agnes to join in on his semi-weekly afternoon poker game in the back room of the bar. They agreed, and Agnes showed far more enthusiasm than I expected. Maybe they were tired of running around. It was a relief they were somewhere safe.

We were in my father's more well-used vehicle, a midnight blue '03 Grand Cherokee. One thing about my father: he didn't cut any corners in his vehicles. The Jeep was loaded.

As I followed Washington toward the East Bank, Coop stuffed yet another piece of gum in his mouth. "Man, I hope this chick is going to be able to help us. This avoid-them-or-die crap is for the birds."

I checked the rear view mirror for suspicious cars. Either there weren't any or I was a really bad judge of dodgeable vehicles. "No kidding. You know, you've really come a long way."

"A long way for what? Not smoking?"

"That, and how you're handling what's going on. Typically you'd be freaking bananas in a situation like this."

Coop slowed his frantic chewing. "Huh. You're right. Maybe laying off the smokes helps. And playing broomball with you and Kate this winter. I learned to whack that ball into submission."

I laughed. "You were our secret weapon with that slap shot we never even knew was in you. Thanks."

He gave me a perturbed look. "You think I'd duck and run?"

"No, that's not—"

"Gotcha." One side of his mouth curled up.

"Smart ass."

"Takes one to know one."

It felt good to banter like we normally did. Like things weren't one big crazy fucked-up mess.

I pulled into a parking ramp and we found our way to Coffman Union and the Starbucks within.

We walked into the café, surveyed the space. Most of the tables were occupied with kids in their late teens, and probably a good number of twenty-somethings, grouped in twos and threes, some sipping their drinks of choice while a few ate and others dozed. A line of patrons waited patiently to order, and another group stood by at the pick-up window. This place was hopping.

Coop said, "Come on." He dragged me through the crowd to one of the few available tables. "You hold our spot. I'll do battle. Coffee?"

"You read my mind. A double shot of espresso, please. I need a kick." I knew espresso didn't contain the amount of caffeine everyone thought it did, but there was something about downing the thick, syrupy stuff that perked me up.

With a nod, Coop was off.

I looked at the tables farther back for a lone woman. No dice.

With a deep breath, I crossed my arms, fingers tapping against my bicep. I was happy not to have to run the rat race of classes and readings and tests anymore. But that was sure a simpler time, when life was divided between partying and whatever classes you weren't too hung over to attend.

Before I dwelled too long on the challenges of higher education, a woman in her late thirties or early forties hurried into the café. She practically skidded to a stop as she searched the crowd. She looked classy and elegant, dressed in a black suit jacket over an ivory shell, paired with black, billowy slacks. They reminded me of 1980s parachute pants. A black leather messenger bag hung over one shoulder. Glossy black boots with narrow heels completed her ensemble.

I stood and waved, hoping this was Luz Ortez.

She saw me, waved back, and threaded her way toward me. She arrived at the table slightly out of breath. "Shay O'Hanlon?"

"Yup, that's me. Have a seat." I stuck my hand out and she grasped it in greeting.

"Luz." She pulled a chair out and sat with a deep huff.

"Thanks for taking the time to meet with us."

"No problem." She tugged the strap for the messenger bag over her head and set the bag on the floor next to her with a half-groan, half-sigh. "That gets a bit heavy after a while." Her hands smoothed her shoulder-length, jet-black hair. It was even darker than mine, but she had more gray strands peeking through. The smell of jasmine wafted delicately off her, tickling my senses.

Coop returned to the table bearing three paper cups. "Good timing," he said as he handed them around. "You must be Ms. Ortez." He smiled at our visitor. "I took a gamble and picked you up some coffee."

Luz met Coop's gaze evenly and took the cup he offered. "Thanks, but please, call me Luz. And who are you, you kind soul?" Luz's slight accent only emphasized her exotic beauty.

"Nick Cooper." He thrust his hand out.

She shook it and held his hand a fraction of a second longer than necessary. "Nick, it's nice to meet you."

I waited for his inevitable correction. No one called Coop Nick.

Coop settled himself at the table without a word, but with a perplexed look on his face.

Luz crossed her legs. "So. How exactly can I help you?"

We should have thought about how to explain things without sounding crazy or guilty. I decided to roll with it. "Coo—ah—Nick and I are grad students."

Coop nodded, but kept his mouth shut.

"We're doing a project on Mexican cartels, specifically in the Juárez area." Liar liar pants on fire.

Luz's face tightened for a fraction of a second. Then she nodded attentively and took a sip of her coffee.

I sucked in some air, hoping it would spark my brain cells into more creative thinking. "The project is what-if scenario." That sounded good. "So we did some research on the internet and found a lot of cartel information is framed in generalities." I paused and swallowed the last of my espresso. "So, let's say there are a couple of factories down south, maybe across the border. They find some way to ship drugs or weapons into the US. The contraband makes it all the way up here to the Cities. Somehow the goods are converted to cash." Not bad. With this imagination of mine, I should take up writing. "The question is, how does it all work?"

Luz stifled a yawn as she considered my words. "It's been a long day." She folded her hands together, elbows on the table. "I think it would be best to start at the beginning. Drug cartels in Mexico did not exist until the late 1980s. A corrupt cop named Félix Gallardo decided to break up the drug trade he ran and divide Mexico into regions. He assigned territories to allow the business to keep running whether or not one arm was metaphorically cut off by the authorities." Luz's words were softly spoken, her voice falling into the lilting musical tones I'd heard on the phone. Her outward focus faded as she warmed to her subject.

I peeked at Coop. His eyeballs followed every move Luz made. Then it dawned on me. He was interested, and not in what she was saying. Freaking peachy. All I needed now was for him to fall into a pseudo-infatuation with our informant, who was some years older than he was.

Luz continued, "These newly formed cartels took over day-to-day operations. They struggled—and continue to struggle—for control and dominance. Alliances were forged, turf wars fought. Right now there are two main factions, two umbrellas, under which the cartels operate. But, accords often change and cartels are known to cannibalize themselves." She looked from me to Coop. "Have I lost you yet?"

Coop shook his head, obviously fixated. "No. Not at all."

"I'm with you, too." I briefly cut my gaze to Coop and gave him a nearly imperceptible shake of my head.

Luz took a sip of her coffee and gently set the cup down on the tabletop. "You asked about the city of Juárez. Right now the Reynosa Cartel controls the area the city is a part of. In the last ten years, there have been a number of changes and adjustments to what used to be the Juárez Cartel."

I asked, "How do you bring a cartel down?" Figured we might as well get to the crux of the issue.

Luz leveled her gaze on me, one eyebrow lifted slightly. It felt like her dark eyes burned into my soul. "Hmm. Good question. Whoever is the head of the cartel is the key. The head of the snake. Do you know what I'm saying?"

Coop said, "You bet," without taking his eyes off the woman. Could he be any more blatant? I resisted the urge to kick him in the shin.

I said, "It seems like the cartels manage to get a hold of a lot of law enforcement personnel and turn them so they're working for the cartel instead of staying on the right side of the law." My mind drifted back to the cop in New Orleans.

"Yes, the cartels can be very … persuasive."

"This Reynosa Cartel," I asked, "do you have any idea who it's run by?"

Luz sat for a few moments considering her answer. "The struggle for power between the Reynosa and Juárez Cartels has been deadly, with numerous losses on both sides. The most recent drug lord is the first woman to hold such a position. She's deadly, strikes like a rattlesnake when angered, or metes out a slower though no less painful punishment if she feels someone deserves it."

From the tone of Luz's voice, this new drug lord was a fascinating subject. "Her name is Miguela Carillo-Sanchez, better known simply as Zorra." She caught the widening of my eyes. "Yes, her name is a take off your American Zorro, and like him, she too has worked to use her ill-gotten funds to help the poor people of her region. She even wears a mask and a cape, along with the gaucho hat when she's in public. She's highly regarded in her own organization and treated with grudging respect throughout the loose coalition of Mexican drug organizations. She's mysterious, very rarely seen. But extremely powerful."

Holy crapola. Zorra was the head of the snake. The same woman Hunk, Tommy, and the mystery man had been talking about. The leader of one of the most notorious drug cartels in North America was after us. Double crapola.

I took a couple of steadying breaths. I sat back in my chair, feeling faint, my heart tap dancing in my chest. We were in seriously dangerous territory, sinking into raging quicksand. Coop met my eyes, and then we both turned our sights on Luz.

"So, you wanted to know how cartels work." Shadows filled in the hollows of Luz's cheekbones, and I distractedly noticed it gave her a patrician profile.

"Yeah," I was barely able to get the word out. I'd better find my backbone, fast.

She said, "The cartels underwrite small-time farmers' operations and various labs and processing centers in Mexico. Then the drugs are delivered many places. A huge amount of the stuff goes into the United States. The cartel coordinates the Mexican end, while a contact linked to the cartel is on the receiving end. Generally mules smuggle a great deal of drugs into the country."

Luz caught the confusion on my face. "Mules are people, not the four-legged hairy beasts you're thinking." She half-grinned, and then her face turned serious once more. "They owe the cartel or are desperate for money and will dare to risk everything, including their lives, to transport the drugs to their final destinations."

Coop's attention was riveted on Luz. In fact, he was so focused I was willing to bet if I waved my hand in front of his face, he wouldn't even blink. I wondered if he was actually hearing what she was saying or if his brain was stuck in Luz-centric loop.

"Then the drugs are supplied by the contact to their own set of distributors." A peculiar look of distaste or disdain twisted Luz's features. "Many times children, kids under eighteen, are used to disperse the end product. These couriers give most of the money they take in back to the contact, who takes a portion and returns most of the cash to Mexico, and the cycle begins again." Luz ended her explanation and sipped from her cup. She set it down and surveyed us with one eyebrow raised.

"This Zorra," Coop began.

Luz nodded.

"Exactly how deadly is she?"

"She's a master manipulator and knows how to work people, to bend wills. Once she has her sights on either somebody she wants to join her organization or someone she wants to be rid of, they're as good as involved or as good as dead."

That was so not what I wanted to hear.

Coop and I thanked Luz for her time. He tried for her phone number, but she politely sidestepped the request. We walked back to the car in near silence, both of us trying to absorb what Luz had said. Coop jammed two sticks of gum in his mouth and worked them hard.

It freaked me out that not only was Zorra a notorious drug lord, but she'd issued a cartel-style warrant for our deaths with a deadline.

Once we climbed into the car and locked the doors, I looked over at Coop. His skin was pale, his cheeks flushed pink. "I think we need help, Coop."

Chomp chomp. "I'm thinking you're right on." He looked out the window, his eyes flicking frenetically from one thing to another. "I feel like they're everywhere, Shay."

"Me, too. But you know what? They're not. We're fine. They don't know this vehicle. We're okay, Coop."

"Maybe." He sniffed and held his forehead with his hand, rubbed his temples with his thumb and index finger. "Who we gonna call?"

"Ghostbusters are going to be of no help." I allowed a fleeting smile. "Let's see what JT says. Maybe she'll have another moment of serendipitous insight."

"I think you're losing it, O'Hanlon."

I pulled out my cell. "I think you might be right, *Nick*. What the hell was that all about?"

Coop's ears began to glow. "We had a connection."

"I think it takes two for a connection, and she didn't look like she was feeling it, Mister Slick."

"Just call already."

I keyed in the contact number JT had given me and caught the time at the top of the screen. It would be about six out there, and she should theoretically be finished for the day. But then, cop types loved their nighttime deploys and practice maneuvers.

The phone rang three times. I was sure voicemail was going to kick in when a breathless "Hello?" came across the line.

"JT? It's Shay."

"Hey babe, how are things going? Did you talk to Harry?" She was panting. The sound of her voice, winded or not, calmed me.

"What are you doing? If you're in the middle of something I can call back."

"No, it's okay, I'm about done with the Yellow Brick Road. Second time today, so I can call it good."

"JT Bordeaux, you like pain. I didn't realize this about you."

A wheezing chuckle came across the line. "S'up? Did you get a hold of Harry?" she repeated.

I told her about the unconventional visit with Harry and the ensuing meeting with Luz.

"So," I finished, "it looks like the head of a drug cartel might be..." how was I supposed to phrase this? "...looking for us."

The labored breathing coming through the phone disappeared. "JT?"

"What if you go to the Feds? I need to come home, Shay. You guys are seriously—"

"Come on, what can you do? Nothing but hold my hand, right?"

I waited. For a moment silence reigned. Then, "Okay. Although you have a very nice hand to hold. Call the Minneapolis FBI field office. Google it, and then look under the Contact Us link for the number. Ask for Rusty Smith. Tell him who you are and that I told you to call him specifically. Explain things and see what he suggests. He's a good guy."

"Okay, I can do that." I nodded, even though JT couldn't see me. "Get back to your torture. I'll call you if anything goes on."

"You damn well better, Shay. It sucks being here when the crap is hitting the windmill at home."

"I know, but you're almost done. And JT?" I was going to do it this time.

"Yeah?"

"I love … the way you breathe." Gah. I'm a loser.

She chuckled, but it sounded strained. "I love the way you breathe, too."

I hung up, kicking myself. What if that was the last time I ever spoke to JT because some big bad drug lord murdered my ass? She should know how I felt. *Shay, you're nothing but a big clucker.*

We found a Caribou Coffee and parked in an available spot in front of the building. Gotta love free WiFi. Coop booted his laptop, secured an connection, and Googled the FBI phone number. After calling the Minneapolis field office and getting a recording telling me to call back during regular business hours (but I could leave a message if I knew my party's extension), I decided to try the DEA. Coop did his magic again, and soon the phone was ringing.

"Thanks for calling the answering service for the Chicago Division-Drug Enforcement Agency. How can I direct your call?"

A live person, hallelujah! "I need to talk to an agent about a situation in Minneapolis."

"Regarding drugs?" The woman sounded about as enthusiastic as Eeyore.

I pulled the phone away and looked at it in disbelief before bringing to back to my ear.

"Yes, regarding drugs."

"Right now, no one is available to speak with you. You can call back tomorrow during normal business hours, or you can leave a message for one of the agents."

How was no one was available? Good grief. "What would happen if I told you there was a major Mexican drug lord coming to Minneapolis in two days?"

"Interesting information, but I'm sorry, there's still no one available to talk to you right now. I can forward you to the tip line."

"Is there anyone I can call here in the Twin Cities?"

Shuffling papers filled my ear. "You can try the Diversion Control field office in Minneapolis." She read off the phone number, which I repeated for Coop to write down.

I thanked her for her great wealth of information and disconnected.

Coop said, "Sounds like she was a font of knowledge."

I dialed the number Eeyore had given me and went through the same recording machine rigmarole, disconnected, and thumped my head on the headrest. "Maybe it would be better to wait until tomorrow morning and try again when real people should be around. But I really don't want to wait."

Coop looked at me for a long moment and blew a double bubble, which he sucked back in his mouth with two loud cracks. "Okay, let's give it one more try. I'll see what other federal offices are located here in the Cities." He went to town.

After a couple of minutes and some mumbling, Coop said, "There's an FBI field office in Minneapolis, which we've tried. An ICE field office is in St. Paul, and … " he tapped some more, "ATF in St. Paul, too."

I tapped my own fingers on the steering wheel. "What is ICE, exactly? I remember seeing something about them being a part of an immigration crackdown not too long ago."

"Hang on." Coop worked the phone. "Man, I could use a cigarette."

"Gum. What you need is more gum." I grabbed the pink pack of Bubble Yum he'd left on the dash, pulled two pieces out, unwrapped them, and stuffed them in his mouth.

"Thanks," he said sarcastically as he worked the new pieces into his already well-chewed wad.

"Okay, here is it. ICE is Immigration and Customs Enforcement. Looks like they deal with immigration issues as well as ... holy cow, they cover a ton of stuff. Human trafficking, cyber crimes, narcotics enforcement—"

"Narcotics! That's us. Give me the number." And please don't let there be any freaks on the other end of the line.

I dialed as Coop read the digits off for me. I held the phone to my ear, ready to hang up as soon as the recorded message kicked in. To my surprise, a man answered.

"Thanks for calling the St. Paul division of Immigration and Customs Enforcement. Agent Farroway speaking. How can I help you?"

I sat for a moment, stunned to silence.

"Hello? Anybody there?" the man said.

"Ah, hi. I'm in shock to be talking not only to a living human being, but to an actual agent. On a Sunday, no less."

The man barked a laugh. "That's what happens to the new kid on the block. So what can I do for you?"

"I have a little problem. I have some potentially useful information regarding a major Mexican cartel leader."

Agent Farroway's tone changed immediately. I imagined him sitting up straight. "What's that?"

As much as I wanted to dump the whole thing on his lap, I didn't feel comfortable letting it rip across the airwaves. I'd feel better if we could explain everything face to face. I told him that, and he said, "It's getting close to quitting time. I really need get home and let my dog out, but I can meet you after that."

I started the truck. "I have a better idea."

EIGHTEEN

COOP, BAZ, DAWG, AND I pulled into the parking lot of a fenced-in, off-leash dog park in St. Paul. Rocky stayed behind, thrilled to be chatting with his flower. I was never going to remember her name. Daisy? No. Petunia? Lily? Tulip. That was it. Good grief.

Picnic tables were scattered throughout a grassy space half the size of a football field. Games of Dog Chase Frisbee and Get the Stick played out in the clearing. A wooded area took up the back half of the park, and the city had installed inviting wood-chip-lined paths that meandered through the trees.

Baz was none too happy we'd dragged him to a dog park. When we entered the park through the double gate, I noticed him doing a weird tiptoe shuffle-dance-step move.

I said, "Baz, what are you doing?"

He didn't raise his eyes from the ground. "Looking out for dog dung."

Dog dung? I said, "Don't worry, this is a pick-up-the-poop park. Your dog poops, you pick it up. It works most of the time."

Baz ignored me and kept up his fancy footwork all the way to one of the tables. Coop and I plunked on the worn-smooth bench seats while Baz actually crawled on top of the picnic table, trying to stay out of Dawg's licking range. "Can't you make that beast keep his tongue to himself?"

I grinned. "He thinks you taste good."

"That tongue," Coop said, "has a mind of its own. What are you afraid of, Baz? A little dog drool?"

Baz ignored our egging. He pressed his lips into a thin line, and cast suspicious gazes toward the dogs closest to us. I figured he was on the lookout for lethal canines who might try to devour him. Or poop on him.

Since it was right around quitting time for most 9-to-5ers, the park was busy with antsy dogs and stiff-from-sitting-too-long owners. I kept an eye on the main gate and watched a solitary man enter with a dog by his side. The dog was as big, if not bigger than Dawg, his short coat rusty with a few large black blobs.

His owner was very tall and stick-man thin. If I didn't know better, I'd have said he and Coop were brothers. Instead of Coop's light locks, the man's hair was bright-red and cut in an honest-to-goodness flat-top. I instantly dubbed him Big Red.

As the pair wandered closer, I realized freckles weren't just dusted across his nose. They were liberally splattered all over his face.

If the haircut wasn't a dead give-away this was our guy, his attire was. He wore a fancy suit that mirrored what Tommy Lee Jones and Will Smith wore in the movie *Men In Black*. Big Red even had similar black shades covering his eyes, although the sun was well on its way down.

I had told Agent Farroway on the phone we'd be with a sixty-five pound Boxer with a huge tongue. I waved. Big Red caught my movement, returned my wave, and headed toward us. I stood and grabbed Dawg by the collar, not wanting a clash of wills if he and the new arrival didn't get along. As Big Red came closer, I watched the dog practically drag his owner one way then another, his nose glued to the ground.

The duo stopped ten feet away, and Big Red pulled off his sunglasses. His eyes were a piercing, electric blue, and they assessed us slowly.

Dawg wriggled beside me, dying to meet the sniffer.

"Ms. O'Hanlon? I'm ICE Special Agent Mike Farroway."

Formal. "Thanks for coming, Agent Farroway. This is Coop," I jerked a thumb toward him, then stepped out of the way and introduced Baz, who was now fully on the top of the table, hugging his knees to his chest, or as close to his chest as his rotund gut would allow.

"Nice to meet you all. This here is Bogey. Shall we?" He indicated the dogs.

Dawg sat politely next to me, his head cocked in curiosity. His upper lip was hung up on a lower front tooth, and his forehead was all crinkled up. His body vibrated with excitement. Although I was pretty sure Dawg would behave, I kept a good grip on his collar.

"Sure." I met Farroway halfway, and our dogs nosed each other. It looked like Bogey might outweigh Dawg by a few pounds.

The sniffing was intense for a minute, but calm. Agent Farroway unhooked Bogey and I let go of Dawg, both of us ready to intervene if necessary. After a couple of rounds of nose to butt introduction, Bogey and Dawg settled down to some serious play.

"I think they're going to get along fine." Agent Farroway crossed his arms and leaned against the side of the table as he watched the mutts. Bogey flopped on the ground upside-down, sturdy legs waving in the air, tail flagging as Dawg thoroughly snuffled him. I thought Dawg's face was a mass of loose flesh, but this dog's folds were many and enormous. His jowls, lips, and maybe even his cheeks piled up in a mound on either side of his face in the dirt. In the next moment, Dawg was beneath Bogey, receiving the same treatment. They were indeed going to be just fine.

Baz spoke up from behind us. "Is that a Bloodhound?"

I turned to him, having forgotten for a moment he was still huddled on the tabletop. If I wasn't so mad at him, I'd have felt bad.

We all looked at Agent Farroway. I thought Big Red fit him better, although I had a hunch he wasn't going to be too receptive if I tried calling him that. Kids can be terrible, and I could just imagine the taunting he probably received in school.

Farroway smiled. "Sure is."

Coop asked, "Had him long?"

Farroway stroked his cheek with an open palm as he thought about it. "I guess it's been two years now."

"Do you use him for your job?" I asked as I watched the two dogs just a few yards away, happily chasing each other around. "I'd think he'd be helpful in your line of work."

"Not exactly. Or not officially, anyway."

Baz, ever tactless, said, "Why not? Looks like he's got a snoot on him."

Something flitted across Farroway's features. He said, "I'm working on that. Actually, Bogey was a reject from Bloodhound training school, and I rescued him. He has the right idea with scents, but gets too caught up in what's going on, like playing with Dawg, there, instead of doing his homework." When Farroway looked at Bogey, his face changed from mostly impassive to all melty. His tone became slightly defensive. "He's got the nose, just isn't as fast a learner as the others. Doesn't make him useless. We've been working on the sly, since he's not officially an ICE hound anymore."

"Your secret's safe with us." Coop said. "Sometimes some of the best people, or dogs, for that matter, have a rough start, but once the tarnish is off, they can do amazing things." I knew he was referring to Dawg, whose junkyard life had been ugly.

"Right," I said. "It's important not to give up. So." I wanted to get on with things. "You're kind of low on the totem pole, huh?"

Farroway nodded. "The lowest. It doesn't get lower. The bottom of the well."

Coop asked, "How long have you been doing the … ICE thing?"

Both Farroway's so-light-they-almost-weren't-there eyebrows lifted, and he stuck his lower lip out. He nodded once, as if deciding something, then said, "A month."

Baz snickered. "You've been a federal agent for a month? A whole month?"

I shot Baz a warning gaze. We didn't need to alienate Farroway, even if he was so new he hadn't had a chance to break in his shoes yet.

Farroway looked down and scuffed his as yet unbroken-in shoe in the dirt. Then he met my eyes and shrugged. "What can you do? You want a Fed on a Sunday, I'm what you get."

The crooked grin on his face transformed him. The kid inside battled with the macho man Farroway tried to project. He couldn't have been more than twenty-five or -six.

He rubbed his hands together. "Tell me what's going on."

I said a silent prayer that Big Red wasn't low dog on a Mexican payroll. "You might want to sit down. It's going to take a while."

Between Coop, Baz, and me, it took forty-five minutes to explain everything to Farroway. He sat with his elbows on the top of the picnic table, chin on his fists, listening with rapt attention.

We finished and sat silently, waiting for Farroway to speak. His eyes were locked on our dogs, who were now lying next to each other, his chewing on a pig's ear while Dawg gnawed on a big rawhide.

He said, "You haven't seen any drugs, but you have a bear full of money."

I nodded enthusiastically.

"And you basically stole this from Fletcher Sharpe's house."

I nodded again, a little slower this time.

"And what you've told me is ultimately hearsay."

My upper lip curled and I bobbed my head once.

His shoulders slumped as he dropped his hands to the grooved, paint-chipped boards of the tabletop.

"I don't know if I can help you right now. My office is hooked in with a bunch of other agencies, and they're all off working a multi-jurisdictional investigation. They left just me behind to cover home base."

Baz said, "They tell you what the investigation was?" Once in a while Baz surprised me with an intelligent comment.

Farroway shook his head. "Nope. The bottom line is this. I think you have some good information here, but I don't have anyone to take it to. As soon as this op wraps up, I'll do what I can. I think you have enough reasonable suspicion that it warrants looking into, but nothing points directly … there's no smoking gun, as the cliché goes."

"What about the fact people are after us?" Coop said. "Want us dead? And the leader of a cartel might be here in the cities Tuesday?"

"That," Farroway said, "is a problem. We have forty-eight hours, give or take, before Zorra arrives. Is there somewhere you can hole up for a few days? At least until I can see what I can do on my end?"

I looked skeptically at Coop, who raised his hands in the classic I don't know gesture.

Baz peered at Farroway with squinty eyes, thankfully keeping his mouth shut.

I sighed. "We could go to the cabin."

"I'm sorry," Farroway said. "If you had more evidence, some drugs, some incriminating video tape … "

Baz sucked in a breath. "Are you sure you know what you're doing? Isn't a bear full of money enough?"

That remark took Farroway back a moment. "If it hadn't been gotten by illegal means, yeah. And," he directed at Baz, "most of the time I at least pretend to know what I'm doing." Then he laughed, easing the tension. "Tell me about this cabin."

I told him the location of the cabin, and we gave him our contact information. He returned the favor, and even included his home phone number. Then he said, "If anything changes, you call me, and I'll do everything I can to help you out."

I shivered in the cooling twilight and hoped that offer wouldn't be too little, too late.

NINETEEN

WE LEFT FARROWAY AND Bogey at the dog park and drove back to Kate's place.

On the way I put in a fast call to the Leprechaun, and asked the bartender for my father. He came on the line after a couple of minutes, his voice all rumbly and deep. Cigars did something weird to his throat, and he could do a voice-over for James Earl Jones when he smoked more than one. From the sound of it, he'd puffed plenty. He said Eddy and Agnes were beating the butts off him and his poker-playing cronies, and they weren't finished playing yet. Just as well, two less people for us to worry about.

At seven-thirty, we pulled into Kate's driveway and piled out of the Jeep. Dawg bounced with excitement beside me. I opened the gate to the backyard, and he tore around the enclosure like his fur was on fire. Then he stopped in the corner near Kate's flowerbed, circled a couple times, hunched over, and deposited a log-sized doogie. He then straightened up, sniffed around, and looked from it to me and back again as if to say, here it is, clean it up.

Coop, who was standing next to me watching Dawg's antics, said, "I'm outta here," and high-tailed it inside. Baz had already headed into the warmth of the house, so that left Dawg and me on our own.

I sighed. This dog ownership thing was sometimes smelly business. I rustled up a plastic bag and took care of things.

Once I'd dropped the bag with its revoltingly warm contents into a garbage can next to the garage, I reentered the yard. Dawg sat near the stoop, patiently waiting for me to return. His butt was on the ground, his legs skewed out to one side. Sloppy and very unmanly. Yet irresistible.

"You're definitely not suave, big boy." I put both hands on his face and rubbed, flipping his lips up and down. His eyebrows shot up and he made a groaning sound that usually meant he liked whatever you were doing.

"Come on, let's get inside, you big fart." I kissed him on the top of the head. He slurped my face, and I hardly minded at all.

I held the screen door open, and Dawg scooted in. I followed at a more sedate pace.

Kate sat sprawled on a black, worn-leather couch in the living room, watching *America's Top Chef*. Rocky worked at a computer on a desk by the window.

Kate looked up from her show and greeted me, while Rocky was so absorbed in what he was doing that he didn't hear a thing. Kate said, "The boys went into the kitchen. I assume you're all hungry?"

She stood and stretched. Today she was wearing a purple top and black cords. A couple of brown stains decorated one side of the front of her shirt.

"Of course we're hungry. Rough day at the Hole?" I asked, trailing her into the kitchen.

"Not bad, busy in the morning. I think we should hire another part-timer."

Fine by me. It'd been a bumpy road for the last couple of years, but things were starting to pick up again.

Dawg followed us and kept nudging me in the back of the legs, his way of letting me know we weren't the only ones with grumbly tummies.

Kate opened up the refrigerator while I scooped up some dog chow and piled it in Dawg's bowl.

Kate's voice drifted from inside the fridge, "What's the news?"

We told her about meeting with up Luz Ortez and ICE Special Agent Mike "Big Red" Farroway. I left out the crush it appeared Coop had on Luz. If Baz hadn't been there, I'd have heckled Coop, but Baz kind of took the fun out of everything, even making fun of an old buddy.

"Well," Kate said as she assembled various items on the countertop, "what are you going to do now?"

Coop said, "Nothing has changed. We still don't have anyone who can really be of help." He crossed his arms and stuck his hands in his armpits. "Farroway says we need more evidence."

"Evidence?" Baz practically spat. "What more can they want? We have a stuffed animal full of dough."

I guess Baz didn't realize how ridiculous that sounded. "I think they want actual drugs or something. He said videotape would be good." I watched Kate move around her kitchen, effortlessly whipping up what I guessed were going to be ham and cheese omelets. I knew better than to ask her if she needed help. She ruled her culinary domain with an iron fist, and unless you were doing dishes, she didn't need you getting in her way.

"Drugs." Kate looked over her shoulder at us as she whipped the eggs in a bowl. "That's something hard to argue."

I picked up the bunny-shaped salt and pepper shakers I'd given Kate for her last birthday and made them hop across the table in front of me as we talked.

Coop grabbed the shakers from my hands and plunked them back down in the center of the table with a bang. "Enough," he said, softening his actions with a laugh. "I'm already jumpy as it is. You're making me nuts."

"No kidding. Thank you," Baz said.

I gave them both a dark look.

Kate turned to face us, wiping her hands on a towel. "So, you guys just need to get more evidence. Find some drugs. Then go back to that ICE guy."

I scrunched my eyes shut. I was tired. Tired of running. Tired of talking. Tired of trying to figure out what to do. I wanted JT to come home and all this to be a cockamamie dream.

I opened my eyes, and unfortunately, I was still sitting at Kate's table instead of waking up from a nightmare. Guess I'd better suck it up.

Coop said, "Maybe we should do a little poking into the office at the Hands On Toy Company. I know most of the managers there. If we went later in the evening, there's usually only one manager on. I could divert their attention while you," he paused and looked at me, "sneak into the office and see if you can find anything."

TWENTY

AND THAT WAS HOW I found myself about to break into the Hands On Toy Company management office a few hours later. As soon as we walked through the front door, the smell of freshly popped popcorn wafted through the air and right into my nose, mixing with the cardboard-like tang of plastic-wrapped games and packaged toys.

The office was located in the rear of the store between the café and the gaming area. The wall around the office door had been painted to look like the entrance to a big top, resplendent with colorful drape-like cloth hanging from above, made to appear tied off like real tent flaps.

Coop pointed out a woman dressed in the requisite red-and-white-striped, puffy-sleeved button-down reminiscent of the shirts the Swiss Guard—the Pope Protectors—wore. It didn't matter if you were a male or a female. If you worked at Hands On, you donned the shirt. I hoped Fletcher Sharpe paid his staff enough money to put up with looking like a Renaissance throwback.

He breathed a sigh of relief. "Good. That's Robin. I won't have a problem distracting her. She likes me." He shot me a lecherous look. "Hot, huh?"

Baz snorted while I checked Robin out. She wasn't classically beautiful, but she had what my mom used to call apple-cheeks and a smile that lit up her entire face as she laughed at something the employee said. Her blonde hair hung in two braids and brushed her shoulders. I couldn't help but think of Pippi Longstocking. I wondered if Robin had red-and-white striped knee-highs on, too.

"She's cute," I whispered.

"Yup." Coop said. "You know what the signals are, right?"

"I do, and he better," I eyed Baz, "since he's going to be on lookout duty again."

"I got it. Geez Louise." Baz scowled. "Can't a guy screw up once and not have it made into a federal case? If your hands are in your pockets, things are fine. If you stretch, that means to hurry up. If you pull your jacket on, that means get out now. If you yell 'come on!' we better run."

Screwed up once, my ass, I thought, but held my tongue with some difficulty. Coop caught my eye. He was thinking the same thing. But this was neither the time nor place to get into a verbal smackdown with mush-brain.

Coop tossed a worn, old sweater over his shoulder. "I'll distract Robin and you two meander toward the back. Make sure the kid working in the café doesn't see you. The code to the back office is 2-3-2-4."

Baz nodded. I looked at my palm, where I'd written the numbers just minutes before sitting in the Bug with Kate, who was primed and waiting right outside as our get-away driver. I'd asked Coop how he got the access number, and all he did was grin.

Coop's smile was absent now as he sucked in a deep breath and let it out slowly. "She's in a good place, there by the board games. It's right where I can see both the front entrance and the office door. Oh." His gaze stopped on a trash can against the wall. He walked over and spit out yet another wad of pink.

While Coop disposed of his gum, I tried to see how many Hands On patrons were still in the building. At a little after nine, most of the younger kids had already been dragged home and stuffed into bed. A few adolescents hung out in the young adult area, playing around with different items and chatting. I couldn't see past the wall where the checkouts were, but the only things on the other side were the gaming room and the café, both of which were semi-enclosed. Should make Operation Great Sneak that much easier.

"This is a bad idea," Baz mumbled behind me.

I ignored him.

Coop returned, and with a nod said, "Here we go."

He marched purposefully toward his target while Baz and I began the trek to our target. A single cashier hung out behind the tills. He leaned against the shelving behind the counter, paging through one of the magazines that lined the checkout aisle. He looked like he might have been two days over sixteen.

Since it was nearly Easter, the place was loaded with stuffed bunnies in a multitude of pastel colors, painted display eggs, little tot's outfits with rabbits and trees and Easter eggs. If tradition was followed, a couple days before the holiday hit, some poor schmuck would be stuck wearing a hot, stinky bunny suit entertaining whiny kids as adults spent their hard-earned money to make this Easter extra-special.

I peeled my eyes away from the holiday displays to grab Baz's jacket as he veered off the Path of Ages toward a display of video games.

He shook my hand off and fell back in step with me. "I was just looking."

I resisted the urge to pop him in the nose. "Well, you need to be looking elsewhere. Come on."

We passed Coop and the manager, who were deep in conversation. Coop caught my eye and raised a brow. We kept going right past them. The employee who'd been talking with the manager had drifted toward the group of kids in the young adult area, either to watch for dastardly doings or to join in the conversation. Maybe both.

As we followed the Path of Ages around the wall dividing the retail area of the store from Café Hobbitude and the Dungeon, I was relieved to see there were six or seven people sitting in the café. The worker behind the counter was busy whipping up something. Two people stood in line waiting to have their orders taken.

The gaming area was quiet, with only four people sitting at one of the tables in the first cave-like room, all intent on the cards in their hands.

The Path of Ages split, with one trail leading into the Hobbitude, and the other to the Dungeon entrance. Nestled between the two was the faux big-top entrance to the main offices. I glanced once more to either side, then shot a quick look behind me. Coop faced me, rather obviously flirting up the poor manager. From the giggles that floated to my ears, she was having a good time.

It was now or never.

"Come on, Baz," I whispered and walked nonchalantly toward the tent flaps. Quickly I pulled on a pair of yellow rubber gloves I'd found under Kate's sink. I handed Baz another pair and pressed the numbers 2-3-2-4 into the keypad attached to the doorknob, praying no one was inside. I held my breath. The lock box made a whirring sound, and then a green light blinked on. I pushed down on the handle and we slipped inside.

The door clicked shut—too loudly, it seemed. Then the hammering of my heart echoed in my ears. My diaphragm kicked in, sucking air into my lungs. The roaring subsided, and my vision cleared. We were in a typical corporate backroom that had a break room cubby on one side. In the main space, five desks lined the walls on opposite sides and a closed door leading to another room, maybe a bathroom, occupied the far end. A large set of gray metal shelves held various office necessities like paper, rubber bands, filing folders, and signage.

Everything was quiet, and the place felt empty.

A teal banner with yellow letters hung high on one wall and read: MAKE THEIR DAY. EVERY DAY. IN EVERY WAY.

Not a bad slogan.

Baz whispered, "What now?"

Yes, what now? I wasn't comfortable poking my nose where it didn't belong until we'd ascertained that the room on the end was unoccupied. "You crack that door and watch Coop and let me know if we need to run. I'm going to make sure we're flying solo here and check the room behind the closed door."

For a minute I was afraid he was going to refuse. Then he said, "Okay. Fine. Let's get this over with."

I rapidly positioned myself at the side of the door frame, like they did in the cop shows. I reached out and twisted the knob on the mystery door. Locked. After all that adrenaline, what a letdown.

So much for that idea. At least if the door was locked, it probably meant no one was inside. Right?

I put my hand to my chest and felt the thumping of my racing heart. I felt pasty and sick.

I said, "Stay there and keep watching for Coop's signals. I'll take a quick look at these desks."

"Best idea I've heard all day," Baz whispered weakly.

The first desk I checked was bare. Nothing in the drawers, nothing on the top. Even the double shelf that sat over the desk was empty.

The second desk was exactly opposite. Its surface was loaded with files on one side, stacked in an alternating pile. One wrong move and they'd be all over the floor. The other side of the desk had a loaded wire basket with a sign reading INCOMING taped to the front. It sat atop another basket with a sign that said YOU ARE OUT OF YOUR MIND. Someone here had a sense of humor.

I picked up a few of the files and sheets of paper, but they all looked like information used for day-to-day business. A photo of two kids and a plain but friendly-looking woman sat in a frame propped on the shelf above the desk. Toy catalogs littered the rest of the shelf and there were even some sheets that looked like blueprints peeking out on the bottom of one pile. I slid one of the lined pages out, and on the sheet was a diagram of a toy. I recognized it as one of the newly released Hands On–branded toys that had come out this past Christmas. I stuck it back in the pile and moved on to the drawers.

Hanging file folders held audit reports and accounting information. I pulled them as far forward as I could, but there wasn't any dope or bricks of cash hidden in the back.

Baz stood behind the door, holding it open just enough that he could see Coop. Or at least I hoped he could see Coop. "How're you doing, Baz?"

"Fine. Hey, someone's a Star Wars junkie. Look at that desk."

"Stop looking in here and look out there," I hissed. Baz obediently turned back to the door.

A credenza next to one of the desks was loaded with action figures, each out of their packaging and standing proudly at attention. There had to be at least a hundred different plastic men, and some women to boot. One accidental bump and the miniature army would topple like a set of dominos. A Millennium Falcon constructed of LEGOs sat on top of a shelf that spanned the desk.

The desktop itself was neatly organized. From the labels on the folders and the printouts of planograms for the store floor, I deduced all this had to belong to the merchandise manager.

I rifled through the drawers but came up empty. It'd been close to five minutes since we'd left the sales floor. I wandered over to the last desk. We needed to get a move on, and I wanted to see what was behind the closed door. I hoped curiosity wasn't going to kill the cat. Or maybe we were mice. That, actually, would be worse.

I softly called to Baz, "I'm going to try the break room."

Baz shrugged and returned to his view in the main store. I pillaged the room in no time flat but found nothing but molding food in the fridge and a holiday edition Toys-R-Us magazine stuffed in one of the drawers beneath a counter built between the wall and the refrigerator. I wondered if the competitor's ad was like contraband and could only be perused on the sly. I crammed it back in the drawer.

"Nothing. This was a waste of time." My watch said nine minutes had now expired. I really wanted to take a gander at what was behind that locked door. With our luck, it would be cleaning supplies.

"Let me try one more thing," I told Baz and walked rapidly to the door at the back of the office.

"Shay," Baz said slowly as he twisted around to watch where I was going. "What are you doing?"

I didn't answer and pulled out my wallet instead. I removed my pliable Minnesota driver's license, stuck the plastic card between the door jam and the door, and wiggled it up and down. It probably wouldn't work, but you never knew. I was ready to give up when I felt the card slide deeper, into something tight. I pushed at the knob, and the door swung open. Open Sesame. How about that?

"Wow, you did it." An unusual trace of respect reflected in Baz's tone. I looked up to see him standing beside me. I gently pushed the door inward, and before I had a chance to yell at him for leaving his post, he crossed the threshold. The room was dark. I stepped inside, felt the wall for a light switch, and flipped it on.

I blinked as my brain caught up to what my eyes were seeing. Two maroon-covered plush-looking chairs sat in front of a desk. It was a huge desk that looked like a scaled-down, old-fashioned horse-drawn circus wagon.

The sides of the wagon were painted maroon, and bright yellow swirls and swooshes decorated the edges. In the middle of the side of the wagon that faced the door, raised yellow letters spelled out the words HANDS ON TOY COMPANY. The roof, which arched over the desk, was a rich, burnished mahogany. Polished, wood-spoke wheels held the body of the wagon off the ground. I walked toward it, intrigued. This sucker was cool.

Behind the desk, a huge four-foot by five-foot picture hanging on the wall caught my eye. The black and white image within the gold-gilded frame showed a young man standing next to a circus caravan, dressed in overalls and a white shirt. The wagon in the picture looked similar to the creation in the middle of the floor.

Apparently Fletcher Sharpe came from carnival stock and was proud of his heritage. On the wall to my right several framed pictures showed a man I finally recognized without a doubt as Sharpe. He was a big redheaded man with a wide, friendly smile. The photos caught him shaking hands with a number of local and national celebrities, including Bruce Springsteen and Prince. Others showed him receiving awards or commendations of some kind.

Once Baz realized no one was lying in wait for us, he rounded the unique desk and started rummaging through desk drawers disguised as barred windows.

"Get your butt back to the door." All we needed was to get busted in the inner sanctum of the circus of Hands On. "Baz!" I said.

Baz ignored me for a moment, then said, "Hey, what's that?"

I turned away from the pictures, surprised to find Baz's butt sticking out from under the desk. I moved closer and dropped to my knees next to him. If you can't beat 'em, join 'em. He pointed to a row of various sized dark spots on the carpet. The floor covering was light tan, and the spots easily stood out.

I poked a finger at it. The substance glistened on my yellow-gloved fingertip.

Baz said, "What is it?"

I reached out to touch another one of the spots when a drop fell from the bottom of the desk and splatted on the back of my hand.

"What in the world?" I pulled my hand into the light, and the dark drop turned a deep, rusty red. It looked like blood. But how would blood be coming out of a desk?

Baz got up and walked around the desk-wagon. He said, "There's a door on the end here." I heard a squeak, then Baz grunted a few times. "Uff. I could use a hand."

I climbed to my feet. "That's an unconventional storage place." I took a more critical look at the mock caravan/wagon/desk. The desktop was probably six or seven feet long and maybe five feet wide. A computer, keyboard, a couple of forbidding ledgers, and some files took up two-thirds of it. The last third, facing the door, was clutter-free.

A cutout allowed a chair to tuck under the desk, into part of the wagon. Baz tugged on a ring attached to a small door. I reached down and grabbed part of the ring. On three, we heaved. The little door popped open. Baz lost his balance and fell on his butt, narrowly missing taking me down with him. I crouched and took a gander inside the desk. I immediately wished I hadn't. Biting back bile, I made a strangled sound.

"What's wrong?"

I pointed at the door, the rubber glove rattling as my hand shook. I whispered harshly, "I think we just found Fletcher Sharpe."

Baz struggled to his hands and knees and scuttled over. He froze for a long moment, then slowly rotated on all fours to face me. His usually pale face was sheet-white, and I was afraid he was going to pass out. His eyes met mine, and they had a wildness to them that I completely understood. With Baz out of the way, I could easily see the brush of red hair attached to the body that had somehow been crammed into the desk. Those splotches under the desk were indeed blood. There was a dead body's blood on my gloves. Holy shit.

"Come on," I choked out, "we have to get out of here. Now."

Without a word, Baz swung the little door shut and stood. His bottom lip was trembling. He looked like he was about to burst into tears. Which about summed up how I felt too.

We both backed toward the doorway, not wanting to turn our backs on the body in the wagon. I flipped the light off, plunging the room into darkness and gently closed the office door. Then we made tracks for the door that led onto the sales floor.

"Give me your gloves," I whispered. Baz tugged them off and handed them over. I pulled mine off as well, then used one to open the door. We bolted through it, not caring if anyone saw us. Luckily, no one was in sight. I race-walked onto the Path of Ages, stuffing the inside-out gloves in my pocket as I charged along, Baz hot on my heels.

We rounded the bend into the retail side of the store. Coop was gone. The manager he'd been talking to stood at the cash registers jawing with the cashier. Splintered thoughts streamed through my mind like multiple shooting stars. Coop must have gone outside for some reason. Or maybe he hit the bathroom.

As we sailed past them, the cashier waved and called out, "Come see us again soon."

"You bet!" I chimed. *Not*.

Baz and I zoomed out the door. The coolness of the night hit me, and I sucked in great breaths of fresh air, trying to purge death from my pores and keep my stomach's contents where they belonged. Baz panted behind me. He gagged a couple of times. Kate was idling next to the curb.

We hit the car like a monsoon, nearly ripping the doors off their hinges in our haste to get inside.

Once I slammed the door closed and heard the back door bang shut, I realized Baz was the only occupant of the rear seat.

Panic made my voice sharp. "Kate, where's Coop?"

I had been too preoccupied with my own terror to notice the strange look on Kate's face, or that she was white-knuckling the steering wheel.

"Kate?" My voice went up a couple more octaves.

"A few of minutes ago two men went into the store and came out seconds later with Coop between them."

Oh no. Oh, sweet lord, no. "Was one of them tall?"

"Yeah, he was. Walked with a limp."

From the back seat, Baz moaned. "We're all dead."

I breathed out a long, "Oh, holy fuck." For once, I was afraid Baz might be right. "Did you get a plate number or anything?"

Kate said tightly, "I tried to do better than that. I snapped a picture of the car with my cell. Got the license plate, too. They dumped him in the trunk."

I cradled my head in my hands, then shook it, trying desperately to clear out the fog. "Go. Anywhere but here."

"You got it," Kate said as she put the car in drive. "What happened in there?"

I pressed my head against the backrest and squeezed my eyes shut. "I don't know what happened to Coop, and there's a body in the back office. Stuffed in a desk. I think it's Fletcher Sharpe."

"You're kidding me, right?" Kate's voice dropped, sounding unusually deep.

Baz groaned in the back again. "No, she's dead serious."

Heavy emphasis on the *dead*.

TWENTY-ONE

KATE WEAVED THROUGH RANDOM streets toward her house as I tried desperately to think of what to do next. Baz whimpered in the back seat, alternately howling that he was going to throw up and then going on about becoming "bloody fish bait." I whipped around and told him to shut up or he could get out and hoof it wherever he damn well wanted. I'd had enough.

The vehicle in the picture Kate snapped looked like a dark-colored Camry or something similar. The first two letters of the plate number was GR, but the third letter was too fuzzy to read. The only digits I could make out on the plate were a 7 and maybe a 5. Or it could have been a 6. Call the cops? They'd probably think I was a crackpot or arrest us for breaking into the office and then they'd lay a murder rap on Baz and me.

As Kate neared her place, my cell phone rang. I grabbed for it and it slipped out of my fingers like a greased eel. I got a hand up and pinned the thing to my chest, then looked at the caller ID and recognized Coop's new number.

I pressed answer, and then almost hung up on him in my shaky haste. "Coop—"

"Shay," Coop's voice was a ragged rasp. "I'm in the trunk of a—" a loud bang cut him off. "They don't know I have another phone—OW. Stupid potholes. Listen, I'm handcuffed in the trunk of a dark blue or black—" another thunk, this one sounding different from the previous banging interrupted him again. "Oh god. Gotta g—" Coop was cut off mid-word, and the phone went dead.

I stared at it, eyes wide. Panic blossomed from the bottom of my feet and rushed toward my brain.

Kate looked at me, eyes narrowed, face tense. "What?"

"I'm not sure." I spoke each word slowly, deliberately, trying not to hyperventilate. "But I don't think it was good."

The phone rang again, and this time I kept a solid hold on it. "Coop," I nearly screamed.

Instead of Coop, another voice spoke. "Listen, you little devil bitch." It sounded like Donny. Or maybe Hunk. Or maybe no one I'd ever heard before. The only thing I knew was that the voice wasn't Tomás. And whoever it happened to be was not happy. "3140 Shingle Creek. Brooklyn Center. Thirty minutes." The phone went dead in my hand.

———

Exactly twenty-five minutes later, after leaving panicked messages on both Dirty Harry and Farroway's cell phones, Kate pulled into the empty parking lot and plugged the Bug into a spot near the main doors of 3140 Shingle Creek Parkway.

Shingle Creek was a curvy road that ran, in part, through an industrial area in northern Brooklyn Center, just up I-94 from downtown Minneapolis. The single-story, white brick building was gigantic, at least two blocks long. There was no hint of the dark-colored car that had whisked Coop away from the Toy Company. I noticed a small sign at the lot entrance that read HOTC Manufacturing.

HOTC?

I hadn't realized I had spoken aloud until Kate said, "Probably Hands On Toy Company." She peered out the windshield. "This must be where they make their exclusive toys."

Kate lapsed into silence, staring straight ahead, her hands clamped on the top of the steering wheel.

Baz had ceased making any sort of sound in the rear seat, and I disjointedly wondered if he'd expired. That would be way too easy an out for him after he brought all this insanity down on us.

My caller had not directed me what our next move should be once we arrived. Were we supposed to wait in the car? Walk around the building? Break the glass in the door and—

The phone I held tight in my right hand rang, and I nearly crapped my pants. I'd hate to face my impending death with a load in my britches.

I stabbed at the talk button and practically slammed the cell against my ear. "Hello."

"Walk behind the building to the first door. Go inside. Follow the hall to the fourth door on the left. Go through it, and go through the door on the other side of the conference room. Walk until you can go no farther."

That was a lot of direction, and I hadn't been able to write a thing down. "Wait," I croaked out. "Tell me again—"

A maniacal snort of laughter cut me off. "Figure it out or your friend becomes ball-less."

The Tenacious Protector stirred in my gut. It filtered everything out. The world shrunk down to just me and the bad man on the other end of the line.

My voice sounded like it was coming out of a barrel. "Listen, jackass. You touch a single testicle on that man and I'll return the favor, twice over." Whoa. *Way to go, Shay. Put the man right over the edge.* Jesus.

The Protector inside me was slowly and irrevocably squeezing rational thought from my mind. Everything in my line of vision was now tinted red as a veil of righteous rage descended. It'd been a long time since I unleashed the Protector in all her glory—so long since I felt this close to losing complete control. Abducting and manhandling my best friend was the last straw. The relief I felt in the power of my growing fury was palpable, and the adrenaline rush made my torso tremble.

The man on the cell continued, "You have five minutes. Make sure everyone in that car comes with you, *bitch*." He sneered the last word and hung up on me. That was becoming a pattern.

I turned to look at Kate, my expression hard, but my demeanor deadly calm. "You've got to come."

Kate nodded, recognizing the signs that I was now fully in TP mode. We'd been friends long enough for her to see my reaction when someone I cared about was in trouble or was threatened. One night back in college, an evening of tutoring one of the U of M's star football players turned into a train wreck.

I had swung in to pick up a textbook Kate had borrowed and instead found Kate pinned to her bunk by the wide receiver.

His muscled weight muffled Kate's shrieks as she struggled to scream for help and breathe at the same time. Blood was flying, but later I was relieved to find out she'd managed to bash him in the nose before my arrival. Out popped my inner lioness, and I took care of business. There was no explanation when the coach benched that wide receiver for a conference game the following night because of an unexplained dislocated shoulder. To the best of my knowledge, the kid hadn't tried to "fix" another lesbian ever again.

I snapped back from the past with a shudder. "You're coming too, Baz."

"Erk," was the only sound he made.

Kate and I climbed out of the car. I yanked open the back door, grabbed Baz by the collar of his jacket, and dragged him from the vehicle.

Once Baz was on his feet, I pointed at him for emphasis. "You will stay between me and Kate." I stuck my face right in his space. "You try anything, you try to run, and—" I jabbed my finger in his chest, "I'll make you sorry you ever asked me for help." I poked him again for good measure.

"Ow," Baz yelped and rubbed his pec. He glowered at me but wisely kept his lip zipped.

I gave Kate a piercing look. "Don't let him get away if he tries to take off."

Though she was slight, there was a lot of stubbornness and determination in Kate's slim body. She nodded.

"Pop the hatch Kate, will you?"

A worn duffle bag lay in the narrow area between the back of the rear seat and the hatch. I unzipped it, and just as I remembered, it held a half-dozen well-used aluminum bats. Kate was the first baseman for the Uptowners, a team we belonged to on a Twin

Cities LGBT softball league. Good thing she hadn't brought the gear in from the last indoor batting practice session.

I tossed a bat at Kate, who snagged it with one hand. Baz wasn't so quick, and the bat I lobbed sailed past him and clattered on the sidewalk.

"Better hone those reflexes, Baz." I secured my own tool of potential mayhem.

I shut the hatch and took a deep breath. "Okay, follow me."

The fricking clock was ticking, and I tried to recall, with a shiver of dread, the exact instructions the man had fired at me through the phone. First door, go inside. Down the hall to the fourth door on the left. Pass through the room and out the door on other side. The devil would be there, waiting for us. My heart pounded triple time.

A sidewalk led around the corner of the building and disappeared into the darkness. I followed the path to the first door, about twenty-five feet from the corner of the building. My two-car quasi-train was right with me. I tugged on the handle, but it didn't budge. How were we supposed to get to our destination when the baddies hadn't bothered to unlock the door?

"Goddamn it." Frustration simmered on the brink of boiling-over. I snapped, "Back up."

Both Kate and Baz stepped off the cement and onto the dead grass that bordered the sidewalk. I raised my bat and swung with everything I had. The sound of the aluminum shattering tempered glass barely registered as reverberations ran up and shook my arms. What should've felt like an incredible release was just one more emotion I stowed away for later. I used the bat to knock out the remaining glass shards so we could step over the frame without skewering ourselves.

Once we'd safely navigated the point of entry, I took a few seconds to regroup. Donny or Hunk or whoever called had to have heard that. But no one was in sight.

A weak light from the exit sign above our heads extended only a few feet down the hall.

"Ready?" I asked Baz and Kate. Kate nodded. Baz stared at me like a startled bunny. I spun on my heel and marched down the hallway, counting off the doors until I hit the fourth on the left. The knob twisted easily under my hand, and I pushed it open.

"Shay, wait a minute." Kate's whisper barely penetrated my hearing. I paused long enough for her to flip a switch, and the room flooded with light. All three of us stood still for another few seconds as our eyes adjusted to the brightness.

We were in a large conference room. At least twenty chairs encircled a huge, rectangular table. A white board covered the far wall, and diagrams of what looked like toys in different stages of development filled the surface.

My brain registered these details, but I was too busy looking for the door that was supposed to be on the opposite side of the room to pay any kind of attention. I stalked toward it, fingers tightening on the wrapped handle of the bat resting on my shoulder. I was ready to end this.

I grabbed the doorknob and heaved, then launched my body through the threshold into the unknown, which turned out to be a cavernous space, dimly lit by two fluorescent bulbs suspended from the ceiling. With the bat held high above my head, I belted out a battle cry that would've curled my Irish ancestor's toes. I charged across the floor toward a cluster of people forty feet away. Kate and Baz whooped it up right alongside me.

Spread-eagled and bloodied, Coop was shackled to a chain-link fence that ran into the darkness. Where the light did reach, I could see cardboard boxes stacked inside the fence. The sight of my best friend, wounded and dangling like yesterday's laundry, was the final straw.

Hunk and Donny stood on one side of Coop. Tomás, on Coop's other side, was behind a tall, red-haired man dressed in khaki pants and a bright green Hawaiian shirt. If I hadn't seen Fletcher Sharpe mashed into his desk, his blood leaking out on the floor with my own eyes, I would've thought it was him.

A woman, obscured in shadow, waited a few feet away. She was dressed in black boots, black cargo pants, a loose cable-knit black sweater, and one of those black-felt Mexican cowboy hats. Her face was an impartial mask.

My brain assessed all that in a blink, and then I was back on task. If I took Tomás out, Kate and Baz could take a few whacks at Hunk and Donny. As I closed in on the group, my shout turned into a high-pitched growl. My eyes locked on Tomás's as my pumping legs carried me toward him.

The woman turned a pair of deep blue eyes on me and calmly uttered, "Shoot him."

Her voice was high-pitched and heavily accented. I shoved those lightning-fast thoughts away as my brain frantically tried to process the meaning of her words.

Tomás moved a half-stride forward, coming even with the Sharpe lookalike. He held something in his hand. That something was a huge, black handgun. In slow motion, he pivoted and pointed the weapon directly at Coop's chest. He'd never miss.

"NO!" I screamed and chucked the bat at Tomás as hard as I could. He ducked, and it sailed harmlessly over his head, clattered against the fence, and dropped to the floor with a hollow clang. I launched myself into the air. Tomás hesitated between completing his orders and turning his weapon on me.

His hesitation cost him. In a textbook flying tackle, my shoulder met Tomás's legs. He flew over me, and then hit the hard concrete with a bone-rattling crash.

Gunfire erupted as I skidded across the floor. I flashed back to a particularly violent broomball game, careening on my back over slippery ice after a vicious hip check from an opposing player. That hadn't ended well, either.

I slammed into a huge though surprisingly light plastic barrel and upended it. My forward motion stopped, but gunfire continued to echo throughout the huge space. I was vaguely aware of some fuzzy-like substance tickling my exposed skin.

Move, Shay. Get up. Find cover.

I rolled to my hands and knees, fought for breath. With each inhale, the fluffy substance coated the inside of my mouth. I spit, nearly gagged. Hands grabbed at my jacket. I panicked, tried to crabwalk away. Too late. After a quick scuffle, my assailant wrapped an arm tight around my throat. Pressed something cold and unyielding to my temple.

The scent of jasmine filled my nose.

Then it clicked. Oh my god. There was absolutely no doubt in my mind this woman was Luz Ortez.

TWENTY-TWO

TEN MINUTES LATER, I was on a metal folding chair in a toy storage room. Teddy bears of all shapes and sizes spilled out of a line of open cardboard boxes. One wall supported stacks of board games. White fuzz clung to my clothes. I looked like a walking snowman.

Coop sat on my right, Kate on my left. Baz was beside Kate. In a surprising turn of events, the Fletcher Sharpe imposter was in a chair next to Baz, having received the same treatment as the rest of us. Our arms, painfully twisted behind our backs, were zip-tied securely. Foul-tasting rags doubled as gags, and I tried to breathe carefully through my nose. I was able to spit out most of the fuzzy crap that tumbled out of the barrel before Hunk gleefully tied the cloth so tightly around my head that the corners of my mouth were pulled back in a farcical grin. Our one saving grace was that we were still alive. The Sharpe imposter was the only one who hadn't yet been silenced.

Sadly, there was no time to relish this fact, because Tomás, Luz, Hunk, and Donny were busy pointing weapons of various sizes at us.

"You lost them in New Orleans," Luz told Tomás. "This time you will not fail." The emphasis was on the *not*.

"*Sí*, Zorra, it is done."

Oh my god, Luz was Zorra? A mild-mannered U of M professor was one of the most feared drug lords in Mexico? No freaking way.

Luz gave her lieutenant a look that would make even the most hardened man squirm. "It is not done. Incompetence doesn't suit you." She checked a delicate silver watch on her wrist. "And we're out of time. They're going to have to come."

She turned her back to him and addressed us.

"How can such a … a … " Luz shot us a derisive look as she sneered, "frustratingly *stupid* bunch of people cause so much trouble? If you so much as twitch, I'll have Tomás break your fingers and then cut out your tongues."

On the bright side, if she was thinking about breaking our fingers and slicing our tongues out, she wasn't planning our immediate exits from this world.

Luz slowly approached me. "Do you understand, Shay?" She prodded me in the forehead with the barrel of her gun, tipping my head back. I nodded frantically against the circular steel pressing against my skin. Then she sidestepped down the line and stopped in front of Baz.

He whimpered.

She said, "This is your doing. Your friend's deaths will be on your head."

Luz moved on to the redhead. Donny was in the process of gagging him. "You should have gone along when we asked nicely,

Mr. Sharpe. It did not have to end this way. Such a shame." My eyes widened in surprise. If this man was Fletcher Sharpe, who was bleeding inside his desk?

Fletcher said, "You have no right to do what you're doing. I run a clean business."

"I will make my offer one last time. It's your choice—live, become rich—or die."

Fletcher spluttered then clearly said, "Go to hell. You're all already halfway there anyway."

Luz laughed in his face. "You are so naïve, Mr. Sharpe. Your business hasn't been clean for a long time. Gag him," she ordered Donny, who quickly silenced the man I now realized was indeed Sharpe.

Luz/Zorra spun around and addressed Tomás. "Load them up. Once the meeting is over and you have taken care of this," she indicated the line of us with a sweep of her hand, "hunt down the two old ladies and the little round man and dispatch them as well."

I didn't have time to digest and analyze what that horrifying comment meant. With Luz's directive, a flurry of activity commenced.

The bad dudes had learned well from their previous mistakes. Hunk and Donny approached with strips of cloth and proceeded to tie blindfolds on the lot of us. When Donny came to me, I shook my head wildly. The thought of not being able to see what was coming panicked me to the core. A howl from deep in my chest leaked from around the gag. I swung a foot at Donny's crotch, but he neatly shifted to my side, out of reach.

"This," he whispered in his high-pitched voice, close enough for me to smell his bad breath but not close enough to head butt, "This is for my ear." Like lightning, the palm of his hand connected sharply with the side of my face. My head snapped sideways, and I grunted at the impact.

"Donny," Zorra said, a clear warning her tone. "There is no time."

He resisted dealing a second blow and roughly tied the blindfold across my eyes. As the light disappeared, it felt like the air in the room went along with it. I tried to suck oxygen through my nose. After a few panicked moments, I managed to calm myself enough to breathe evenly again. Passing out wasn't going to help anyone.

Once the blindfolds were secured, I was yanked to my feet and led along for what felt like forever. I could hear shuffling, so I presumed the others were also being led somewhere. The air suddenly felt cooler. We were outside. The sound of a door sliding open told me there was as van of some kind nearby.

Before we were piled inside, Luz told Tomás she would meet them wherever we were going. I reasoned that that left Hunk, Donny, and Tomás with the five of us trussed up like Easter hams.

Tomás's voice said, "Let's go."

Without the use of my arms for balance and with the added impediment of the blindfold, getting into the vehicle was a challenge. The step in was knee-high, and after two attempts I heaved myself inside. On the upswing, someone gave me a shove and I landed with a bounce on a bench seat and tipped over. The side of my head hit the metal wall on the side of the van.

Tomás growled, "Move already, *pendejo*."

I righted myself and attempted to slide over to make room. Someone pushed into my side. They moaned, and I recognized Baz's distinctive utterance. I tried to move even closer to the metal side of the van.

Then I heard a scuffle outside, a couple of bangs, some cursing, and two fast impacts of a fist hitting flesh followed by more cursing. Someone let out a pained, muffled howl. I cringed, heart in my throat. Knowing I couldn't do a thing about what was going on outside nearly made me cry out in frustration. I hurt for whoever was on the receiving end, and wished it were Baz instead of one of the other captives. This was all his fault anyway. He huddled against me, whimpering, way too close for comfort. Body odor wafted from him in waves. If I could've wriggled an elbow free, I'd have happily applied it to his ribs.

The vehicle rocked as each person entered. My cheek still stung from the run-in with Donny's palm, and the plastic on the zip ties cut into my wrists. My hands were already falling asleep. Plus it pissed me off that the gag was making me drool on myself. I rested my head against the side of the side of the van and tried to think a way out of this.

The side door of the van slammed shut. Our doom was sealed. The front doors opened and closed. Some low conversation floated to my ears, although I couldn't make out anything clearly. The van roared to life, and the seat beneath me began to vibrate.

I tried to remember the turns the van took, but I should have known by now that such attempts were only good in theory. Luz's words haunted me instead: *Hunt down the two old ladies and the little round man and dispatch them as well.* The phrase thundered through my brain like a skipping record on full volume. The Tenacious Protector inside bridled at the thought, sending impotent adrenaline through my veins. My heart rate ratcheted up, and it was all I could do not to throw what would amount to little more than a toddler's tantrum. It would get me nowhere and probably hurt a lot, given my hands and blindfold. I forced myself into a state of agitated calm.

I realized a funny thing: time is hard to gauge when you can't see anything. It could've been anywhere between ten minutes or a half hour when the vehicle creaked to a stop and the engine was cut. One of the front doors opened, and the van rocked as some-one stepped out.

Tomás said, "You two stay here, and *dios mio*, make sure they do not go anywhere. I will be back."

"Sure, boss," Hunk rumbled.

The side door rolled open and stopped with a distinct click. Cold air swirled around my head, clearing my brain a little.

"You don't move," Hunk addressed us. We obeyed. In less than five minutes, Tomás was back. "We will bring them inside."

"But boss," Donny said, "they'll hear everything."

"It does not matter. I don't want them out of our sight. And as soon as this is done, so are they. "

I really didn't like being talked about in the past tense.

Minutes later, after some gun barrel encouragement, we stum-bled across a bumpy, rough surface and entered a building. Herd-ing five blindfolded, bound prisoners through a maze of hallways wasn't an easy task. At some point, we crossed from a hard floor onto carpeting.

"Stop," Tomás said moments later. "Turn to your left and sit."

Feet shuffled and the back of my legs banged against some-thing hard. Someone pressed down on my shoulder, and my butt landed on a hard, narrow object. I grunted in surprise as similar sounds issued from both sides of me. I wasn't sure if Baz was next to me anymore or not.

"Hunk, Donny," Tomás directed, "do not let them move."

The air was heavy with a myriad of odors. Mold and rot. The faint, stale smell of popcorn and hotdogs. Sweat. Kind of like the locker room in high school.

Many voices I didn't recognize interrupted my olfactory rumi-nations. By the sound of the echo, we were in a large, empty space.

A number of the voices sounded Hispanic. They weren't close enough that I could make out what they were saying, though, and I couldn't tell if there were five or fifteen.

Wonderful. Just what we wanted to be knee-deep in—a meeting of drug lords. Why, of all places, would they pick Minnesota as a location to gather?

Then I recognized Luz's voice as she raised it in greeting. A rapid exchange in Spanish ensued. The deeper baritones of at least seven or eight different men mixed with Luz's at an alarming rate.

Poor Coop. His crush turned out to be worse than bad news. We'd both fallen for her act like starving fish finding a worm.

The volume level dropped, and an expectant hush fell. I strained to hear what was going on. Dim light seeped in the edges of my blindfold, but I was still effectively sightless. The rag in my mouth was disgustingly soggy, chafing the corners of my mouth. An unfamiliar feeling settled into my gut, and the feeling shook me to the core. Hopelessness. Then, unbidden, Eddy's voice floated through my mind. "Where there's a will, there's a way. Don't give up. Never surrender."

Shay, listen to her, I chided myself. *You have too much to lose to die tonight. You haven't told JT you love her. You can't die before you actually say those words to her face and not to your pillow.*

Luz interrupted my personal lecture on perseverance. "*Buenas noches, mis amigos.* In deference to our non-Spanish-speaking partners, I will conduct this meeting in English. I would like to thank you for taking the time to travel from your respective homes to this very important moment in our history. This is an unusual venue in a cold climate, and this is precisely why we are here. The unexpected keeps us safe. It also allows our Canadian counterparts to participate."

A rumble of *buenas noches,* good evenings, and one *buenas tardes* filled the air.

Luz continued, "We are here to find a way to proceed together, as a group. One instead of many. This will allow all cartels to not only succeed, but surpass prior victories and accomplishments. *La policía,* the FBI, ICE, and others continue to interrupt our shipments, find our tunnels, confiscate our money, halt our movers. If we can all find a way to make this new Canadian alliance work, we will have power in numbers. We will be unstoppable." She raised her voice on the last word.

The audience broke into excited chatter. Luz let it go for a few long moments. Then she said loudly, *"Por favor."*

The chatter subsided.

"We are here to come to a joint agreement that will bind the Reynosa with the Hermocillo, Monterrey, Guadalajara, and Villa-hermosa organizations with the Manitoba cartel. This agreement will be called *Seis Hermanos.* The Six Siblings."

Excited voices rose again.

Oh my god. We were witnessing—or hearing, at least—an attempt to pull together six major players in the Mexican and now Canadian drug trade. If this alliance actually could function without the players killing each other off, Luz wasn't kidding about the unstoppability of *Seis Hermanos.*

I shuddered as I considered the implications. Already the sophistication in drug importation had risen to all-time highs, even with the relatively limited resources singular cartels had. I couldn't conceive of what power they would hold if this plan came together. It would certainly be a huge blow to law enforcement efforts in the US and all over the world.

"Silencio, por favor," Luz commanded. The attendees obeyed.

Before she had a chance to say another word, an explosion ripped through the building. Order immediately dissolved into chaos.

Instinctively, I ducked and hurled myself off the bench, into whoever was sitting to my right. We hit the floor in a tangle, and the initial impact knocked the air from my lungs.

Three more explosions ripped the air. The concussions from the blasts hit me like a physical force. I rolled around the floor, hit my left leg on something very sharp, then bashed into someone, all the while trying to suck air through my nose. I tried to scuttle sideways, toward whatever my leg had run into. An unending growl leaked from around the gag in my mouth as I heaved myself to my knees. My momentum tipped me forward, and my forehead smacked into something hard as I fought not to meet the floor with my face. The force of the blow knocked my blindfold askew, partially uncovering my right eye.

The lighting was dim, cast from a few bulbs high in the ceiling that still worked. Immediately in front of me stood a bench ten or twelve feet long. To my right, Kate, Baz, and Sharpe huddled on the ground. On my left, Coop was pitching a fit on the floor, futilely attempting to free his arms. A quick look behind me revealed a three-foot tall fence that looked suspiciously like the boards that encircled the rink in a hockey arena.

Beyond the bench was a counter with breaks at intervals for foot traffic. The din increased as a barrage of gunfire added to the mix. My ears rang painfully from the deafening explosions.

Please don't shoot us, I prayed. I frantically hunted for something to use to get the blindfold completely off.

Donny and Hunk weren't in my one-eyed line of sight. I hoped they had run off to help with whatever was going down. I fixed my attention on Coop. He was now on his side, hands still behind him. His chest expanded and contracted as he sucked air.

In his struggles, his t-shirt had ridden up. His sweat jacket spread open on the floor. The belt Eddy'd given him at Christmas was woven through the belt loops on his pants, and on his over-sized belt buckle was a Boxer dog's head. The docked ears jutted up in two sharp points. When I first saw the thing, I told Coop he'd better be careful not to pierce his belly when he bent over.

The cacophony in the building increased. I dove between Coop's legs, aiming for the buckle's ears to dislodge my blindfold. In my desperation, I forgot I had nothing to slow my descent, and crashed nose first into his family jewels.

My ears rang from the impact. Coop's body went completely limp. *Please don't let me have killed him with a face to the crotch*, I thought. Then I felt a tiny movement as his left thigh contracted and a high-pitched keening burst out of his mouth. The sound didn't drown out the gunfire, but it was close. *Thank you, god of the love sack, thank you.*

With my mind back in survival mode, I carried on with my original plan. I scooched up the buckle, face pressing into Coop's gonads every time I tried to move. He was going to kill me later if we lived through this.

Once my eyes passed my target, I was confronted by the sight of a faint trail of light-colored hair that ran from beneath his belly button down into his pants. Never in a hundred years did I ever think I'd be up close and personal with this part of Coop's anat-omy. In fact, this would be what a chick would see if she were about to give him—I immediately forced that thought into obliv-ion and dragged the blindfold across the buckle.

The tip of one of the ears jabbed me in the head wound I received in New Orleans and reopened with Agnes's vodka bottle. I bit hard on the material in my mouth. The pain was worth it, though, because the blindfold caught on the dog's metal ear, and I tugged my head down harder. The cloth shifted slightly higher.

The gunshots had ceased. Aside from an occasional shout, the silence was a welcome break from the racket of deadly violence. I wondered if someone was standing over me with a gun, ready to pull the trigger and bury one in my back. That thought motivated me to try again. Finally, the blindfold rested commando-style on my forehead, exposing both eyes to the world. Paranoid panic swept through my body. I flipped myself over Coop's leg, ready to try to kick the person about to execute us. The relief that swamped me when I saw no one was about to cancel us from the show of life was sadly short-lived.

Someone with a bullhorn bellowed, "This is Immigration and Customs Enforcement. I encourage you to put down your weapons and surrender peacefully. We have you surrounded. I repeat, you are surr—"

Gunshots interrupted the bullhorn guy, who I hope ducked. More shouting and yet another deadly salvo followed.

When I rolled over Coop's leg, I'd landed with much of my body weight pressing on my wrists. The plastic of the zip ties cut into my skin. I struggled to sit up, and blood ran into the palms of my hands. I achieved a semi-vertical posture, my legs stretched in front of me. Coop was curled up on his side, still trying to recover from my unwitting assault on his nether region.

Movement to my right caught my attention. A figure with a gun in one hand and a buck knife in the other crouched low behind the boards. The head popped up over the boards, and then muzzle flash of gunfire lit the darkness for a split second. More gunfire exploded from somewhere close by. Then the figure dashed toward us. I couldn't run. I closed my eyes and braced myself for an inevitable knife or bullet.

Then that someone was right next to me, talking rapidly. My brain wasn't computing. I opened my eyes. Luz crouched beside me, yelling repeatedly, "Turn over!"

Right. As if I was going to give her an easy out and let her kill me as I faced away from her. I flailed in a fury, swinging my head, my legs, anything to try to strike her.

She tackled me and expertly flipped me on my stomach, using her body weight to hold me down. Really? The bitch was too lily-livered to murder me while I watched?

One side of my face was squashed into the damp carpet, the mold smell invaded my nostrils, choking off my only source of air. Luz's fist was next to my nose, gripping the knife. The knife looked even more deadly up close. Her cheek was pressed against my ear, and she was hollering. My brain caught broken phrases: "Don't move," "Cut you," "Can't help," and "Stubborn girl."

Then the weight of her was gone. I felt the slide of metal against my hair, and I inanely wondered when Cartel drug lords had taken to scalping people. There was a momentary increase of pressure on the gag in my mouth, then it fell away from my cheeks. Before I could comprehend that my mouth was no longer corked up, my hands sprang free as well.

I spit the gag out. Almost as if they had a mind of their own, my hands braced against the floor. I prepared to push myself to my feet. Then Luz landed on my back once again, and I hit the carpet hard, the air whooshing from my mouth. I was going to be seriously flat-chested if I lived through this.

Her hand twisted into the hair on my head. She pulled me tight against her. This time the words she yelled in my ear registered.

"Shay! Shay, listen. I'm not going to hurt you! I'm FBI."

TWENTY-THREE

I FELT LIKE I'D gone deaf. I saw the scene in front of me as if through the end of a long, narrow tube. I didn't move, and Luz shook my head like a rag doll's. "Shay, did you hear me? I am *not* going to hurt you."

The pain of her practically yanking strands of hair from my head stunned me into awareness. I nodded, which was not easy to do with the grip she had. A switch flipped on somewhere inside me, and I was back in the moment. My senses opened, the tunnel effect fell away. Once more I could hear people shouting and intermittent gunfire. My hands and cheeks tingled painfully as circulation returned.

Luz was a Fed, not a drug lord? She was probably lying, and planning to use us for cover to make her escape. Although she *had* cut me free ...

She breathed in my ear, "Stay here. Stay down. Don't move until I say. Do you understand?" She shook me again, and I nodded weakly.

Satisfied I wasn't going to play pop-goes-the-weasel, she crab-walked over to Coop, who was still lying sprawled on his back a few feet away. With a flick of her wrist, she neatly cut off his blindfold, his gag, rolled him on his side and freed his arms. Her dark hair partially obscured Coop's face. She said something in his ear. I saw him bob his head in acknowledgement. In a blink, she moved on to Baz then Sharpe then Kate and gave them the same treatment. In less than a minute, she'd freed us all.

Luz scuttled back. "Okay. Follow me. Stay low."

There wasn't a whole lot of choice. If we trusted Luz, there was a chance she was telling the truth. If we didn't trust her and stayed where we were, it was only a matter of time until someone stumbled across us and finished the job. I, for one, decided to take my chances with Luz. The rest of our rag-tag group apparently felt the same. The five of us waddled like ducklings after their mother. Luz tucked the knife away but still had her wicked-looking gun in hand. She took care not to expose the top of her head above the much-scuffed boards. I mimicked her moves.

On my right, raised rows of bench seating created tiered spectator stands. Some of the metal benches were intact, and some were missing entirely. We were definitely in a hockey arena that had seen better days.

Silence filled the cavernous space once again. I was terrified someone would hear our panicked panting or desperate shuffling, or simply observe our attempted escape and blast away right through the boards. Miraculously, we made it unscathed to the end of the rink. I saw the gate and knew we were on the end of the arena where the Zamboni usually enters. The garage-like space beyond the rink was typically filled with resurfacing equipment and other large items that needed storage. The opening into the space was pitch black, and the weak lighting above our heads barely dented the darkness.

Luz whispered, "Hang on to me. Tell the others to hold on as well."

I nabbed the cloth of her jacket in an iron grip and whispered the instructions to Coop. He took hold of the back of my pants, then relayed the message back. Luz paused only a second to make sure everyone hooked up. Linked together, we plunged into the inky unknown.

My eyes struggled to adjust to the relative blackness of the space. The smell of mildew and neglect was even more evident here. Someone grabbed my arm. Kate whispered in my ear, "I'm right here with you." Good.

From what I could tell, the Zamboni was long gone and left in its place was the offal of the rink. We crept past castoff seats, benches, and other pieces of the inner workings of the building that littered the floor. Garbage was strewn haphazardly all around.

Occasional spurts of gunfire still echoed from the rink itself. We made our way deeper into the space, and I ceased being able to see much of anything. I wondered how Luz had any idea where she was going. My heart was beginning to slow to a survivable pace. We might have a chance to escape this dump after all.

A voice some distance behind us said loudly, "Zorra, where are you going?"

The voice was vaguely familiar, and I tried to place it as my heart rate soared again to near-stroke level.

Luz froze, then whipped around. Air whooshed by my arm. I judiciously let go of her clothing, dropped into a crouch. My eyes adjusted to the dark enough that I could see Luz step forward and sideways, away from us. She continued to move until she was within a few feet of the men.

The speaker was clearly backlit against the opening into the rink. At least in that we had a definitive advantage.

"Mudd, leave now, and I will not shoot you." Luz sounded calm and sure.

"Now Zorra, would you shoot an unarmed man? I guess it's a good thing he's not unarmed then." With those words this Mr. Mudd stepped to one side, exposing Tomás, large gun in hand, pointed directly at Luz.

Holy shit.

Kate and Coop were nothing more than black blobs in the dark, hunkered down next to me. Baz and Sharpe were completely out of my sight, which was fine by me.

I nudged something with my left foot and shifted my weight onto the balls of my feet. Reaching down, I groped around til my fingers closed over something long and narrow. I picked it up and slid my hands over the top half of a broken hockey stick. Tape long ago wrapped around the top of the shaft was still sticky and the broken end was jagged and sharp.

The fates spoke loud and clear. I wasn't about to abandon someone who'd just saved our necks. Besides, there weren't a whole lot of options on the table.

Luz kept up a steady stream of chatter that I didn't have the attention to listen to.

I elbowed Coop and whacked him with my improvised weapon.

"Where did you get that?" he whispered.

"On the ground."

In a breath, he was feeling around the floor himself. I fumbled to find Kate, caught her sleeve, and pulled her toward me.

"Feel for something to use—" She interrupted me by pushing something into my gut. I got a hand around what felt like a pipe. I grabbed a handful of cloth on each of them, pulled my two friends toward me and whispered, "Back door. I'm on the right. Coop, you go left. Kate, come around down the middle. Watch all the junk on the floor."

They immediately crept away, completely disappearing in the gloom. We were about to begin the play of our lives.

I backed up, moving sideways, then shifted to the right. My lungs froze as I reentered the firing zone maybe ten feet behind Luz.

"Zorra," Tomás was saying, "you are done. How I have waited for this moment."

Luz's tone was mocking. "You have planned a coup so you can take over the most powerful cartel in the world? Tomás, I trusted you."

"Trust?" His voice cracked. "What kind of trust do you show?"

"I am simply doing what you failed to do. Because you are inept—"

Luz and Tomás continued to exchange barbs while Mudd looked on silently. No more sounds of battle echoed from the rink. I didn't know what that meant.

In moments, I was out of the firing line. My lung function returned, barely. Images of JT flashed through my mind. Damn it, I was going to get the chance to profess my affection for her even if I had to kill someone to do it.

Thankfully, the two men remained silhouetted against the light. It made them that much easier to target. I was relieved to have come this far without tripping and falling flat. Hopefully that same luck shone on Coop and Kate.

Then I was directly even with Mudd and Tomás, on their left side, about fifteen feet away. If the play was going to go down correctly, Kate had made an even wider loop around the two men, while Coop should be on the opposite side in the same position as I was.

Mudd was saying to Luz, "I can't believe you're an agent. Tomás, can you?"

Luz's voice was steady. "I told you, Kelvin. I am not a plant."

"Then what are you doing with those people? The people you sent us out to dispose of?" Tomás's tone was icy.

"And where are they?" Mudd rocked back on his heels, his hands clasped in front of him.

To Luz's credit, she didn't flinch. "Drop the gun, Tomás."

"I no longer take orders from you. I give them." With no warning, he fired two shots in rapid succession. Horrified, I heard Luz's body hit the ground. Rational thought fled and the Protector once again took over. I charged the men, shouting at the top of my lungs, "NOW!"

Before Tomás could react and point his gun toward me, I was on top him. I swung that broken stick at Tomás's head with every ounce of strength my body possessed. The impact jarred my forearms all the way to the elbow. The man dropped like a rock. His gun arced through the air, into the darkness.

Coop roared toward us, his arms over his head, a length of pipe in his hands. I clobbered Mudd in the neck with a reverse scorcher. Mudd gurgled as he took the brunt of my blow in his Adam's apple. Coop followed up quickly with a healthy swat of his own. Mudd dropped. With a dual roar, Kate and I leaped over the sprawled bodies of the two men and dove for Tomás's weapon in tandem.

Kate chanted, "Oh god, oh god, oh god, " as we frantically felt up the trash-strewn floor for the gun. My fingers brushed against the barrel and I snatched it up. I bounced back to my feet and swung around. My hands barely shook as I aimed in the general direction of the two downed men and snarled, "Score two for the home team."

TWENTY-FOUR

TWENTY MINUTES LATER, THE now-defunct Columbia Ice Arena in Fridley was lit up like a massive Christmas tree. Cops and agents of all stripes swarmed the building and the grounds, tagging bodies of former cartel leaders and their lackeys, triaging the wounded, and cataloging evidence.

Coop, Kate, Baz, Fletcher Sharpe, and I each sat in separate cruisers, all parked near a group of no less than eight ambulances. Already five or six had screamed off into the night, carrying wounded from both sides of the battle.

We had shivered in the chilly night air under silver, crinkly blankets asking questions and generally sticking our noses where they didn't belong until someone realized what we were doing. Then we were quickly isolated—away from each other and away from secrets we weren't meant to hear.

Luz had been loaded in one of the first ambulances to leave, thanks to the stink we made. She was unresponsive after taking a slug above her collarbone, near her neck. The paramedics said the bullet barely missed her jugular, but she'd lost a lot of blood. Her Kevlar body armor stopped the second bullet Tomás fired. It would have been a fatal shot if the vest hadn't done its job.

Regardless, the paramedics quietly told me her outlook was bleak.

Kelvin Mudd was treated for a nasty neck wound before being crammed into a squad. Tomás "Tommy Tormenta" Rios-Torres, his eye swelling closed beneath a huge lump on his forehead, was in yet another cop car. Before the police separated us, Coop told me he recognized Kelvin Mudd as the man who was with Hunk and Tomás in the basement of Fletcher Sharpe's house the night we accidentally broke in. I knew I recognized his voice.

I shivered against the cold vinyl of the seat. Those rescue blankets—or whatever the shiny pieces of tin foil were called—were a waste of taxpayer dollars. The officer who'd stuck me inside the car had been kind enough to start the engine and let it run with the heat blowing, but the thick plexi divider made it difficult for the warmth to reach me.

Thoughts of Luz floated through my mind. How at first I thought she was a mild-mannered teacher. Then I though she was a feared drug lord who'd held a gun to my head and ordered us dispatched. Then she saved our asses. Nothing made sense.

At least it was over. JT would be home in a few days, and boy was she going to get the loving of a lifetime.

I sighed, and it turned into a huge yawn. Weariness swirled through me. I leaned my head back against the seat and closed my eyes.

———

The next thing I knew, somebody was opening the car door. I was disoriented by the scenery until I realized I was no longer at the arena. Instead, the car had pulled into the newly finished FBI headquarters in Brooklyn Center. Ironically enough, the building was a stone's throw from Sharpe's manufacturing plant, where this mess had started just a few hours before.

A disheveled young man dressed in a rumpled, dark-colored suit had opened the back door. I clambered from the car and hurried to keep up with his long, silent strides.

We entered the building. The new smell hadn't yet worn off, and for some reason it gave me a sense of normalcy. I didn't mind the scent of newly installed carpet and freshly applied paint. It made some people sick, but it always gave me a renewed sense of hope. Like a fresh start.

The lobby had a vaulted ceiling. I guessed it would be bright and airy in the daylight.

I trailed the man into an elevator, and he punched the button for the third floor. I leaned with a sigh against one wall. He stood looking straight ahead.

Just to try out some conversation, I asked, "Where are my friends?"

He looked me in the eye for the first time. "On the way. You'll be free to go as soon as we get your statement." He had a kind voice, hoarse from stress or yelling, or a combination of both.

"Do you know what happened to the woman who was shot? She was one of the first to leave." I wasn't sure if he'd tell me even if he did know.

The man didn't say anything. I prompted, "Her name was Zorra, or maybe Luz?"

A muscle bulged in his cheek, which was baby smooth. He was just a kid. His lips narrowed, and he forcefully blew out air through his nose. "If you're talking about the woman drug lord, she died on the way to the hospital."

I half-expected those words, but hearing them spoken aloud was like a fist to the solar plexus. I opened my mouth to say something and closed it before anything came out. But I had to know. I whispered, "I thought she was one of yours."

The agent considered my words. His Adam's apple bobbed below his collar and bounced back up. "Nope. She was one of the most powerful drug lords in Mexico."

I shook my head. Luz's words clearly echoed in my mind. "She really wasn't FBI?" Maybe for some reason she had second thoughts about killing us and lied to get us to follow her.

He shot me an impatient look. "She really wasn't. Where'd you get that idea, anyway?"

"She said she was."

The elevator binged and the door slid open. He half laughed and said, "You can't believe anything a drug dealer tells you."

———

My watch read 2:23 a.m. when I shuffled out of the elevator and dropped into one of the beige easy chairs scattered in clumps throughout the lobby. I had answered questions until I was blue in the face, and then answered more. I was talked out.

I scrunched down and rested my head against the back of the chair. My body felt boneless, my arms too heavy to bother trying to lift. Everything hurt. I didn't want to think anymore. I wanted to sleep for a week. I considered calling JT even though it was so late, just to hear her voice, but I didn't have the gumption to dig the phone out. The way my body felt reminded me of my aches and pains after the broomball tourney Kate, Coop, and I played in a few months earlier, but five times worse. I was completely wrung out.

A few minutes later, the elevator pinged. Kate emerged, along with a fresh-faced, solidly-built blonde dressed in faded jeans and black t-shirt covered by a navy windbreaker. Bright yellow letters spelled FBI on the left chest of the jacket. Of course: I got the grumpy guy, and Kate'd got to have a cute female Feeb twist the screws on her thumbs.

They approached. I was too drained to do more than utter, "Hey."

"Hey." Kate looked at me for a moment. "You're toast."

I nodded.

"Agent Louden here," she indicated the woman, who nodded at me, "is going to take me home and pick up the money bear for evidence. Want to come?"

Did I ever. The thought of crashing into a soft bed nearly brought tears of relief to my eyes. I heaved a noisy sigh. "No. Thanks, though. I'm going to wait for Coop."

"Okay." Kate turned to leave, then swung back. She dug in her pocket a moment, and threw her keys at me. Reflexively, I snagged them out of the air. It was nice to know my reflexes weren't entirely gone.

"The car's only a few blocks away if you want it." She shrugged. "If not, we can get it tomorrow."

I gave her a half-grin. "Thanks."

Kate and Agent Louden disappeared out the front door into the darkness.

Fifteen minutes later, the elevator pinged again and disgorged Coop.

"Over here," I called.

He looked rough. His lip was split, there was a cut on his cheekbone, and he limped as he walked toward me.

"Looks like you've had a tough night."

"You're not looking much better." He eased himself gingerly down in the chair next to me. "That cut on your forehead looks pretty raw. And your chin is really red."

A red chin? I tried to think where that had come from. No one had smacked me there lately. Then I remembered. An unbidden laugh burst from my mouth.

Coop raised his eyebrow.

"Oh," I giggled. "I think it's—" My giggles dissolved into a roar of laughter. "Face burn—" I gasped, "From your crotch. I was using your buckle to get my blindfold off. I'm sorry if I hurt your ... " My gut convulsed with laughter. The level of my mirth sounded like I really wasn't sorry, which wasn't true at all.

Coop watched me struggle for control, tried to keep a straight face, and lost it. We both melted into quivering lumps of human flesh as we howled the stress of the night away.

I tried to catch my breath and wiped the tears from my cheeks. "I really am sorry."

Coop snickered, but managed not to fall into hysterics again. "I know. It's okay." He shifted uncomfortably. "But it'll be a while before the 'nads recover."

We both heaved great sighs and lapsed into silence.

After a couple of minutes I said, "Kate gave me the keys to her car. It's pretty close, I think. We could walk."

Coop considered my words. "Wanna wait for Baz?"

I considered that. "I'd really like to ditch the little rat here."

"Could."

"He and Sharpe ran when Tomás confronted Luz." Oh. Luz. Saying her name made me wonder if Coop knew.

I was about to ask when he said quietly, "She didn't make it."

"I know."

A heavy silence fell. There wasn't much more to say. When Coop and I got some sleep and some distance from this thing, we'd talk.

Coop said, "What should we do about Baz?"

I crossed my arms and shrugged. "Let's wait."

"'K."

Baz was sprung a little after three. We trudged to the car. Every time Baz tried to say something, I shushed him. After a while, he got the message. At some point, we'd have to hash this whole mess out with him, too. If I tried now, though, the fury he made me feel would come out in some very inappropriate yet savagely satisfying ways.

Kate's car was right where we left it outside the plant before going in to find Coop. As much as I wanted to go home and sleep like the dead for a week, we needed to talk to Eddy and Agnes. Resolutely, I pointed the car toward Northeast Minneapolis and the Leprechaun.

———

Three cars sat in my father's small, potholed lot when we pulled in. Winter and snowplow blades were hard on gravel parking lots. I'd been after my dad for the last few years to have it paved, to no avail.

The bar appeared locked down and dark, as did Dad's apartment above. I had a key, and I let us in the back. I hadn't bothered calling ahead because I didn't want to wake anyone, but with the three cars outside, I guessed that wouldn't have been a problem.

I led the way through the kitchen. The smell of pizza was strong, and to a lesser extent, the odor of stale cigarette smoke and booze. I was starving. "I think I could eat a whole pizza."

Coop said in a near moan, "I really, really need a smoke."

Baz grumbled from behind Coop, "I really, really, really want a drink."

Interesting how smells triggered different responses. If I had my way, the answers to those three vices would be hell yes, hell no, and maybe.

We exited the kitchen through the swinging door and entered the main part of the bar. Here, the odors of alcohol and smoke were pungent. Light glowed from an open door in the rear of the bar that led into a large room where special functions, large parties, and my dad's poker games took place. I suppressed a laugh. Of course they'd still be playing poker. Crazy people.

Not wanting to startle anyone, I called out, "Hey, Dad," and we threaded through the tables toward the light.

"Hey, honey," his voice drifted from inside the room. "Come on in."

When I crossed the threshold, I shook my head. Should have known. A low-hanging light surrounded by a Bud Light shade lit up the players.

My father, Eddie, Agnes, and three men I was vaguely familiar with sat around a green felt-covered poker table, cards in hand. After playing poker for hours on end, they still looked bright-eyed and feisty.

Clouds of smoke hovered above their heads and curled in wisps around the fluorescent bulbs. A cigarette smoldered in my dad's hand, and two of the three men puffed on cigars. Eddy had a stogie clenched between her teeth. At my entrance, she rumbled around the cigar, "It's about time you kids showed up. I hope you've been staying out of trouble."

TWENTY-FIVE

On Tuesday, the front page headline of the *Minneapolis Star Tribune* read:

Operation White Stag Bags
Mexican and Canadian Cartel Leaders

Well over a year in the offing, Operation White Stag netted six feared drug czars. It all came down to a shootout in Fridley's old Columbia Ice Arena, best known for its moment on the big screen in the movie The Mighty Ducks. *The mysterious female drug cartel leader, known only as Zorra, was among those killed in a firefight that lasted...*

The story went on, but my eyes kept straying back to the phrase "among those killed." I still found it next to impossible to believe that the mild-mannered woman Coop and I met at Coffman Union was the infamous Zorra. It also bothered both of us she'd claimed to be FBI when she came to our rescue after issuing the warrant for our demise. We'd talked about it at length, but none of us came up with a reasonable answer. Whatever the truth was, it would be buried with her.

We tried a number of times to engage Baz in our amateur debriefings. He wouldn't return any of our calls or texts. Agnes told Eddy that Fletcher Sharpe wasn't pressing charges against Baz, but he would spend the next six months in the county lock-up on work release for violating the conditions of his probation. They'd know more after his court date in a couple of weeks. I hoped he felt some seriously major remorse after dragging all of us into his deadly nightmare. And I hoped (but seriously doubted) he'd stop swiping stuff. Next time it probably would get his ass killed for real.

Fletcher Sharpe returned to the limelight as a tragic innocent in a tale that enmeshed his beloved business with the illicit drug trade. The police were able to prove that Sharpe hadn't been aware that his director of product development, Kelvin Mudd, had been a key player in a major drug-running scheme.

The bruises were beginning fade a little by the time Friday rolled around. At least they wouldn't glow like neon signs when I picked up JT that evening at the airport. When we spoke on the phone after our terrifying and perplexing ordeal was over, I filled her in on only the basics of that deadly night. I wanted to tell her the most horrifying parts face to face.

It drove me nuts wondering who the guy bleeding out in the circus desk was. I checked every media outlet I could think of to see if there was any coverage of a body found in a desk at the Hands On Toy Company. I came up with zip.

In the last few days, a slew of exhausting, confusing emotions buffeted me, with anger leading the pack. But right now the only one I had left was impatience.

JT's flight had landed at 7:45 p.m. I looked again at the time on my brand-spanking-new iPhone. It still said fifty-three minutes after seven.

I waited near the glass-enclosed exit from the terminal proper into baggage claim. Arriving travelers began to trickle down one of the two sets of escalators that ran on either side of a flight of stairs. A TSA official sat at a podium inside the glass enclosure carefully monitoring the exiting passengers and the people milling about the baggage area.

The low ceiling on the baggage claim level cut off the view of the top two-thirds of the escalators and steps. As the escalator rolled, each passenger was slowly revealed from the bottom up. Watching, wondering if this next person would be JT, rivaled the excitement that used to course through me on Christmas morning.

Two women with builds similar to JT's had already stepped off the escalator and come through the automatic doors. My heart sped up both times as I watched them descend.

A pair of black boots rolled into view, followed by long legs encased in dark blue jeans. My heart ratcheted up a couple notches again. Then came a familiar, well-worn black leather motorcycle jacket hanging open over a faded black shirt. My blood pressure rose some more. When her head appeared, there was no doubt. The chestnut hair pulled back in a sloppy ponytail, the angular features, and the delighted grin that spread across her face as she caught sight of me definitely belonged to JT Bordeaux.

My pulse roared, thundering so loudly in my ears that the rest of the airport faded from my senses. My eyes locked on target, and that target hit the bottom of the escalator and strode purposefully through the sliding doors toward me. When she came within reach, I launched myself at her. I didn't give a damn who might be watching or what they might think. This was about heart and love.

JT dropped the duffle bag she was carrying and her arms came up, squeezing me tight. For the first time in what felt like forever, I felt whole. Her scent surrounded me like a balm and for the first time in a very long time, tears rolled down my face.

Warm, strong hands cupped my cheeks, tilted my head back.

"Shay," JT whispered, worry etching her face. "Are you crying?" Her eyes narrowed at the sight of the cut on my forehead and the fading bruises.

My lips caught hers in a searingly fast kiss. I broke away and rested my forehead on her shoulder, preparing to unleash the gathering storm within.

"Shay?" She said sharply. "What's wrong?"

I lifted my head and looked in her eyes, seeing affection, concern, and apprehension. I pressed a finger to her lips and whispered, "I love you, JT Bordeaux."

———

"You," I said with a huff, "have way too much luggage." I dropped the last bag on the floor next to the other three in JT's large entry and kicked the door shut with my foot. Her red-brick, two-story colonial revival overlooked Lake of the Isles. The only way she could afford the joint on a cop's salary was because she'd inherited it from a wealthy relative. JT was a fortunate woman.

Dawg bounced around, racing from the foyer to the living room and back. He stopped periodically and enthusiastically head butted JT, slurped her hand, and then did it all over again. I understood how he felt.

"I know I do. But I needed my stuff." JT laughed and rubbed Dawg's cheeks. Slobber flew through the air. "You missed me, didn't you, boy?" He nailed her square on the nose with his oversized tongue. "Ugh," she said as she straightened and wiped her face on her sleeve.

"We both missed you."

JT met my eyes, and it was like drowning in bowls of liquid chocolate. I shook myself, needing to stay focused. When JT found out we'd been in the middle of a gun battle between the feds and some of the most dangerous drug runners in North America, she was going to blow a gasket. It might be some time before the granite that was about to show in her eyes melted back into the warm pools I loved.

I inhaled, put my hand on the back of the sofa and squeezed. "JT, we need to talk."

She was in the process of throwing her jacket across the arm of an easy chair. She paused mid-toss. "What is it?"

"Come on, let's sit down."

She followed as I circled the couch and sat, one leg tucked under me. JT mirrored my position, worry creasing her smooth forehead, pulling her expressive eyebrows toward each other.

Dawg came over and put his head in my lap. I fiddled with his soft ear and looked absently out the picture window.

"Shay," JT said gently. She hooked my chin and tugged until I met her gaze. "Spill it."

I licked my lips, took a deep breath, and spilled. Everything.

An hour later we'd shifted positions. JT and I were cozy in one corner of the couch, and Dawg snored, stretched out across the other two-thirds.

Her hand rested on my shoulder as she considered my words. Up to now, she'd done nothing but listen carefully and ask clarifying questions.

"Well," she said after a few moments of pensive silence, "I think you absolutely did the best you could with what you had." She kissed the top of my head.

"You're not going to blow a cork?"

"If blowing a cork would help in some way, I would. I am angry. Angry with Baz for putting you all in this position. I'm angry with Kelvin Mudd and his cronies, and with all of the drug lords in Mexico. But," as she spoke, her arm tightened around me, "I'm absolutely furious you could've been killed, and there wasn't a goddamn thing I could've done to prevent it."

"JT, babe, can you ease up a little?"

That broke the tension, and she loosened her hold but didn't let go. I leaned my cheek against her chest, listened to her heart pound. My own thumped merrily along with hers, beat for beat.

I said, "The one thing that really bothers me about this whole thing is Luz. Zorra. Whatever her name is." I straightened and propped my head on my hand against the couch. "None of it makes any sense."

"Sometimes things don't make sense. No matter how hard you try to make them."

I nodded. That was true, but I didn't have to like it.

"So," JT continued, "I think we should set all of this on the shelf and get back to my homecoming." Her eyes glinted. "I believe you said something earlier I'd like to hear you say again."

I rolled and straddled her lap, hands propped on the top of the couch on either side of her head. My eyes met hers, and the granite I'd expected to be reflected back at me was absent. In its place was something deeper than anything I'd ever seen before.

"I love you." It was even easier the second time.

She smiled and raised a dubious brow.

"I. Love. You." This time I punctuated each word with a kiss. This love stuff wasn't so hard after all.

She beamed.

I repeated it a third time and you know what? They, whoever they were, were right. The third time is a charm. I thought my heart couldn't be more full until JT said hoarsely, "Shay, I'm in love with you, too."

TWENTY-SIX

SUNDAY MORNING DAWNED PARTLY cloudy and found me at the Rabbit Hole. JT was off to play a little catch-up at the cop shop after weeks of being gone. Kate was on a well-deserved day off, and Dawg sprawled upside-down, sound asleep on his bed in the corner of the café. There was no shame in his game. The breakfast crowd had dwindled to a trickle, and Eddy and I stood behind the counter chatting.

Rocky had bussed tables through the morning rush, and once things quieted I sent him off to Eddy's living room. I'd set up my laptop and pulled Facebook up so he could talk to his flower—or rather, Tulip—during down times. I swear I was never going to remember her name. And thanks to Eddy, he was also the proud owner of a brand-new stuffed rattler from the Hands On Toy Company. He named it Doodlebug Two. Creative, Rocky wasn't. Dear, he was.

The front door swung open, the attached bell chiming merrily. I broke into grin at the sight of our latest patron.

JT walked up to the counter, leaned over, and planted a big one right on my kisser.

Eddy came around the counter and held her arms out to JT, who dutifully gave her a hug. Eddy gently patted her cheek. "What are you doing in this dive, stranger? It's been a while."

"Yes, it has." JT smiled. "I hear I can't leave without you getting into trouble."

Eddy nodded. "You can say that again, child."

The door opened and bells jangled again. This time Agnes bustled through the door.

"Yo, Aggie," Eddy called.

"Yo, yourself," Agnes said as she approached. "When are you going to stop talking like those rascal kids?"

"I'll stop talking like the kids when my bones are too old to move."

"Aren't they already?"

I cleared my throat. Loudly. "What can we get you to drink, Agnes?"

Before she could reply, JT waved a hand at me. "Hang on, Shay, just a second." She leaned conspiratorially toward Eddy and whispered something in her ear. Then they high-fived each other.

Agnes peered at me in question. I leaned my hip against the counter and shrugged.

Eddy stepped behind me, untied my apron, and yanked it off.

"Hey!" I made a grab for it and missed.

Eddy poked me. "Skedaddle. I'll stay here and take care of things."

I shook my head. "It's Sunday, and it—"

"Shush, you." Eddy grabbed my arm and dragged me around the counter. "I got Rocky in the back, and Agnes will be here to help. Won't you Aggie?"

"Why not? I got real good making those little shot things the last time—"

"Are you kidding?" Eddy pushed me toward JT but looked at Agnes. "You pulled those espresso shots and drank 'em all. You were so wired—"

"I can't help it I have no tolerance for caffeine."

"Vodka, neither."

I allowed JT to lead me through the café, between tables of amused customers, and out the door.

Her forest-green Durango was double-parked. Very cop-like.

"Into the back you go," she said.

"Where—" I stopped cold when I saw Coop sitting in the front passenger seat, looking rumpled, like he'd just been awoken and dragged from bed. Baz was in the rear, a scowl on his face, arms across his chest like a petulant child. Kate was beside him looking very Kate-like.

I crawled in next to Kate as JT settled herself and started the engine.

"All right. What's going on?"

Coop twisted around to look at me, eyes bloodshot. "No idea. The devil woman showed up at my door and wouldn't leave until I got in the car." It looked like he'd had a few late nights, probably celebrating the fact that he wasn't dead. And from the smell of cigarette smoke that wafted from him, he'd lost his latest battle in the war to quit smoking.

I said to Baz, "And what about you?"

He seemed to be wearing a permanent scowl. "Pushy, isn't she."

A laugh burst unbidden from deep in my chest. "She has her moments. Kate?" I elbowed her.

"Your woman showed up and asked me to go away with her. I would've gotten excited if I hadn't been all wrapped up and cozy with Lane."

I raised an eyebrow. "Lane?"

A dimple in Kate's cheek deepened. "Yep. Remember the FBI agent who took me home?"

I did.

"She hasn't left yet. Unofficially, of course."

I laughed. "Of course. Way to keep a secret, there, lady-killer. You need a couple more days off to rest and recover?"

Coop turned around and said, "It's a good thing the girl's an FBI agent so she has the stamina to keep up with you."

Man, he was snarky today.

Kate's lips curled into a smirk, and she simply sat there looking like the cat who swallowed a whole tank of tasty goldfish.

I gave her a leer, then said to JT, "Really, what are we doing?"

She caught my eyes in the rearview mirror, her expression impassive. "Sit back, relax, and enjoy the ride."

Forty minutes later, a few miles somewhere south of Shakopee in a densely wooded area, JT turned into a gated drive. The privacy fence around the property had to be ten feet tall, made of white planks with medieval, spear-like extrusions running along the top edge.

JT pressed a button on the call box. It squawked. She said something, and the estate gate slowly rolled open. We followed a curvy drive a quarter-mile or so through a thick stand of trees. Even with most of the leaves dropped for the winter, I couldn't see the house or any other buildings until we crested a small hill. The trees gave way to a sizable single level ranch house and three-car garage. The top of a small red barn with white trim and a couple of other buildings were visible behind the house.

The drive circled a white, two-tiered fountain that would probably be back in business soon, once the threat of one last freeze dissipated.

JT put the car in park and cut the engine. "Come on." She exited the SUV and marched toward the front door. We trailed along behind.

She rang the bell, and after a moment, the door swung open.

A short, round woman with gray-black hair wrapped up in a bun and rosy round cheeks stood beaming at us. She wore a yellow peasant dress with poofy sleeves and colorful embroidery along the edges. Black slip-ons encased her feet.

"*Buenos días!*" She clapped her hands once and beamed. "Please, come in. We have been expecting you." Her voice was heavily accented.

Expecting us? Even this cuddly grandmother-type knew more than we did. If she was another cartel leader, I was going shoot JT with her own gun. On second thought, maybe I'd take Baz out first, and then shoot JT.

We followed the woman from the spacious entry down a hall. Interior beams were exposed high above, giving the large house a roomy Southwest feel. We trod on rust-colored tiles through an arched doorway into a living room. Colorful handmade pottery artistically arranged on glass shelving rested against one wall. A huge picture window overlooked the front yard. A burnished piece of metal artwork stretched across another wall, composed of a sun setting behind two saguaro cacti, with the impression of low mountains in the background.

"*Por favor*," she said, clasping her hands to her chest. "Take a seat. Please." A huge smile nearly squeezed her eyes shut. "I will return in a moment."

The woman swooshed from the room. I shot JT a look, but it was like trying to read a rock. A couch and love seat squared off across a low, multi-color tiled coffee table. Padded leather wing-back chairs flanked either side. The furniture looked like it had been hand-carved. Thick cushions were covered with red and brown upholstery that resembled a Native American blanket I had as a kid. I sat with JT on the love seat, and the boys each settled in one of the wingbacks. Kate took one corner of the sofa.

"JT," I asked, "What exactly is going on?"

"Just wait." She put a calming hand on my leg and gently squeezed.

I sat back with a disgruntled sigh and crossed my arms.

A couple of minutes later, footsteps echoed in the hall. Then the woman returned, assisting someone behind her. Then she stepped out of the way.

I blinked. Holy shit. The dead was walking.

"Luz?" Coop breathed, poised to spring from his chair.

Baz sat stiffly, his forehead puckered and his mouth open in a ridiculous O.

I shot JT a look. A proud and satisfied expression was written all over her face.

Luz, or Zorra, or whoever this woman was, slowly entered the room. Her left arm was immobilized against her body, and white gauze covering the wound in her left shoulder peeked out from under a pink tank top. Turquoise sleep pants covered her legs, and she wore thick knit socks.

247

Luz shuffled to the couch, and the woman helped her to the cushions.

"*Gracias,* Mama," she said with a grimace. "This is my mother, Estella," she added to no one in particular.

Estella straightened and asked, "Can I get you all something to drink?"

After taking stock of our hydration needs, Estella bustled out of the room.

Luz looked me square in the eye. "I suppose it is only fair to tell you the truth of what's going on."

I wasn't sure if I was relieved, pissed, curious, or confused. Probably a little of each. This woman ordered our executions, held us at gunpoint, and prodded me and Baz in the head with the muzzle of her pistol, for cripe's sake. I could still feel the impression of the barrel on my forehead. But, then she freed us and tried to help us escape. And then she was shot dead. This was serious mass of fucking contradictions. How on earth did JT know that, a) Luz was alive, and b) where she was? And did she also know who had been crammed into Fletcher Sharpe's ridiculous desk?

I leaned against the back of the couch. As Rod Serling was fond of saying, "You've crossed over into the Twilight Zone." Now we just needed the eerie music to go along with it.

Luz (I just couldn't think of this woman as Zorra) tucked her legs awkwardly under her. "First of all, I want to thank you." She gazed from me to Kate to Coop. "You saved my life."

Kate, ever honest, said, "No we didn't. That guy shot you. We didn't stop him in time."

Luz closed her eyes at the memory. "No—well, yes, he did shoot me. Twice. Thank goodness for Kevlar. But Tomás is nothing if not thorough. He'd have made sure I was dead if you hadn't attacked him."

Estella returned at that moment with our beverages and doled them out. She set a full pitcher of reddish-purple liquid on a side table. She'd offered up homemade sangria as one of the options, and we'd all taken her up on it with the exception of my always-in-control cop and the bullet-riddled bad girl on narcotics.

I took a sip, nodded in appreciation. Nothing like a little happy juice in my empty engine. Breakfast had been some time ago. "Estella, this is really good."

The others murmured their agreement.

"You talk." Estella's gaze settled on her daughter. "And thank you for allowing *mi hija* to return to me. *Gracias.*" She retreated.

Luz inhaled quickly and blew out long. "Let me start from the beginning."

"Good idea," I muttered.

"My father and mother—who are good, kind, hard-working people—came here to Minnesota from Monterrey, Mexico, in the late sixties. They were undocumented but wanted a better life than they'd be able to have in Mexico. They got good jobs, worked hard, and my father started a cash-only furniture company, selling by word of mouth. He made this furniture." Luz waved a hand at what we were sitting on. "He was very good. Anyway, I was born in Minneapolis. And always getting into trouble."

Somehow, I could buy that.

Luz continued, "When I was thirteen, I took a little joy ride in a neighbor's car. For the third time. And was busted. For the third time. A now-retired Minneapolis detective realized I was a decent kid with a wild streak. He took me under his wing."

My cup runneth empty. I corrected that and sat back down, my attention riveted once again on the not-dead dead woman in front of me.

"With his influence," Luz said, "he found ways for me to funnel excess energy in less-illegal avenues. As I grew older, I became interested in a career in law enforcement. When I graduated from college with a double major in politics and Mexican studies and a minor in criminal justice, the FBI was on my doorstep, waiting to sign me up."

I asked, "So you are really FBI?"

Luz nodded. "I am. Or I was. I'm officially retired. And I'll explain. You see, the glitch hit during my background checks. It came out that my parents were not in the country legally. A high-ranking FBI agent offered to fix the situation and allow them to stay in Minnesota as citizens if I agreed to infiltrate the Reynosa Cartel. The cartel was vulnerable because the leadership kept killing each other off. There was so much unrest, the essence of the organization was threatened by neighboring cartels who would have loved to take it over."

Damn. That was a lot to put on a kid.

Baz asked, "Why did they think you'd be able to do it?"

"Because," Luz explained, "I was the right mix. The right mix of Mexican, stubborn, and native Spanish speaking. At least that's what they told me."

JT's hand was back on my leg, but she'd eased up on her grip. I think she was no longer afraid I might attack Luz.

"I agreed to the FBI's terms. My parents had done everything they could to make my life better than they'd had. I couldn't let them be sent back. So I went through training at Quantico." She looked at JT. "Where you just were, I heard."

"Yup."

Luz nodded. "I made it through boot camp and was sent off to specialty training. I learned to alter my facial appearance with high-tech prosthetics provided by the movie industry and improved upon by FBI forensic scientists. The alterations were subtle but effective. Soon I was a master of disguise. I accomplished the infiltration faster than anyone expected."

This was something right out of a thriller novel. I was riveted.

"I began feeding critical information back, and major players in non-Reynosa cartels were picked up left and right. After a couple of years of success, the FBI followed through on their end of the deal by orchestrating the naturalization of my mother and father. They also called an end to my covert activities. By this time, I had worked my way halfway up Reynosa's organizational ladder."

Luz shook her head. "The danger fed my inner wild child, and I took great satisfaction in helping to make both Mexico and the United States a safer place. I really enjoyed the work. I convinced them to let me continue my work."

Good grief. I was practically having a heart attack listening to the story, much less living it.

Baz asked, "How many people did you kill?"

A ghost of emotion flitted across Luz's face. "I never personally killed anyone. Let's leave it at that." Her voice was tight. "After some back and forth, ICE became involved in a joint operation with the FBI. My boss signed off on my assignment, with one caveat: Due to the very nature of my attempt to rise up the chain of the Reynosa Cartel command, they added a Dangerous Actions clause. DA clauses are far and few between," she acknowledged JT's nod, "but pay handsomely if the agent manages to live though the assignment. The upshot of the clause holds that in order to keep my cover intact—and also to protect the FBI and ICE from culpability if something happened to me while I was so deeply mired within the Reynosa organization—I was on my own while on Mexican soil. There'd be no US bailout. There was some degree of safety for me in the United States, and that was why I made so many trips home to Minnesota."

I topped off everyone's sangria again. I was starting to get a slight buzz, and it felt good.

Luz rubbed her face with her hands and dropped them into her lap. "I slowly moved further up the Reynosa ranks, wresting the top spot from the former drug lord, Antonio Luis Sanchez. Sanchez was a tough character who survived numerous assassination attempts from both within his own organization and without. When someone finally managed to oust him, and that someone was a woman, I became legendary, not only within the Reynosa organization, but throughout Mexico."

Kate ran a hand over her mouth. "Did you have him killed?"

"Everyone assumes I had Sanchez killed." Luz smiled. "Instead of fertilizing the earth, I coordinated Sanchez's delivery into FBI custody. Eventually, he cut a deal and sang like a robin in spring, giving up intimate cartel information that greatly assisted me. He gave law enforcement a huge edge. All this happened on the condition ICE would place him and his family in witness protection through the FBI."

Coop had been following the story, watching Luz carefully. "So how did this Zorra thing come up?"

"I adopted the familiar persona of Zorro, altering it slightly to Zorra. I dressed in black, on occasion wore a black mask over my eyes, and topped the costume off with a Gaucho hat. As Zorra, I ruled the Reynosa Empire, running it from behind an elaborate cover of smoke and mirrors in an attempt to keep my true identity hidden.

"Only recently, I accepted an adjunct teaching position in Mexican Studies at the University of Minnesota. I had worked my dual charade for too many years and helped to put hundreds of cartel members away. I had finally done enough. I wanted to come home."

I retrieved another tipple. "I'd say you've done enough." My lips were going pleasantly numb.

"Yes." Luz nodded. "Operation White Stag was going to be my coup de grâce, and once it was over, Zorra would disappear as quickly as she'd risen. The Columbia Arena bloodbath was the result of a many months of multi-jurisdictional collaboration directed, in part, by me on the cartel side and by one of the top agents in ICE. The op took agents from many places, including Mike Farroway's office."

The light bulb flicked on. Farroway's bristly red hair flashed in my mind. Why hadn't this clicked sooner? I didn't want to know but was compelled to ask. "Was he in Fletcher Sharpe's desk?"

JT nodded, her face grave. "Yes. Apparently after you talked to him, he decided to do some investigation on his own. He was in over his head before he even had a chance to react. Everyone else was wrapped up in Operation White Stag."

I felt terrible. If we hadn't dragged him into this, he'd still be alive. Based on the crestfallen look on both their faces, Coop, and Baz, to his credit, felt the same.

Luz spoke again. "When I met with you and Nick on campus, I had no idea you were the ones causing Tomás so much grief. I was shocked when you and Nick were dragged into Sharpe's manufacturing plant bound and bloodied."

Kate eyed me and mouthed, "Nick?"

253

I raised both brows and shook my head.

"Shay," Luz said, her tone sincere, "I'm so sorry I had to threaten you with my weapon. And you," she bobbed her head at Baz, "as well. But I could do nothing to alert Tomás or any of the other cartel leaders that something was very wrong. Every second I was trying to figure out how to get all of you out of there."

Coop asked, "When we saw you at the warehouse and later at the ice arena, your appearance was altered?"

"Yes," Luz acknowledged. "I changed both my clothes and my face through prosthetics and contact lenses. It's subtle, but enough of a difference to make it work."

I said, "So when Kelvin Mudd and Tomás confronted us behind the rink, they were addressing Zorra, not Luz. Your invented identity remained intact."

Luz said, "Yes, it did. That's thanks to you. Then Tomás shot me."

I shuddered at Luz's words, my brain flashing back to the moment I saw the fire explode from the end of Tomás's pistol. I quickly slugged down the last of my third—or was it my fourth?—cup of sangria and refilled. The pitcher was almost empty.

Luz sighed. "Word was leaked that Zorra had been killed, which wasn't true, along with other cartel leaders. Also killed was Lieutenant Pomerantz, the corrupt missing-persons head from New Orleans. Another eight were wounded in the firefight. Hunk and Donny were arrested, uninjured, after they were pulled from beneath a set of bleachers where they hid like the cowards they are. Three escaped and are now on the FBI's most wanted list."

JT squeezed my hand and said, "I have a question I wasn't able to get a full answer to."

Luz's nearly perfectly arched eyebrow arched higher.

"How exactly did Kelvin Mudd fit into this?"

"He was Sharpe's director of product development and the main man who coordinated the shipments of drugs from Mexico. He ran the goods through Hunk and Donny, who in turn used an unofficial gang of underage kids, of all people, as drug runners. The runners converted the drugs to cash, received a cut, and gave the rest of the money back. Hunk and Donny then kept their own cut and handed the remainder over to Kelvin Mudd. Mudd also kept a portion and devised a way to stuff toy animals full of cash. Then he shipped them back to Mexico as an export. An associate of the Reynosa Cartel picked up the toys once delivery had been made to Sharpe's manufacturing plant located outside of Juárez, Mexico."

"Wow," Coop said. "That's seriously complicated."

My brain felt woozy.

Luz's mother picked that moment to check on us. "You must stay for a late lunch," she declared as she cleared away the cups and now-empty sangria pitcher. "It will be ready in twenty minutes." She issued the mandate and exited without waiting for a response.

Kate's eyes opened wide. "She doesn't take no for an answer, does she?"

Luz smiled. "No. She doesn't."

Coop said, "What kind of food does she cook that a vegetarian can eat?"

Luz appraised him with hot eyes for a moment. "We'll find something to fill you up."

Whoa. Sparks were flying.

A dimple in Coop's cheek deepened, but he didn't respond.

JT said, "I heard through the rumor mill that Mudd sang like a lark and implicated Hunk and Donny, who then ratted out their underage runners. It's going to be a major shift in drug dealing here in the Cities. Thanks directly to you, Luz."

Luz gracefully accepted the comment. "Thank you, JT. And I hope you're aware what an amazing individual Shay is. She has a sense of honor and decency you don't see often any more. And these friends of yours … " she waved her hand at us, "are true and good."

JT looked at me, her eyes full of warmth. "Yes, I certainly know just how special Shay is. And the rest of these yahoos aren't half-bad either."

Kate asked, "Luz, what will you do now?"

Luz gazed out the window for a moment. "My mother will stay here. It's safe enough. We have guards patrolling the fence-line and good security. I may leave for Europe or Australia for a while and return when this has blown over and something else has caught the attention of the media. I'll have to give up my teaching position, but that's a small sacrifice to be alive." Luz's eyes bore into Coop when she added, "But I'll definitely be back."

Coop returned her gaze with an alarming intensity. "You look me up, okay?"

Oh jeez. We could light a lamp with the voltage that zinged between the two of them.

"I absolutely will."

A motion caught my eye, and I turned a little too fast. My head stopped but my brain kept going. Baz had something in his hand, and he was nervously playing with it. I squinted. "Baz, what is that?"

Baz looked at his hands as if he'd just realized there was something in them. "Oh, nothing." He tried to stuff the object into his pocket.

"Baz." The warning in my tone was clear. "What is it?"

He met my gaze and held the item out. It was a Star Wars figurine of Darth Vader. I turned it over a couple of times and gave it back. Something niggled, foggy, in the back of my mind, made worse by the strange look on his face. I said suspiciously, "Where'd you get that?"

He didn't answer but did have the grace to look guilty.

"Baz." I gave him the evil eye as I recalled where I'd last seen figurines like those: in the business office of the Hands On Toy Company. After all this, the little bastard had taken something else. Was he nuts?

My sloshed innards started to quiver. "Did you swipe it?"

"I'd never do that." Baz attempted to look insulted.

"Bullshit!" I exploded. "You've been doing it your whole life. And look what it's gotten all of us into, you moron." My fingers dug into the cushion beneath me. I shifted my weight forward. I couldn't believe after all we'd been though, he would do it again. Stupid thinking on my part. Okay, tipsy thinking.

He scowled and then flipped me the bird. "Shay, kiss my ass."

If I had taken a moment to think about it, I'd have been surprised Baz actually had the balls to say those words to me. Instead, I lost it and lunged, intent on wrapping my hands around his neck and squeezing until he turned blue.

JT brought me up short with a fist twisted in the back of my shirt. She either had fast reflexes or had suspected I might lose my cool, considering the source of my ire.

Baz cringed, and held a hand out toward me, palm up. "I don't know what happened. I—it—I found it in my pocket."

The Star Wars Incident broke up the meeting, and JT thought I needed some air. I think she figured if she could keep us separated, there would be no bloodshed in the Ortez household today.

———

Fresh, cool air cleared my brain to some degree. JT and I strolled in silence behind the ranch house, past the barn and a fenced pasture where three horses grazed. My blood pressure slowly returned to normal.

The two other outbuildings were a storage shed and a workshop where Mr. Ortez made his furniture. I knew this because the words carved in a wood sign above the door read ORTEZ FINE FURNITURE.

"I wonder where Luz's dad is," I said.

JT navigated a muddy area of the path we followed. "He died of a massive heart attack eight months ago."

"Oh." Ouch. I stuffed my hands in the pockets of my jeans. It made it all that much more important Luz was alive. Her poor mother.

"How do you know so much about all of this?"

JT grabbed my belt loop. She said, "It helps to know certain people, and dropping a name from my new FBI contacts didn't hurt either."

"You work fast."

The path petered out and turned into a deer trail that cut through the woods behind the house. Birds that were either too stupid to leave the state for the winter or who had recently returned chirped overhead. The air lacked the city pollution factor I was used to, and it plain felt good to breathe.

It was far too easy to fall into a comfort zone and not pay attention to the larger issues in the world. These last few days were a testament to that fact. I reached for JT's hand and laced my fingers through hers.

After a few hundred feet, the trail opened to a small meadow that was a little larger than the size of a running track. It would make a perfect escape in the summer.

I was feeling better, less woozy, and I didn't think I was on the verge of murder anymore. "Thanks for having my back in there. I had a bit too much sangria, and … Thanks."

"You've had a hell of a time. Makes sense you might struggle."

We came to a stop near the center of the meadow. I pulled JT into my arms. "Thanks for being you."

She kissed the tip of my nose. "Anytime. Thanks for not getting killed."

I grinned. "Welcome."

"Mike Farroway's dog—"

"Bogey," I supplied. "He was a nice mutt. Flunky Bloodhound, Mike said. I'm sorry he won't have Mike anymore." I felt the mist of guilt begin to descend and fought to keep it at bay. My head knew I wasn't responsible for what happened to Farroway. He was doing his job. But my heart and my gut felt quite differently. One day, I was going to have to dissect that situation and come to terms with it.

JT leaned her forehead against mine. "I'm going to take him for a while. At least until they figure out what to do with him."

Her eyes were beautiful. And right now they were the warm mahogany I loved. Her dark hair was loose and cascaded around her shoulders. I tucked a wayward strand behind her ear. "You have a good heart."

"I try." She stepped away, grabbed my hand, and we continued our circuit around the meadow. "There's something I want to ask you." Her tone belied nervousness.

She was intently studying the ground we were traversing.

I eyed her. "Spit it out."

"I don't want to scare you—"

"JT! What?" Where was my woman's usually glib tongue? I was the one who had a hard time with the L word, the one who was used to lovin' 'em and leavin' 'em. Was she about to cut me loose? I stopped dead in my tracks, heart in my throat. JT still held my hand, and when I stopped, the momentum swung her around to face me.

My eyes widened in alarm. "What?"

In a blink, JT processed the emotions pouring off me. She stepped into my space, cupped my face with her hands and held my head still. "Shay, it's okay." Her eyes pierced my heart, her voice hoarse with emotion. "I was going to ask you if you might be interested in staying at my place."

"Well, yeah, tonight I planned—"

"No."

I snapped my mouth shut.

"Staying permanently. As in living there."

I released the breath I'd been holding in a whoosh and slapped a hand to my chest. "Perm—oh my god, I thought you were going to dump me. You about gave me a stroke."

"Oh, Shay, no. I'm so sorry. No." JT pulled me tight against her.

It felt like my heart might leap through my skin. I whispered into her neck, "You scared the crap out of me."

"Not my intent." Then she pushed me to arm's length. "I figured since we spend most of the time there anyway, and your place is so small, and Dawg would have a playmate, and Rocky could move into your apartment—" I silenced her with my mouth.

When we broke apart, I wasn't the only one sucking air.

"I don't know." I took a deep breath. "I'm barely used to the idea of telling you I love you. Moving in together is huge."

I adored that forlorn look JT got whenever she was within reach of what she really wanted but something blocked her from getting it. She was usually pretty sneaky about finding a way around the problem. Probably why she was such a good cop.

"Will you think about it?"

"Yes." I pulled her in for another smooch.

She braced a hand on my chest and dodged my lips. "Is that 'yes, you will move in with me' or 'yes, you'll think about it'?"

I squinted at her, a million thoughts charging through my mind. I'd leaped that humdinger 'love' hurdle just to be taken aback by the prospect of domestic bliss in one abode. With two dogs. I always believed that kind of life wasn't for me. My white picket fence dreams flew out the window the first time I kissed a girl. Lately, defining moments kept blasting at me like hundred-mile-an-hour straight-line winds. Maybe the time had come to go with the flow. *Live in the moment, Shay.*

"Okay. I can't believe I'm gonna say this. I'll move in with you."

We sealed the deal with lengthy lip lock.

Life. It's a crazy, precious thing. You never know what's going to come hurtling your way. But damn, it's good to be alive to see what happens next.

THE END

April McGuire, Back Porch Studio

ABOUT THE AUTHOR

Jessie Chandler is the vice president of the Twin Cities chapter of Sisters in Crime and a member of Mystery Writers of America. In her spare time, Chandler sells unique, artsy T-shirts and other assorted trinkets to unsuspecting conference and festival goers. She is a former police officer and resides in Minneapolis. Visit her online at JessieChandler.com.

WWW.MIDNIGHTINKBOOKS.COM

From the gritty streets of New York City to sacred tombs in the Middle East, it's always midnight somewhere. Join us online at any hour for fresh new voices in mystery fiction.

At midnightinkbooks.com you'll also find our author blog, new and upcoming books, events, book club questions, excerpts, mystery resources, and more.

MIDNIGHT INK ORDERING INFORMATION

Order Online:

- Visit our website www.midnightinkbooks.com, select your books, and order them on our secure server.

Order by Phone:

- Call toll-free within the U.S. and Canada at
  1-888-NITE-INK (1-888-648-3465)
- We accept VISA, MasterCard, and American Express

Order by Mail:

Send the full price of your order (MN residents add 6.5% sales tax) in U.S. funds, plus postage & handling to:

> Midnight Ink
> 2143 Wooddale Drive
> Woodbury, MN 55125-2989

Postage & Handling:

Standard (U.S. & Canada). If your order is:
> $24.99 and under, add $4.00
> $25.00 and over, FREE STANDARD SHIPPING

AK, HI, PR: $16.00 for one book plus $2.00 for each additional book.

International Orders (airmail only):
> $16.00 for one book plus $3.00 for each additional book

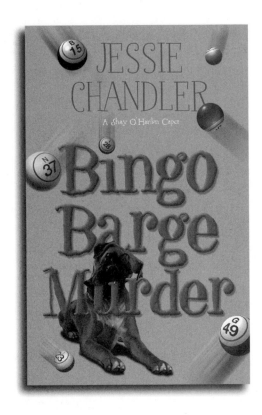

Bingo Barge Murder
A Shay O'Hanlon Caper
Jessie Chandler

Shay O'Hanlon's life as co-owner of The Rabbit Hole, a quirky-cool Minneapolis coffee shop, is well caffeinated, but far from dangerous. All that changes when her lifelong friend Coop becomes a suspect in a murder case. The victim? Kinky, the unsavory owner of The Bingo Barge, a sleazy gambling boat on the Mississippi. The murder weapon? Kinky's own bronzed, lucky bingo marker. Digging for clues to get Coop off the hook unearths X-rated videos, a sweet junkyard pooch, and Mafia goons on the hunt for some supremely valuable nuts.

When Shay's sixty-something-year-old friend is kidnapped and held for ransom, it's up to Shay to rescue her without help from the police. But brushing off the beautiful and relentless Detective Bordeaux—with sparks flying between them—isn't so easy.

978-0-7387-2596-3, 240 pp., 5³/₁₆ x 8   **$14.95**

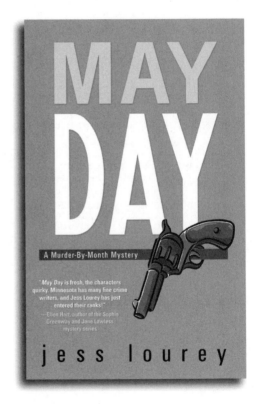

MAY
DAY

A Murder-By-Month Mystery

"*May Day* is fresh, the characters
quirky. Minnesota has many fine crime
writers, and Jess Lourey has just
entered their ranks!"
—Ellen Hart, author of the Sophie
Greenway and Jane Lawless
mystery series

jess lourey

May Day
A Murder-By-Month Mystery
JESS LOUREY

Minneapolitan Mira James has been taking it easy since college graduation—too easy. Due to a dead-end job and a cheating boyfriend, the Twin Cities have lost their charm, and Mira decides to begin a new life in rural Battle Lake. Right away she is offered jobs as an assistant librarian and part-time reporter and falls into an unexpected romance with a guy who seems to be the perfect man until he turns up dead between the reference stacks her tenth day on the job.

Anxious to learn more about the man who had briefly stolen her heart, Mira delves into the hidden mysteries of Battle Lake, including an old land deed with ancient Ojibwe secrets, an obscure octogenarian crowd with freaky social lives, and a handful of thirtysomething high school buddies who hold bitter, decades-old grudges. Mira soon discovers that unknown dangers are concealed under the polite exterior of this quirky small town, and revenge is a tator-tot hotdish best served cold.

A hip, humorous, and gripping account of small-town murder, this novel is the first in a series of cozies featuring Mira James, an urban woman with rural Minnesota roots.

978-0-7387-0838-6, 240 pp., 5³⁄₁₆ x 8   **$14.95**

Mama Does Time
A Mace Bauer Mystery
Deborah Sharp

Meet Mama: a true Southern woman with impeccable manners, sherbet-colored pantsuits, and four prior husbands, able to serve sweet tea and sidestep alligator attacks with equal aplomb. Mama's antics—especially her penchant for finding trouble—drive her daughters Mace, Maddie, and Marty to distraction.

One night, while settling in to look for ex-beaus on *COPS*, Mace gets a frantic call from her mother. This time, the trouble is real: Mama found a body in the trunk of her turquoise convertible, and the police think she's the killer. It doesn't help that the handsome detective assigned to the case seems determined to prove Mama's guilt or that the cowboy who broke Mace's heart shows up at the local Booze 'n' Breeze in the midst of the investigation. Before their mama lands in prison—just like an embarrassing lyric from a country-western song—Mace and her sisters must find the real culprit.

978-0-7387-1329-8, 336 pp., 5³⁄₁₆ x 8 $13.95

An Odelia Grey Mystery

SUE ANN
JAFFARIAN

"PLUS-SIZE
READING PLEASURE—
TRY THIS ONE ON!"
—Lee Child

TOO BIG
TO MISS

Too Big To Miss
An Odelia Grey Mystery
Sue Ann Jaffarian

Too big to miss—that's Odelia Grey. A never-married, middle-aged, plus-sized woman who makes no excuses for her weight, she's not superwoman, just a mere mortal standing on the precipice of menopause, trying to cruise in an ill-fitting bra. She struggles with her relationships, her crazy family, and her crazier boss. And then there's her knack for being in close proximity to dead people...

When her close friend Sophie London commits suicide in front of an online webcam by putting a gun in her mouth and pulling the trigger, Odelia's life is changed forever. Sophie, a plus-sized activist and inspiration to imperfect women, is the last person anyone would ever have expected to end her own life. Suspecting foul play, Odelia is determined to get to the bottom of her friend's death. Odelia's search for the truth takes her from Southern California strip malls to the world of live webcam porn to the ritzy enclave of Corona del Mar.

978-0-7387-0863-8, 336 pp., 5³⁄₁₆ x 8 $14.95

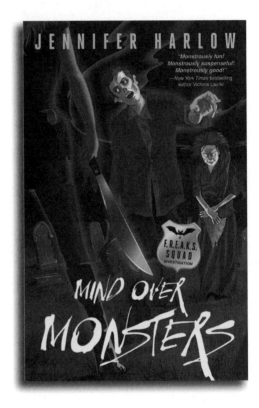

Mind Over Monsters
A F.R.E.A.K.S. Squad Investigation
Jennifer Harlow

Very few people know the truth about Beatrice Alexander. She's no ordinary schoolteacher with a fondness for classic movies. Beatrice can move objects with her mind, an embarrassing and dangerous skill that she's never learned to master—or embrace. After nearly killing her brother by accident, she joins F.R.E.A.K.S. The Federal Response to Extra-Sensory and Kindred Supernaturals is a top-secret offshoot of the FBI that "neutralizes" ghouls, trolls, and other monsters threatening humanity.

Beatrice has no desire to become Buffy the vampire slayer. But F.R.E.A.K.S. offers training to control her power. Also, she doesn't feel like such a freak next to the other supernatural members, including a cute former detective who's a werewolf and an unbearable vampire determined to seduce her. Despite a natural instinct to flee from hideous, bloodthirsty zombies, Beatrice must prove herself on her first mission to find a cunning necromancer.

978-0-7387-2667-0, 288 pp., 5³⁄₁₆ x 8   **$14.95**

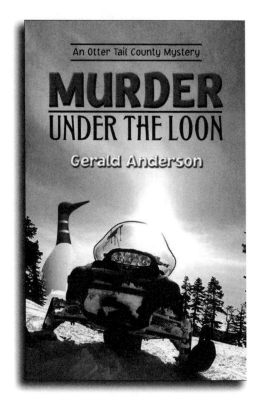

An Otter Tail County Mystery

MURDER
UNDER THE LOON

Gerald Anderson

Murder Under the Loon
An Otter Tail County Mystery
Gerald Anderson

A dead insurance-company president found frozen under a giant loon? Uff da! Life is usually quiet and cold in the average-sized Minnesota town of Fergus Falls. If Miss Marple had been born in the Midwest, you'd find her as the Hershey-dunking, slightly balding, Norwegian sheriff, Palmer Knutson. With one solved murder under his belt, Sheriff Knutson would rather his upstart deputy Orly Peterson look into the incident. But with a mysterious lack of footprints in the snow, the sheriff becomes worried that this is more than just a snowmobile accident.

Excited to retire, the president of Hofstead Hail Insurance was about to announce his replacement to the company during a weekend retreat at a winter resort. Could any of the four employees or their spouses, who had scrambled into parkas and Norwegian sweaters to learn who was to be the lucky choice, commit murder? With old-fashioned greed, ambition, and jealousy—things are starting to look pretty interesting up in da nord country.

978-0-7387-1095-2, 240 pp., 5³⁄₁₆ x 8 $13.95